THE DISHONEST MURDERER

By the same authors
also in large print

Murder Is Served
Murder Within Murder

A MR. AND MRS. NORTH MYSTERY

THE DISHONEST MURDERER

Frances and Richard Lockridge

Thorndike Press • Thorndike, Maine

Library of Congress Cataloging in Publication Data:

Lockridge, Frances Louise Davis.
   The dishonest murderer : a Mr. and Mrs. North mystery/
   Frances and Richard Lockridge.
     p. cm.
   In large print.
   ISBN 0-89621-239-4 (alk. paper)
   1. Large type books. I. Lockridge, Richard, 1898–
   II. Title.
   [PS3523.O243D57 1989]   88-33282
   813'.54–dc19   CIP

no pr,

Large Print edition available in North America by arrangement
with Harper & Row Publishers.

Cover design by Cynthia Bowen.

THE
DISHONEST
MURDERER

I

Friday, December 31
9:05 P.M. to 11:35 P.M.

There is nothing to worry about, Freddie Haven told herself. There is nothing to think about twice. You are not a young girl, she told herself; not a child, full of imaginings, making much of little because it concerns this man. You are a grown woman, contained and poised; you were married, in those other days, to a man whose eyes laughed and whose voice had confident laughter in it, and this is not, cannot be, the same thing. This is a grown-up thing, made of warm affection, of shared understandings; this is more loving than being in love. In this there cannot be the quick excitement, the unreasoning fear and unaccountable delights. This time you cannot be frightened about nothing.

Freddie Haven looked at herself in the dressing table mirror. After a second she began to comb her hair. It was deep red hair; in some

7

lights it was almost too dark to be called red. Satterbee hair. Freddie was used to knowing that it was beautiful, and unexpected. It clung to the brush, fell from the brush in soft waves; it lay sleek round her head, the ends curling under at the back, as her fingers twisted them. "You look fine, Freddie," she told herself. "You're a fine looking young woman. You're a credit to Bruce."

Even if it had been Bruce, she told herself, there would still be nothing beyond explanation. He had changed his plans. That was all. For some reason he had taken an earlier train from Washington. A hundred things could have brought him; he had interests in so many things. There was no reason he should tell her of a change in plan which did not affect her. At ten o'clock — "tennish" — he would come to the party, as he had said he would. Nothing had changed that mattered to them, or he would have let her know.

Even if it had been Bruce — but, of course, it had not been. Was she going to be that way again? Was she going to see Bruce in every big man, with shoulders set a certain way, seeing him where he could not be? She remembered, her hands idle again, looking into the dressing table mirror, seeing nothing in it, how often, how cruelly often, she had seen Jack — in a room, on the street — long after she knew she would never see him again. She was not going to get once more into that sort of turmoil. This had been — what did one say? — a "fancied resemblance."

She took the incident out of her memory and looked at it. She had been coming home in Aunt Flo's car from having tea in Aunt Flo's big, square, irretrievably institutional house in the Navy Yard. They had come across Brooklyn Bridge and, leaving it, gone through Foley Square, then up Lafayette Street. They had gone along fast, with almost no traffic; she had been warm and furred in the back of the big car, looking without attention at almost deserted sidewalks, hardly noticing where they were. And then she had seen this big man who, for an instant, had looked like Bruce Kirkhill. She had seen him only momentarily while the car stopped for a light. Almost as soon as she had seen him, the light changed and the car started.

Now, thinking back, she tried to decide what it was that had made her think the man was Bruce. She tried to make what she had seen vivid again in her mind. A big man — yes, big as Bruce Kirkhill was big. He had been walking south, on the east side of the street. He had been alone; she was almost sure he had been alone. He had been walking with his overcoat unbuttoned, whipped by the wind. She remembered, now. It was that which made her notice him, become conscious of him as she had not been conscious of other men she must have seen and had been unaware of seeing. It was cold; it had grown colder during the afternoon. The cold had bitten into her, with the peculiar damp penetration of cold in the Navy Yard, when she had come out of Aunt Flo's house and gone through the back yard to the waiting car. But this man was paying so little attention to the cold that he did not bother even to button his overcoat.

There must, she thought, have been something in the way the man walked which had made her think of Bruce, and then, fleetingly, identify this man as Bruce. It had not been his face, she realized, looking at the scene she had re-created. She had not tried to see his face until she thought of Bruce in connection with this man, and then the car started and, although she turned and tried to look back, it had been too late to see the face of the man. So it must have been something in the way he moved, something in the rhythm of his body.

She was relieved to discover how intangible it all was, thus thought through, thus reexamined. The man had been about Bruce's size, something in his movements had suggested Bruce. That was all there was to it. She had not seen his face and now, as the picture came clearer, she saw something else which she should have seen from the first. It could not have been Bruce. Even from a distance, even seen momentarily, there had been a kind of shabbiness about the man. Although she could not fully explain it to herself, the word "shambling" came to her mind along with the word "shabby." Then she laughed. She would never tell Bruce — or perhaps one day she would tell Bruce, so that they could laugh together? — that for an instant, in the last hours of a year, riding home in a car from the Navy Yard, she had thought a shambling, shabby man was somehow like Bruce Kirkhill. Like Senator Bruce Kirkhill, the never shabby, the inconceivably shambling — the man who was so surely going places, and with whom she was going.

She stood up in the warm, softly lighted room. She crossed the room, slim in a golden evening dress, her square shoulders high and white, and pulled aside one of the heavy curtains which shut out the night. She could look far down, now, into Park Avenue. There was a kind of blur in the night, the street lights below her were dimmed. It's snowing, she thought; it's begun to snow.

There was a brief, emphatic knock on her bedroom door. She smiled before she spoke. How like her father was that one quick, deci-

11

sive rap. It was polite – never would Vice Admiral Jonathan Satterbee dream of entering another's bedroom without first knocking. But it did not, it would be absurd to argue that it did, request admission. It announced that the admiral was about to enter. As she said, "Come, Dad," she wondered whether anyone had ever kept the admiral waiting, once he had announced his presence. Not her mother, she was certain. Not she, certainly.

Vice Admiral Jonathan Satterbee, U.S.N. (Ret.), was a tall, straight man. He opened the door, now, and stepped emphatically into his daughter's bedroom. He was in evening clothes, perfectly fitting, in all respects civilian. But one looked, subconsciously, unavoidably, for the strips of gold above the wrist. Vice Admiral Satterbee had lived a life in uniform. It was natural that civilian clothes, conscious of their lesser status, should try, on his tall, spare body, to look as much like uniform as possible.

Vice Admiral Satterbee regarded his daughter. She smiled at him.

"Pass inspection, sir?" she said.

He smiled, very sightly, not as one much used to smiling. But the smile softened his face.

"Very satisfactory," the admiral said. He nodded.

"Darling," Freddie said. "Is that the best you can do?"

"My dear," her father said, "you are a very fine looking girl. Very beautiful. As you know."

"The dress?" Freddie said. "The dress, Dad?"

He looked at the dress.

"Fits very well," he said. "Don't catch cold. Where's Marta?"

"Resting," Freddie said. "She's helping with the coats and things. I told her to rest. Why?"

"Not on station," the admiral said. "You coddle her, Freddie."

Freddie only laughed at that. The admiral accepted the subject as dismissed.

"Tie all right?" he said. He held his chin up a little higher; it was a chin which lived high.

The tie was perfect. Watkins was an artist with a bow. As Dad knows perfectly well, Freddie thought, as she always thought. But she went to the tall, erect man and reached up and pretended, but only pretended, so as not to mar perfection, to adjust the bow a little.

She stepped back and smiled up at the admiral, and he patted her arm lightly, gently.

"You're a good child, Winifred," he said. "You coddle everyone."

It was a special moment; because it was a special moment, he called her Winifred, which had been her mother's name. She did not say anything, but she put both her hands for a

13

moment on his arms. Almost at once, before the touch became a caress, she dropped her hands.

"By the way," he said. "Invited a young couple to drop in." He paused. "This publisher fellow," he said. "Going to bring out this book you know. North."

Freddie said, "Of course, Dad."

"Still think the other plan might have been better," the admiral said. He looked down at his daughter. "Ought to feed people," he said.

"Dad," Freddie said. "It's always awkward. It sounds fine, but it's always awkward. And I know I wouldn't like to be one of the late ones. You wouldn't either."

The admiral seemed to entertain momentarily, and to dismiss at once, a preposterous thought. Freddie watched her father's expression, and her smile did not show. The darling has never considered that, she thought; if some were to come to dinner, others to drop in later, the category of Vice Admiral Jonathan Satterbee was preordained. His was a confidence beyond conceit.

"Better this way, darling," she said. "Really better."

The admiral made a sound which was, as much as anything, "wumph."

Probably, Freddie Haven thought, he knows perfectly well that it isn't only the awkward-

14

ness. Aunt Flo and Uncle William, not yet "ret."; the commodore; Captain and Mrs. Hammond; Aunt (by courtesy) Angela; Mrs. Burton, the "Dowager Admiral," whose for some time lamented husband had, in the year before his retirement, achieved Cominch. All very cultivated and delightful, all very Navy, all very — well, call it familiar. Those would have made up the dinner party before the party to which the others, the lesser, the non-Navy, might be invited. And there, of course, Bruce Kirkhill would have presented a hostess's problem, as well as a fiancée's. Had there been a dinner, he could hardly not have been invited. (By her; the admiral's position would have been equivocal.) But Senator Kirkhill and the "Dowager Admiral" would, undoubtedly, have presented a problem. Mrs. Burton had little use for politicians.

"Better this way, Dad," Freddie repeated, and the admiral said "Wumph" again, but with moderated emphasis. He is a darling really, Freddie thought, and patted one of the arms which should have been to the elbow in gold braid.

"Suppose you've heard from Kirkhill?" the admiral said, changing the subject with authority.

"No," Freddie said. "He's coming on the Congressional; going to the Waldorf to change, coming on. It's all arranged."

The admiral said "Wumph" again and seemed about to continue. The hesitancy was untypical. Freddie said, "Yes, Dad?"

"Nothing," the admiral said. "I'm — I'm fond of you, Freddie. Know that, don't you? You know what you're doing?"

"Of course," Freddie said. "We've been over it, Dad."

"Well," the admiral said, "he's a politician, you know."

"Darling," Freddie said. "Please, Dad. We *have* been over it. Bruce is a senator — a United States senator."

The admiral said "Wumph," doubtfully.

"And," Freddie said, "you like him. You know you do."

The admiral briefly raised square shoulders.

"Nothing against him," he said. "As a man. Seems all right. Good war record." He smiled, with his lips only. "Set in my ways, Freddie," he said. "Probably there's nothing to it."

She was puzzled by that. She looked an enquiry. She thought, surprised, that her father had not meant to say the last — not out loud, not to her.

"Nothing to what?" she said. "What is it, Dad?"

The admiral said "eruh," as one word, which he did on those few occasions when he was

16

uncertain. He resumed command at once.

"Prejudice against politicians," he said, with finality. "What do you people say? An allergy." She said, "Oh."

"And I'm fond of you," he said. "Don't want you to make a mistake. Damn those monkeys."

She knew what he meant by that. Damn the "monkey," the hideously courageous, horribly skillful "monkey" who had crashed his plane against the bridge of a destroyer off Okinawa; against the bridge of Commander John Haven's destroyer.

"That was another day," Freddie said. "A fine day. It won't come back, Dad. There's no use."

She looked up at him.

"This isn't a mistake, Dad," she said.

The admiral said "Wumph" once more. He patted her bare shoulder. She thought, for a moment, that he was about to say something further; she had a feeling, not easy to explain, that he had more to say about Bruce, was hesitating to say it. But there was nothing tangible to indicate this, and when the admiral spoke again it was merely to ask her if she were coming down. She shook her head, said there were finishing touches.

"Can't see where," her father said, looking at her with approval. "I'll go down, then." He patted her shoulder once more. He was more demonstrative than usual, she thought; more

17

anxious that she should know his fondness for her. It was as if he were, secretly, uneasy about her. She watched him turn, go out the door, and felt her own previous uneasiness returning. She tired to shake it off, to persuade herself to accept the obvious. Fancied resemblance; fancied implication in a sentence; imagined note of concern in her father's voice. One led to the other; one heightened the other. If she had not imagined Bruce in a big man walking somewhere on the lower east side, glimpsed briefly, with a shabby overcoat open on a cold night, she would not have gone on imagining. "Probably there's nothing to it," her father had said, and seemed to hesitate when she asked an explanation, but then had given her an explanation entirely reasonable. There was nothing to any of it.

She returned to her dressing table and the finishing touches. For several minutes she was able to occupy her mind with them. But then the slight feeling of uneasiness, the ridiculous feeling of anxiety, came creeping back. She could not keep it from creeping back.

Well, she thought, if I'm going to be this way, I may as well call Bruce and — and know he's all right. He would, she thought, be at the Waldorf by now; he would not yet have left to come to the apartment.

She went across the room to her desk near

the bed and took up the telephone of her extension. Then she heard her father's voice, speaking on one of the other extensions, and instinctively started to replace the receiver.

" – as of tonight," she heard her father say. "Circumstances have changed. Send me your bill and – "

She had replaced the receiver by then. But she stood looking at it. "As of tonight." For no reason, no explicable reason, the words entered into, became part of, her anxiety. She lifted the receiver again.

A man's voice she did not think she had ever heard before was speaking.

" – to you," she heard the voice say. "What we've got begins to make it look like there was something to it. But it's up to you, Admiral. He's going to be your son – "

"That's all," her father cut in. "That's enough. I've told you what I want. I'll expect your bill."

"Sure," the other voice said. "Sure, Admiral. Whatever you say."

"Goodbye," the admiral said. She heard the click of his replaced receiver.

She put the telephone back in its cradle and stood for a moment without moving. She stood erect, as her father had taught her, her square shoulders high, her slim body motionless in the moulding golden dress. She looked at noth-

19

ing; saw nothing. She could feel a kind of tightening in her mind. Her mind seemed to be tightening, almost quivering, under repeated, inexplicable, tiny blows. It was as if something were flicking at her mind, something invisible were stinging it.

"Going to be you son – " Son-in-law, the man must have been going to say when her father, his voice firm with authority, sharp with impatience, cut him off. Bruce – it was, again something about Bruce. "Probably there's nothing to it," her father had said. That had been something about Bruce. The shambling man seen from the car window – but that could not have been Bruce Kirkhill.

Something was happening to the day, the last day of the year; something was happening to her, to the order of things, to tranquility. It had been a day like any other day, with the difference that it, more than most, had slanted upward toward the evening, toward the party and the drinking in of a New Year; toward the party which was, tacitly only, for her and Bruce. It was to be the first party for both of them, for them as a unit.

There had been the not arduous responsibilities of a hostess with an adequate staff, in an apartment more than adequate to any probable party. There had been lunch at the Colony with Celia, and Celia's young, happy excitement about almost everything, and Celia's admiring eyes. Remembering the way Celia looked at her, Freddie smiled faintly, her shapeless anxiety momentarily lessened. Anyway, it was going to be fine with Celia; Celia's admiration of this not too much older woman who was to be her step-mother was evident and undisguised. Celia might have been eight, instead of eighteen, when she looked at Freddie Haven. Sometimes it was almost embarrassing. No one, Freddie thought, and least of all I, can be what Celia thinks I am.

There had been the luncheon, which was pleasant, and the tea at Aunt Flo's, which was not unpleasant. Tea had meant sherry, with an alternative of scotch, and The Benefit had been rather thoroughly discussed, according to democratic procedures. (This meant that Aunt Flo, and the Dowager Admiral, had been duly authorized to do what they would have done anyway: take matters into their firm and capable hands. The meeting had, as was inevitable, been less that of a committee than of a staff. That it even so much as authorized was a pleasant, gently absurd, fiction.)

And then this slow disintegration of the day had set in; this uneasiness had begun. It was, Freddie thought, like one of those morning moments when you awakened, lay contentedly for a little time and then became conscious of a vague dissatisfaction, as if you were already in the shadow of some impending disappointment. Such things meant nothing. The feeling vanished when you remembered some tiny thing – you were committed to an engagement which promised badly; you had undertaken to do something which, now, you did not want to do. This anxiety was hardly sharper than that passing premonition of disappointment, but this, for all its shapelessness, had a center – Bruce. Bruce whom she could not have seen shabby on the lower East Side; Bruce about whom her father's half formed hint, half finished sentences, could mean nothing.

Freddie Haven took the telephone up, found the telephone number of the Waldorf-Astoria in her memory, and dialed. She asked for Senator Bruce Kirkhill and waited.

"Senator Kirkhill is not registered, modom," a young woman's voice said.

That was wrong; that was merely inefficiency. Freddie said as much, courteously, without emphasis. There was a mistake; Senator Kirkhill was unquestionably registered.

She was passed along. A man's voice was less detached. The man recognized the possibility of error. He went and, after a minute or two, returned. He was sorry; Senator Kirkhill was not registered. A suite was reserved for him, however. He was expected. A message for him would be happily accepted.

"No," Freddie said. "Thank you. Is there a Mr. Phipps? Howard Phipps?"

The assistant manager checked again. A Mr. Phipps there was. She was asked to wait. A young woman's voice said, "I'm ringing Mr. Phipps." There was the sound of ringing, continued over-long.

"I'm sorry, modom," the girl said. "Mr. Phipps's room does not answer. Would you wish – "

"Thanks," Freddie said. "Don't bother." She hung up.

What it all amounts to is that he took a later train, she assured herself. There's nothing strange about it. There can't be anything strange.

Her desk clock told her it was almost ten. "Tennish" would not mean ten o'clock to anyone, except possibly Aunt Flo. Still – She looked at herself in a long mirror, nodded, and went out of the room and down the stairs to the lower floor of the duplex. Marta and the new maid were in the foyer, sitting side by side on straight chairs. They stood up as Freddie came down and she grinned at them.

"Carry on," she said. "As you were."

Marta giggled without making a sound, her shoulders shaking slightly. The new maid looked politely puzzled.

"Yes'm," Marta said, and sat down. She pulled at the sleeve of the other maid. "Carry on," she said. She giggled again, soundlessly. "You're in the Navy now."

Freddie went on into the living room. Marta, she suspected, would tell the new maid that it was all right to joke with Mrs. Haven; that Admiral Satterbee was another matter. "The admiral don't notice lessen it's wrong," Freddie once had overheard Marta tell another new maid. It was true enough, Freddie had thought; it applied to the lower ranks, as well as to those who might be identified with the enlisted personnel.

She said good evening to Watkins, who was supervising a waitress, who was polishing already polished glasses. She went on into the kitchen and told cook that everything looked wonderful, and filched a shrimp from an iced plate of shrimps. "Now Miss Freddie," cook said. "Leaves an empty space." Freddie shuffled shrimps, filling in the space. Cook had been around a long time; she had been known to be stern, within reason, with the admiral himself. A buzzer sounded faintly.

"There's people, Miss Freddie," the cook said, and Freddie went out to meet people. She went rather quickly, and only when she heard Aunt Flo's voice did she realize that she had hoped the voice would be Bruce's. She greeted

24

Aunt Flo and Uncle William, not showing that she had wanted them to be Bruce Kirkhill. Tactfully, after the greeting, she enquired about the driver. Uncle William sometimes forgot. "The boy's all right," Uncle William assured her. "Told him he could take in a movie." He beamed at his niece by marriage. "You look fine, Freddie," he said. "How's Johnny Jump-up?"

It was always odd to hear her father called that. The theory was that they called him that in the Pacific: "Old Johnny Jump-up." There had been a time when Admiral Satterbee's task force had jumped apparently out of nowhere, disconcerting the Japanese. Freddie, with the best will in the world, had never been able to believe that her father was, widely, known by so irreverent a nickname. As Uncle William used it, she noticed that the term was invisibly bracketed by marks of quotation.

Admiral Satterbee came out of the library, greeted his wife's sister and Admiral William Fensley and, firmly, led everybody to Watkins and the scotch. With glasses filled, Admiral Satterbee drew Admiral Fensley out of the feminine and into the professional circle.

"This new flat-top, Bill," Freddie heard him say. "What d'y think?"

"Hell of a big target," Bill, a battleship man to the end, assured him. "Wait till — "

" – of course," Aunt Flo said, "there's always the question of the reviews. You remember, dear, when the League took over that play that looked so good before it opened, and then all those critics said – "

It was ten minutes before the buzzer sounded again and Freddie, still being invited to worry about the reviews of the play the League was planning to use as a benefit, brought back her wandering mind and – found she was listening again for, but again not hearing, the voice of Bruce Kirkhill.

They came with some rapidity, thereafter, since Navy people are habitually punctual and these were, for the most part, Navy people. They came, they took drinks; the Navy men tended to coagulate and were, by her as hostess, gently, not too obviously, redistributed. There was enough to do as the big living room filled slowly; there were enough small things to think about, details to keep an eye on. But now, as time passed, as tennish became elevenish, it was increasingly difficult to keep her mind on pleasant chat, to shape her lips into a welcoming smile, keep interest in her voice. Because, still, Bruce did not come.

It was a few minutes after eleven when a couple she did not know appeared at the door of the living room and paused there, with the slightly bewildered, rather anxiously amiable

26

expressions of people who know no one present and wait to be, as it were, adopted. That was, at any rate, the expression on the face of the man, who wore glasses and who, as he stood there, absently ran the fingers of his right hand through short hair already faintly pawed. The expression on the face of the slight, trim woman beside him was more difficult to analyze. She appeared to be, above everything else, interested in the room — in the people, in all of the scene — and to have a bright intensity in her interest, as if it were all new, freshly seen and to be taken in gulps. There was nothing appraising about the slight young woman's expression. She merely seemed pleased to see so many things, so many of them alive.

Half smiling. Freddie Haven turned from the group she was hostessing and began to move toward the couple which was waiting to be adopted. Then she realized her father, who was tall enough to see over most people, had seen over a good many, noticed the couple at the door, and was moving toward them. He moved with purpose, as he always moved; he caught his daughter's eyes and, with a movement of his head, asked her to join him. They converged on the couple at the door and the man of the couple began a smile of greeting.

" 'Evening, North," Admiral Satterbee said, in what was inevitably a voice of command,

27

while he was still a stride or two away. He held out his hand. "Glad y'could make it."

The man with the slightly ruffled hair took the admiral's hand, and Freddie, approaching, hoped he would have no cause to wince. The admiral's hand-shake was frequently firm; it was apt to be particularly so with people he did not know well. It was one of the small things which Freddie Haven knew, tenderly, about her father. He was firm with people he knew only a little. Because, Freddie thought, he had once — oh, long ago — been shy. You would never know it now.

Mr. North did not wince. He released his hand, made polite sounds, and said, just as Freddie reached them, "Pam, this is Admiral Satterbee. My wife, Admiral."

"How do you do?" Pam North said, in a clear, light voice, and almost as if she were really asking. "Sideboys."

The tallish man beside her grasped at his hair. He said, "Pam."

"All I could think of at first was sideboards," Pam North said. "But that didn't sound right. To pipe you aboard."

"Oh," Admiral Satterbee said. "Oh — yes. Yes, of course."

It did not seem entirely clear to her father, Freddie thought. She had joined them, by then.

"Mrs. North," the admiral said. "Present my daughter. Freddie, Mrs. North. Mr. North. Told you about them. North's going to bring out this book of mine."

"Miss Satterbee," Mr. North said and Mrs. North smiled and Freddie had an odd, vagrant sense of pleasure which was disproportionate to anything in the expression of this slight young woman with the attractively mobile face. But Freddie felt, without being able to explain why she felt so, that she had been approved of, frankly and with pleasure. Freddie felt that she must be looking even better than she had hoped. She also felt that, intangibly, she had been outdistanced.

She shook her head and said that Dad always forgot, never made little things clear. "Mrs. Haven," she said. She also said she was so glad the Norths could come, and asked if the Norths knew everybody. Mrs. North's eyes widened a little momentarily.

"Oh no," Mrs. North said. "Nobody, really." She paused, as if she had just heard herself. "Here, I mean," she said. "But it's all right, because we do have to go on almost at once."

Freddie said she hoped not; Admiral Satterbee said, "Nonsense, come and have a drink, North."

Mr. North went, obediently. Mrs. North

looked up at the taller, somewhat younger woman.

"You mustn't bother with us, you know," Pam North said. "We do have to go on. We're meeting some people. But Jerry said – "

Pam North stopped, then. Freddie Haven waited, suddenly grinned.

"Go on," she said, feeling that she had known this Mrs. North for much longer than minutes.

"Oh," Pam said, "that I ought to see a real admiral. That it probably would be educational." She spoke unhesitatingly, without any indication of embarrassment. "So few authors are admirals," she added, paused, and said: "Or so few used to be, now it's hard to tell. Like all the people who knew Roosevelt."

Again, for an instant, Freddie Haven felt outdistanced. It was, she thought, like trying to read a sentence in its entirety, not word by word. But even as she thought this, she realized she had caught up.

"Is it?" she said. "Educational?"

"Probably," Pam North said. "Was his hair once like yours?"

"Yes," Freddie said. "Satterbee hair."

"Look," Mrs. North said. "You must just park me somewhere, you know. It doesn't have to be another admiral or anything. Because you've got to hostess, of course."

It was undeniable; Freddie Haven admitted it

30

with a smile, without words. She decided that this Mrs. North probably would enjoy, would really enjoy, the Dowager Admiral. She thought, indeed, that Mrs. North probably would enjoy most things. She took Mrs. North to the Dowager Admiral's group, was pleased to see the slight widening of Mrs. North's eyes and, as she slipped out of the group after a polite moment, realized that she had not, for some minutes, worried about anything. She realized this when the shadow of disappointment returned, for a fraction of a second merely as that, then as more tangible anxiety.

It was well after eleven and Bruce Kirkhill had not come. Now her mind sought little explanations to cling to – he had taken a later train, and the train was late; he had come earlier for a meeting of some sort, and could not get out of it. Not good enough, her mind answered. Not nearly good enough. He would have telephoned. Tonight he would have telephoned, of all nights, because this was their party, because –

She heard a voice she recognized in the foyer, went from the group she was in almost without apology and crossed the room.

"Howdie!" she said. "Howdie! Has something happened?"

The man she spoke to was no taller than she. He was square faced; he had wide-spaced eyes

31

and an expression of candor. Now he looked at Freddie Haven, smiled at her, shook his head and raised trim eyebrows.

"Happened?" he said. "What do you mean, Freddie?"

His voice was low and musical; it seemed, perhaps almost too large for the man. But Freddie Haven, used to it, and to him, did not remember she once had thought that.

"Bruce isn't here," she said. "He isn't at the hotel."

The open face opposite her own was momentarily shadowed, as if by perplexity. The shadow vanished quickly.

"A slip-up," he told her. "Of course he's at the hotel. I —" He broke off.

"Did you see him there?" Freddie said.

The man shook his head, slowly.

"Actually," he said, "I didn't see him. I got in this morning, you know. I checked on the reservations and checked in myself. I didn't get back to the Waldorf until after ten and just changed and came on, figuring he'd be here already."

"I'm worried," Freddie said. "It isn't like him. He hasn't called."

"My dear," the man said. "Nothing happens to the chief. He could have been tied up in Washington, so far as that goes."

"And not have wired? Or telephoned?"

"Well —" he said. "Anyway, nothing's happened to him." He smiled, widely, "The chief can take care of himself," he said. "You ought to know that, Freddie."

She said, "Of course," but the worry was still in her voice. It was still in her mind.

"I'll check the hotel," he said. He smiled again, making little of it. "Maybe he dozed off," he said.

Freddie Haven took him to the telephone in the library; stood beside him as he dialed the hotel, asked to speak to Senator Bruce Kirkhill.

He listened and said, "Nonsense."

"Of course he's registered," he said. "Let me talk to the manager. This is the senator's secretary, Howard Phipps. It's important."

Phipps turned to smile at Freddie Haven. "Pull rank on 'em," he said. "If — yes? Oh —"

He talked quickly, with authority, then with an increasing puzzlement in his voice. Finally he said: "Ask him to call me at" and looked at the number on the telephone and repeated it. "Vice Admiral Satterbee's apartment," he added. He hung up. For a moment his face was shadowed again; then he became, in an instant, very cheerful.

"Not there," he said. "Hasn't checked in. But don't worry. Nothing happens to the chief. Hell — probably he's out there now, looking for you." Howard Phipps jerked his head toward

33

the living room. "Come on," he said. "Probably he thinks you've stood *him* up."

But Bruce Kirkhill was not in the living room. It was almost eleven-thirty, the year was running out; for Freddie, the party was running out. But the party was still there; it was still her party. She went on about the party, smiling, being a hostess. Her lips tired, forming the smile. Her voice tired, saying nothing gaily; her mind tired, straining for a familiar voice from the foyer. Not many were coming, now.

"I *am* sorry," Mrs. North was saying. "It's a lovely party, but we do have to —" Mrs. North's voice stopped. It started again. "You're worried, Mrs. Haven," Pam North said. "Aren't you? Something's happened?"

"I —" Freddie began, and almost went on, because there was so much reality, so much friendliness, in Mrs. North's question. But then she only smiled and shook her head.

"I'm sorry," Pam North said. "Of course it isn't. Jerry says I —" Then, in turn, she stopped, and smiled and shook her head.

"It's a lovely party," Mrs. North said after that. "We hate to leave, but I'm afraid —" She left the sentence unfinished and smiled again. Mr. North was beside them, and the admiral. The admiral looked at Freddie, quickly, worry on his face. She shook her head at him. She

34

said, to Mr. and Mrs. North, the things a hostess says, and found, suddenly, that she meant them. She did not want this friendly slim woman, who so outdistanced you if you went from word to word, whose interest was so oddly bright and undisguised, to leave the party. But she walked with the Norths to the foyer and watched them go. The old year had less than half an hour left for its running out.

II

Friday, 11:35 P.M.
to Saturday, 2:10 A.M.

Freddie turned back toward the living room, and Celia was waiting for her. Freddie changed her expression when she saw Celia's face, wiping the look of worry from her own. Celia was slender and very young, her blond hair hung rather long, almost to her shoulders. She had blue eyes which now sought reassurance.

"You're worried about Dad," Celia said. "Where is he, Freddie?"

"Held up somewhere," Freddie said, making her voice light, casual. "Seeing a politician about another politician."

"Somewhere," Celia repeated. "You don't know, then? You haven't heard anything?"

"He's all right, Ce," Freddie said. "Nothing happens to the chief."

"Howdie said that to you," Celia told her. "But I know Dad planned to be here. Early if

36

anything. I'm worried, Freddie. But Curt says —"

"It's nothing," Freddie said, too quickly. "Of course it's nothing, dear. Whatever Curt said is right. Howdie's right."

"He'd telephone," Celia Kirkhill said. "Dad always — always remembers. Doesn't he?"

"Not —" Freddie began, and realized that would be wrong. "Usually," she said. "But he's all right, Ce." She made herself laugh. "After all," she said, "we've got to let him be late now and then, Ce. We can't —" She raised her square white shoulders, let them fall, let them finish the sentence.

"Curt," Freddie said then, glad of the chance, to a tall young man who came to stand beside Celia Kirkhill, to whom, as Freddie spoke, Celia turned instinctively, her face lighting. "You haven't got a drink! I'll get Watkins."

She looked for Watkins, saw a maid with a tray of champagne glasses. It was almost time, then. Her head summoned the maid. "What time is it, Curt?" she said.

"Tu-twenty minutes of," Curtis Grainger said. He was tall and thin, his hair, blond as Celia's, was short, upstanding on his long head. "Almost t-time."

It was not exactly a stutter; it was a kind of hesitating, uneasily, on the brink of a word. Once, she supposed, Curtis Grainger must have stammered rather badly. He had grown stern with himself. The sternness was evident on his young face when the face was quiet. It vanished when he looked at Celia.

"Y-your father's going to miss the year," he said, and his smile was the youngest thing about him as he looked down at Celia Kirkhill, reached out to put an arm around her shoulders. He looked over her head at Freddie Haven. "The baby's worried," he told her. (He said, "The bu-baby's wh-worried." After he had hesitated on the brink of a word he said it rapidly, clipping it.)

Freddie said she knew. She said it wasn't anything.

"Of course not," Curtis Grainger said. "I've been telling Ce. As my father says, the senator's indestructible." He grinned, disarmingly. "My father ornaments it," he said.

"I'll bet," Freddie said.

The buzzer had sounded in the foyer. She was conscious she was listening; that she had frozen in listening. She heard one of the maids move to the door, heard the door open, her ears straining.

"Good evening, miss," Freddie heard Marta say, and heard a voice she knew, speaking quickly, accenting the words. "*So* late," the voice said. "Has *every*body —?"

Breese Burnley came into the living room

quickly. She wore a white dress, her shoulders bare, a thin, flat circle of diamonds about her lovely throat. As always, now in spite of her disappointment, Freddie Haven was conscious of surprise when she looked at Breese. It was difficult to grow accustomed to such perfection – such perfect perfection. Surely, coming out of a snowstorm, one strand of all the black, artfully arranged hair, would be at odds with art; surely one of the long eyelashes over deep blue would have lost its curl.

"Darlings!" Breese said. "I'm *so* late. *So* sorry."

Breese Burnley looked at Freddie with a perfect smile, at Celia, at Curtis Grainger. Then, almost without hesitating, only slowing a little as for a grade crossing, she looked on beyond them, her smile still perfect, still ready. It was sometimes difficult to speak to Breese Burnley, so rapidly did she pass you, go on to the person beyond.

"Hello, Breese," Freddie Haven said, feeling that she was calling the words after Breese, although Breese herself had not moved. Celia said, "Hello," and there was little expression in her young voice. Curtis Grainger said, "Hello, Bee-Bee," making himself utter the difficult nickname, the obvious nickname, without trace of stammer. He wants, Freddie thought, to give her no hold on him, not even the hold of this tiny weakness, this meaningless vocal uncertainty.

"*So* late, darlings," Breese said again, looking beyond them, still smiling at them. "And I *did* hurry."

"Still time for a drink, darling," Freddie promised her. "I'll —"

"Darling," Breese said. "As if you didn't have *enough!* I do it myseps." It was a catch word of hers, "myseps." It stemmed from baby-hood. "Breese will do it herseps," Fay Burnley said of her daughter, admiringly. Credit where it was due, Freddie had thought. Breese did it herseps, all right. ("B-B indeed," Bruce had said of Breese. "A five-inch shell")

Now Breese, patting Curt's arm in passing, patting it with almost no trace of lingering, went on — went on, slim and perfect, infinitely provocative to the male, very beautiful, very certain because of her beauty. The three of them watched her go. There was a faint smile on Freddie Haven's lips. "Our only Bee-Bee," Curt said, not bothering, now, to enunciate with precision the difficult nickname.

The smile was insecure on Freddie's lips. It faded away. She was conscious that Celia was looking at her again. The girl's eyes were demanding something.

"You're worried, Freddie," Celia said. "You're worried too."

It was a statement, yet it demanded answer.

40

The girl's eyes demanded honesty.

"Yes," Freddie said. There was nothing to add to it.

They could not stand there, so near the door from the foyer, so detached from the others. Freddie put an arm around Celia's shoulders, drew her toward the party. Everyone seemed very contented, very full of conversation. Voices were lifted a little, to be heard over other lifted voices. Uncle William's aide had found a pretty girl, and was looking beyond her toward Breese Burnley. Breese had found champagne. She had also, Freddie noticed, found Howard Phipps. She was talking to him and, so far as Freddie could tell, from a little distance, listening to what Phipps said in return. They must be talking about Breese, Freddie thought, and made a tiny mewing sound at herself for thinking it. Miaow, Freddie thought, without uttering the sound.

"Bruce!" she thought then, smiling at people, walking toward her father with her almost full glass held carefully. She thought the name with a kind of explosive force, as if she could make Bruce hear by thinking his name hard. "Bruce! Where are you?" Almost, she found, she listened for an answer.

Her father was talking to Uncle William, rank appropriately meeting rank, and she heard the words "damned Reds" and then Vice Admiral

Satterbee interrupted himself and turned away from William Fensley. (Who was, after all, only a rear admiral, even if not yet "ret.")

"Haven't seen Kirkhill," Admiral Satterbee told his daughter. The accusation in his voice was, she was sure, only a token of concern. Her face must show her anxiety, then.

"Stood me up," she said, keeping it light. "May I toast the year with you, Dad?"

Her father said, "Wumph." He sounded angry.

"No excuse," he told her. "No excuse I can see. Where is he?"

"Please, Dad," Freddie said. "He's tied up somewhere."

"No business being," her father said. "Supposed to be here, isn't he?" He drew his brows down. "Unless —" he said, and stopped, thinking better of it. He looked at his daughter's face.

"Sorry, Freddie," he said. "Don't worry."

"It's all right, Dad," she said.

"You'd have heard," he said, meaning, clearly enough, that she would have heard if something had happened to Bruce. It didn't follow, she thought; it was not sufficiently consoling. But she managed to smile and nod. Then she remembered.

"You started to say something," she told her father. "You said 'unless,' and stopped. And you

42

were —" She had started to go on, to ask whether he had been talking about Bruce on the telephone to a man whose voice she had never heard, which was not a voice, in texture, in rhythm, like those of the people in the room. But this was not the time for that. Watkins was standing by a window, looking at his watch, ready to open the window, to let, as it would seem, the New Year in, to let the roar of the city carry it in.

"Nothing," her father said. "If — perhaps later, Winifred. It's almost time."

He took out his watch to prove it. He showed her the watch. Its faint tick was a rattle in the throat of the dying year. What a thing to think! What a *way* to think!

Then the roar started. The whistles started, the bells, the indescribable sound, underlying all identifiable sounds, which was the sound of people. Someone shouted on the street below; someone, farther away, fired a gun — an automatic, she thought — rapidly. In the room there was a kind of quiver in the air, a sudden stirring.

Her father, facing her, was raising his glass and she raised hers, to touch it. The tiny sound of touching glasses was momentarily, clearer than any other sound.

"Happy New Year, Winifred," her father said.

"Happy New Year," she said. "Happy New Year, Dad."

Her voice did not falter; she did not let it falter. They drank as the bells sounded, as sirens mourned the old year in metal-throated lament, as the tiny sound of clinking glass was repeated.

They drained their glasses, father and daughter, oddly alike in square shoulders, the way they stood, the way they moved, carrying on a custom which meant nothing. ("A toast's to be drunk, Freddie," her father had said, long ago, perhaps when first they had drunk together, as two Satterbees, her mother dead. "If you mean it, drink it." She had never known where her father acquired this rule, or whether he invented it.) Now her glass was empty when she lowered it from her lips.

Her father leaned down and kissed her, then. He kissed her lightly, on the cheek, and patted her bare shoulder.

The next hour or so meant nothing, could not afterwards be remembered. She became a hostess again, keeping the party alive after its climax; seeing that champagne was passed unhurriedly, without interruption. ("Never rush people," her father's rule was. "Never leave them with empty glasses.") She seemed to remember, afterward, that Breese Burnley and Howard Phipps were together a good deal of the time; that they had been together at midnight, drunk the New Year in together. She knew that Celia Kirkhill and Curtis Grainger were always together; she remembered how often, being near them, she had seen Celia's face turned toward hers, with a question in it; how often she had shaken her head. But, oddly, the tension of her own waiting had lessened after midnight. Apparently she had set that hour as an arbitrary one, the hour by which Bruce Kirkhill must appear. As the night had built toward that hour, her tension had built. But when the hour had passed, when nothing had happened, the unreasoning quality had gone out of her anxiety. She was still worried, but now she felt more than worry, a kind of emptiness. It was as if she had been defrauded; as if she had reached out for something and, where this thing, this wanted thing, should have been there was merely nothing. With emptiness not showing in her face, she moved from group to group; she went with Uncle William and Aunt Flo to the door, when they left half an hour after midnight; she had, with a fleeting expression, let Uncle William's aide know she sympathized as he went along, dutifully, to see that the car was there, the blue-jacket who drove it on hand and competent. (The aide came back, after about five minutes, looking very pleased. He rediscovered the girl he had discovered on arrival. They continued to drink to the New Year.)

The party dwindled, eroding away. It reformed as it dwindled; a halved group joined a group similarly depleted; the revived unit, again diminished, merged with another. Soon there would be only a single group, large at first, then growing smaller. Soon there was. A dozen people remained. Celia, who was staying at the apartment instead of returning to her hotel; Curtis Grainger, who remained very close to Celia, who looked at her so often, with protective concern; Breese Burnley and her mother, Fay; Phipps, who now, as the group shrank, left Breese to her mother and turned to Freddie herself; a scattering who did not wish the party to end as yet. Uncle William's aide was one of the scattering, and the girl he had found. (The girl was the daughter of Captain Arrhhhh, on duty in BuPers in Washington, or of Commander Arummmm, assigned to the Third Naval District.)

The scattering diminished. Uncle William's aide, who was handsome, suave, very savvy, took the girl away, after casting one last, quick glance at the perfection of Breese Burnley. A civilian who had been in the Navy once, but only as a reserve, went suddenly, perhaps having had almost too much champagne. The dozen became nine; the nine became only what you might call "themselves." "Now we're by ourselves," Freddie thought, instinctively, and then, momentarily, wondered why she so united them. The answer was instant. They were all people about Bruce Kirkhill. He was their center.

They would not have made a group, save for Bruce Kirkhill, to whom all of them were something. It could be made to resemble a Shakespearian cast, she thought. Senator Bruce Kirkhill. Celia, daughter to the senator; Winifred Haven, called Freddie, fiancée to the senator; Vice Admiral Jonathan Satterbee, father to the senator's fiancée. (She had them out of order; women last in the Shakespearian cast.) Mrs. Fay Burnley, housekeeper to Senator Kirkhill, cousin to the senator's first wife, mother to Breese; Breese Burnley, photographers' model, daughter to the senator's housekeeper and – Freddie stopped herself. If there had once been a closer tie between Breese, "Bee-Bee," and the senator, it did not any longer matter. What Bruce had done before they met, what, at any rate, he had done in that particular quarter was of no concern to her. They were not children, rushing inexperienced into each other's unskillful arms. Breese Burnley, then, daughter to the senator's housekeeper. Howard Phipps, secretary to the senator. Curtis Grainger, in love with the senator's daughter.

The last, Freddie thought, her hostessing done, piling up thoughts to fill emptiness, is inadequate. Curtis Grainger, in love with the senator's daughter; also son of Julian Grainger, utilities man ("big" utilities man), who made no secret of the fact that he thought Senator Bruce Kirkhill a menace to the American system, to free enterprise, basically to democracy itself. (The free enterprise in question was very worried about a flood-control power production development which might, if not stopped somehow, become the most dreadful thing, "another T.V.A." Senator Kirkhill, dangerous man that he wa, vociferously did not share Mr. Grainger's view. In the Senate he was the leading, and most efficient, advocate of this new "socialistic" development.) Curtis represented his father in New York; he did not, it appeared, share his father's views. At least, ideology formed no barrier between Curt Grainger and the senator's daughter.

They sat there, these people who, in this one aspect of their lives, were linked together, and waited. They were members of a cast waiting for the star; they were the people about Hamlet, with Hamlet missing. They drank very little; they said very little. They were, Freddie thought, waiting for the door buzzer. The maids had been sent to bed; Watkins, a little gray, waited, standing. "Go to bed, Watkins," the admiral said. "Thank you, sir," Watkins said, and went.

"But where *is* he?" Fay Burnley said, her voice aggrieved, as if the others were keeping something from her; as if all of them knew but she.

Fay Burnley spoke a little as her daughter spoke, with words heavily emphasized, darting at words. She had not always done that, Freddie thought. She had picked it up from her daughter, probably. She had decided that that was the way people spoke, the way the best people, the most knowledgeable people, spoke. She was in several respects a little like her daughter, only not so perfect, not capable, as Breese was when she chose, of posed quiet. One felt of Mrs. Burnley that she was, always, trying not to flutter.

She was in her forties. She had been Bruce Kirkhill's housekeeper — so was hostess better? — for a good many years. Ever since her husband died, Bruce told Freddie once. Her husband had been, long ago, Bruce Kirkhill's closest friend. And Fay was a cousin of Bruce's first wife. "It seemed like a good idea," Bruce had told Freddie. "On the whole, I guess it was. Of course, Bee-Bee was a little thing then. So high." Freddie could remember Bruce showing how high.

"Where *is* he?" Mrs. Burnley repeated, with

emphasis. Long earrings swayed; blue eyes — so like her daughter's, yet so unlike — were almost violently alive, almost improbably bright.

"We don't know, darling," Breese said. She was relaxed, leaning back in a deep chair, each line of her perfect body ready for the camera. (Miaow, Freddie thought. Miaow, Winifred Haven.) "Really we don't know."

"He's all right, Mrs. Burnley," Howard Phipps said. "Nothing happens to the chief. Something's held him up is all. Something's come up."

"You don't *know*," Mrs. Burnley told him. Her voice was suddenly sharp. It was intended, Freddie thought, to put Howard Phipps in his place, whatever his place was. Phipps shrugged; he shrugged for the benefit of the others, at this unreasonable attack.

Then, very suddenly, Celia began to cry. She did not cry loudly, she did not cry for others to notice. She had a small face, and it crumpled suddenly. Although she was not crying for others to notice, they all noticed her.

"Celia. *Darling*," Fay Burnley said. "Of *course* he's all right."

"Phipps," the admiral said. "Call the Waldorf again. Perhaps he's there."

Phipps took the order. He went to the library and left the door open behind him. They could

50

hear his voice and they listened; they all looked at the open door and listened. The words were not distinct, but the tone was enough.

"Never mind," he said. "I may call later. Hold the rooms."

Phipps came back, shaking his head. His face, darkened by a heavy beard which the closest shaving could not wholly eradicate, was serious.

"Hasn't checked in yet," he said. The "yet" was the saving word; the "yet" was supposed to make it casual, to imply, somehow, that the delay was small, calculable. Not yet; in five minutes or so, in half an hour, the word said.

"Wumph!" Admiral Satterbee said. "Where *is* the man?"

Nobody answered; nobody had an answer. The admiral looked at this daughter, looked at her with concern, searchingly.

"I'm all right, Dad," she said.

Celia was crying again. Curtis Grainger put an arm about her, held her close. He looked at the others, his glance insistent, demanding.

"We've got to d-do something," he said. "T-try to find him."

"Darling," Breese Burnley said. "How?"

Admiral Satterbee did not, Freddie knew, much approve of Bee-Bee. But now he nodded.

"Quite," he said. "What, Grainger?"

51

He waited, gave Curtis Grainger an opportunity.

"Can't go to the police," the admiral said, when Curt made no use of the opportunity. "Man's a senator. Get in the papers." He spoke of the word "papers" with a peculiar inflection, as if the word soiled his tongue. "No idea about security. No idea at all. Mix us all up in it."

"The pu-police wouldn't −" Grainger began but the admiral cut him short by saying, "Nonsense!"

"Civilians," he said. "Politicians."

It seemed to be stalemate.

"We can't just *wait*," Mrs. Burnley told them, with indignation. "Just *sit* here."

The admiral looked at her without favor. He appeared to consider the look enough.

"Darlings," Breese Burnley said. Her tone seemed to reflect calm, almost amusement. "Darlings. Bruce is a couple of hours late and everybody's in a dither. In a tail-spin. Beginning to talk of going to the police. Really, darlings. Can't a man be a little late? Even the great man?" She looked at Howard Phipps. "Even the chief?" she said.

There was nothing in her voice, nothing beyond inflections carefully cultivated, nothing but a careful avoidance of implication. But the admiral glared at her.

"If −" he began.

52

"No, Dad," Freddie said. "It's all right."

"Not all right," the admiral told them all. "Party *for* him. Him and Freddie. No man's going to report late, unless —"

He stopped.

"Unless what, Dad?" Freddie said. "I think you're right. I'm afraid you're — unless what?"

"I don't know," the admiral said. "Something urgent. Perhaps he's in some tight spot. See what I mean?"

"No," Howard Phipps said. He seemed indignant "I don't see what you mean, Admiral. The chief's in no spot."

The admiral merely looked at Howard Phipps. His glance was measuring. But when he spoke, his voice was, for him, mild.

"Just suggested it," he said. "I don't know anything, Phipps."

"Dad," Freddie said. "You're sure you don't? Don't — think you know something?"

"Wumph," the admiral said. He looked at her, looked away. "Said I didn't," he told her. The words had finality. But, Freddie thought, the words did not express truth; the words reiterated a lie. The admiral did think he knew something, did think that Bruce was not with them because he was in some "tight spot."

Now wasn't the time; the admiral was not to be driven, even by his daughter. Not now, not with these others, could she bring up, demand explanation of, the telephone call she had overheard. Now she could do nothing. Now none of them could do anything, except wait. Even Curtis Grainger tacitly admitted that by silence. He held Celia close to him, his head bent over hers. She still was crying.

Then the door buzzer sounded; sounded once, briefly.

All of them turned toward the door leading to the foyer. Celia raised her head and looked toward the door; Phipps turned in his chair; Fay Burnley, whose back had been toward the door, twisted full round. Their faces, all their faces, for an instant were blank, fixed held a kind of meaningless surprise and expectancy. It was as if they had been caught so, unready, by a photographer's flash bulb.

Then Freddie was on her feet, moving quickly, leaving the others. They focussed their eyes, then; they watched her, watched a slender young woman in a golden dress, walking with her shoulders high, her body erect.

It will be Bruce, Freddie Haven thought. Bruce has come. After all, he's come. It wasn't anything. But even as she thought this, she felt anxiety mounting again, becoming fear.

She was at the door, she reached for the knob. She made herself reach for the knob. She made herself turn the knob, pull the door toward her.

It was not Bruce Kirkhill. She had, and now she realized this, known it would not be Bruce. He rang in a quick sequence – buzz – buzz – buzz. Not like this; not once, briefly.

The man was tall, dark, in a dark gray overcoat. He took off a gray slouch hat. His face was thin and sensitive, now it was grave.

"Is Miss Kirkhill here?" he said. "Miss Celia Kirkhill?"

She did not say anything. She could not say anything.

"I'm from the police," the man said. He said it hesitantly, unhappily. "I'm a detective sergeant." He looked at Freddie Haven. His eyes were dark and, now, troubled. "Detective Sergeant Blake," he said. "You're not Miss Kirkhill?"

Wordless, Freddie shook her head. Then she managed to speak.

"She's here," she said. "Come in. It's – it's about – her father?"

"I hope not," Sergeant Blake said. "I hope not, Miss –"

"Haven" Freddie said. "Mrs. Haven. Celia's here, Sergeant." Then, again, she said, "Come in, please."

Sergeant Blake came in. He dropped his hat on a chair. He did not remove his overcoat. It was damp, Freddie noticed. It was still snowing, then. The thought was meaningless, out of place.

She went ahead of Sergeant Blake into the living room. Celia was already on her feet. Her hands were clenched; a handkerchief was clenched in one of them. Curtis Grainger was rising, to stand beside her. But he did not touch her. He let her stand alone, facing the tall, dark man in the damp overcoat, the man who looked at them with a troubled face.

"Miss Kirkhill," he said to Celia. "You are Miss Kirkhill? Senator Kirkhill's daughter?"

The girl nodded. She nodded quickly, so that he would go on quickly.

"There's been an − accident," he said. "I've ben sent to ask you −"

"Father!" the girl said. "An accident to Father?"

"We don't know," Sergeant Blake said. His voice was gentle. He was, Freddie thought − thought through a swirling of thoughts, in a kind of blackness through which thoughts swirled − trying to be reassuring. "That's why I've been sent. We'll have to ask you to − to look at −" He stopped.

"He's dead!" Celia said. *"Dad's dead!"*

Blake shook his head, quickly.

"We hope not," he said. "That is, a man's dead. It may not be − not be your father, Miss

Kirkhill. We hope —"

Now it was blackness which was swirling; swirling, narrowing, hemming Freddie in.

"Winifred," a voice said, beyond the blackness. "Winifred!" It was her father's voice. She reached out for it with her mind, reached for its solidity in this swirling blackness. With a terrible effort, she forced the blackness back. She could see them again, see her father, moving toward her; see Blake turning his head toward her. It had been only seconds, then; only seconds of fighting the blackness.

"I'm all right, Father," she heard her voice saying. "All right."

It was Celia who fainted. Curtis Grainger caught her, held her in arms, found a sofa to lay her on.

Blake looked at Freddie. There was concern in his expressive face. There was also puzzlement.

"I am going to marry Senator Kirkhill, Sergeant," she said. She made her voice steady. She was conscious, as she spoke, how carefully — with what desperate care — she had chosen the tense. "I am —" But it was not true.

"Probably this man isn't the senator," Sergeant Blake said. "You understand that, Mrs. Haven? You must —"

"Hope that," Freddie said. "Yes, Sergeant."

Fay Burnley was bending over Celia, keeping

the girl's head down, rubbing her wrists, talking to her.

"It isn't your father, honey," she said. "Of *course* it isn't. Of *course* it isn't Bruce."

"The girl can't go, Sergeant," the admiral said. He spoke with finality, with command. "You see that."

But Sergeant Blake shook his head.

"I'm sorry," he said. "Sooner or later, I'm afraid, she'll have to, you know. If it should be the senator — well, she's next of kin."

"Not now," the admiral said. "We all knew Kirkhill. We'd all — know. I'll go myself."

Sergeant Blake hesitated. He looked at the girl, motionless on the sofa. He reached a decision.

"Very well," he said. "The other can come later. If it's necessary." He looked at the admiral. "You would be sure?" he asked.

"I'll go," Freddie said. Her father looked at her. "Yes, Dad," she said. "I — I can't just sit here. Just — wait. You and I, we'll go." She tried to smile. "Please, Dad."

The admiral looked at her a moment without speaking. Then, abruptly, he nodded.

"You and I," he said. He turned to the sergeant. "You have a car?" he asked.

Sergeant Blake nodded.

"Then," Freddie said. "Now?"

Sergeant Blake nodded again. He said, "Please."

It was going too quickly, Freddie thought. It was ending too quickly. It took too little time to get a coat, too little time down in the elevator, too little time in the car to the police mortuary. There was a wait, then, in an anteroom, and now, strangely, the waiting was too long, although in fact it was brief. Sergeant Blake had left them; then he returned. He held open a door.

A man in white pulled back a sheet which had covered a face.

The blackness swirled in again, she fought it back, fought out of it. She heard her voice.

"Yes," Freddie Haven said. "Yes. It is Senator Kirkhill."

She felt her father's arm around her shoulders. But the blackness was going away. She was not going to faint. It was merely a kind of numbness. It was as if this were happening, had to be happening, to somebody else.

III

Saturday, 3:25 A.M. to 5:05 A.M.

There was really nothing difficult about inserting a key into a keyhole. You held the key very firmly, approached the keyhole slowly, deliberately, with confidence, and the key went in. That was all there was to it; you did it dozens of times a day. Well, you did it several times a day. It was, Jerry North decided, probably the basic operation of civilization. Civilization was distinguished from non-civilization by keyholes and keys to put into them; a man's place in the world was assured, or at least not hopelessly precarious, so long as he had a ring of keys in his pocket and those keys, or a majority of them, fitted keyholes to which he had unchallenged access. If you were in a very assured position, you had a great many keys; probably if you were of the mighty, you had so many that a servant carried your keys for you. But the key to your own front door was the basic key, and all you had to do was hold it very firmly in your right hand, move it toward the keyhole with assurance, twist it to the right, so –

"Jerry," Pam said. She was leaning against the corridor wall, waiting. She had seemed to be fast asleep. "Jerry," Pam said, "why don't you open the door? I want to go to bed."

"What," Jerry North said, with gravity, with precision, "do you think I am doing, Pamela?"

"Chinking," Pam said. "Clinking. Making funny noises. Why don't you use the front door key?"

"I –" Jerry began, haughtily. Then he looked. "Naturally I'm using the front door key," he said. It was true now, at any rate. He had, perhaps, while thinking about civilization, momentarily tried to unlock the apartment door with the key to his office desk, but now he was using the proper key. Pam had no business –

"You," Jerry told Pamela, "are sound asleep."

"I certainly am," Pam said. "I can go to sleep right here. Leaning against the wall, waiting for you –"

Jerry put the key to the apartment door lock into the keyhole of the apartment door lock. The trouble with civilization, he thought, was that it gave you too many keys; it imposed the strain of remembering which key entered which keyhole. All over the world, he thought, as he turned the key (so, to the right) men are suffering nervous breakdowns because they have too many keys, too many keyholes, minds too limited to cope with variation so multiplied. He was, he realized, on the verge of a thought of profundity; just beyond the fingertips of his mind was, in all probability, Solution. He would have to tell Pam –

He pushed the door and it opened. Three cats sat in a semicircle regarding the Norths. Pam North moved to Jerry and he put an arm around her.

"Carry me over the threshold," Pam said, sleepily. "Start the New Year –"

Jerry lifted her in his arms. The cats looked at them in astonishment. Sherry, the blue-point, a creature of almost over-acute sensibility, bristled, cried in fright, and plunged under the sofa. Gin, sparked by Sherry's excitement, growled questioningly, but stood her ground. Only Martini, their mother, wiser in the way of these troublesome charges of hers, sat unmoving, her enormous round eyes fixed, her whiskers slightly curled.

Jerry kissed his wife, not casually, tightened his arms around her and then put her down.

"You know," he said, "standing out there – there's something wrong with that lock, incidentally – I almost had something –" He

62

nodded to her. "Almost had it," he said. "Now it's gone."

"Jerry," Pam said. "Tomorrow? I want to go to bed."

"It was about civilization," Jerry said. "And – I don't know. Keys and keyholes. Like the rats, you know? The ones that jumped at little doors and finally got confused and –"

"Listen, darling," Pam said. "I'm terribly tired of those rats. All my life I've heard about those rats, jumping at doors." She paused. "All my life," she said, "I've wanted to go to bed. And you want to talk about rats."

Jerry North ran the fingers of his right hand through his hair. He said, "Oh."

"All your life," he said, "you've wanted – what did you say?"

"I want to go to bed," Pam said, and then stopped and looked at Martini, who had rolled over on her back, with her feet in the air, and was looking at them between her forelegs. "Wants to have her belly rubbed," Pam said. She sat down on the floor and began to caress Martini. "Is the major cat," Pam said. "Is the cat major. Is –"

Then the telephone rang. It rang with horrible loudness, with a kind of anger. Martini swirled from under Pam's hand, rolled to her feet, dashed into the hall, from whence the ringing came, and looked up at the box which held the doorbell.

"Confused," Pam said. "It's the telephone, Martini. It's – Jerry, it's the *telephone!*"

Jerry had the telephone in his hand. He said "Yes?" to it.

But the telephone continued to ring.

"Jerry," Pam said. "The other telephone. The house telephone. Who on earth?"

Pam North was on her feet. She was almost as quick as Martini had been. She was in the hall, at the house telephone on the wall. She said, "Yes?"

"Mrs. North?" a woman said. Her voice was young, now it was hurried, strained.

"Yes," Pam said.

"This is Winifred Haven," the woman in the lobby downstairs said, the words hurried. "May I come up?"

"Why," Pam said. "Of – of course, Mrs. Haven." But it was hard to take the request as a matter of course; hard to keep surprise out of her voice.

"I know," Freddie Haven said, answering the tone. "It's – it's impossible. But –" She seemed about to go on, to change her mind. "I'll come up, then," she said.

Pam turned back to the living room. Jerry was still holding, still looking at the wrong telephone. His look was reproachful.

"Simplification," he said, in a grave, distant

voice. He returned the wrong telephone to its receiver. "Too many everything. Keys. Telephones —"

"Jerry!" Pam said. "Mrs. Haven's coming up. Your admiral's daughter."

Gerald North came wide awake at once. He looked at his watch. He said, "What the hell?"

"I don't know," Pam said. "She's excited. Something's happened."

"At twenty-five minutes to four," Jerry North said. "In the *morning*."

They heard the elevator stop at their floor. The sound of its doors reverberated down the corridor. They heard heels tapping down the corridor. Pam went to the door and opened it and Freddie Haven, coming toward her, said, "This is awful. Unforgiveable."

The strain was in Freddie Haven's eyes; as in her voice, as in her face. Her face was almost colorless; it was marked with weariness, with shock.

"It's all right," Pam North said. "Of course it's all right." She held the door open.

Jerry was on his feet. He did not look sleepy any longer. His face grew intent as he saw Freddie Haven's face.

"It's all right," he said, reinforcing what Pam had said. "What is it, Mrs. Haven? The admiral —?"

She stood, holding her fur coat around her,

as if even in this warm apartment she still was cold, her face drained of color save for the brightness of her lips. The red hair was so deep that it was almost some different color, some new color. She shook her head, without speaking.

"Sit down," Pam said. "Sit down."

The young woman shook her head again, but it was not a response. She sank into a deep chair, leaned back a moment with her eyes closed. Then she sat up, quickly, nervously.

"Bruce is dead," she said. She looked at them. "Senator Kirkhill," she said. "He's — he's been killed. It's — horrible."

"Oh!" Pam said. "I'm — I'm —"

"Somebody killed him," Freddie Haven said. "The police say somebody killed him." She looked at them, shock living in her eyes. "Meant to kill him," she said.

Pam North made coffee, then; Jerry North brought brandy. While they waited for the coffee, Freddie started to speak, but Pam had shaken her head, said, "Wait!" They drank coffee, brandy in it. Some color came back into Freddie Haven's face.

"Now," Pam said.

They waited a moment while Freddie Haven, shock slowly leaving her brain, her body, arranged her thoughts. Then she tried to smile. The smile was unreal, tormented.

"I want you to help me," she said, finally, her words chosen. "Mrs. Burnley — somebody — said you were — that you —" She paused, the words lost.

"That we were detectives?" Pam said. "Investigators? Something like that?" She shook her head. "We're not," she said. She looked at Jerry North.

"We know a police lieutenant," Jerry said. "A man named Weigand. We've been — involved. But your friend is wrong. We're not detectives. I'm a publisher. Pam's —" He paused and looked at his wife. Pam was what? Housewife? True, legal — ridiculous as description. "Pam's not a detective," he said.

Freddie Haven looked from one to the other. She looked at Pam North.

"I thought, tonight," she said. "I thought you — saw things, understood things. That I was worried, that something was wrong. Afterward somebody said —" She broke off. "I was going to be married to Bruce," she said. "They say he was — murdered." She looked at them, as if there were an answer to this.

Jerry North had been standing, looking down at her. Now he sat down in a straight chair.

"Mrs. Haven," he said. "Listen. Will you listen?"

She nodded, her eyes on his face.

"If that's true," Jerry said, "if Senator

Kirkhill was murdered, the police will find out about it. Find out who did it. That's what you want? That's why you came to us?"

She shook her head.

"No?" Jerry said. He felt thrown off.

"That's only part of it," she said. "Can I tell you?"

Jerry hesitated, he wanted to say "no." "Of course," Pam said. "Listen, Jerry."

"It's about my father," she said. "He – I'm afraid he – he knows something he hasn't told the police. Isn't going to tell the police." She looked at Jerry. "He's a dear," she said. "He's – an innocent."

Jerry North looked at her blankly. Innocent? He repeated the word aloud and she nodded.

"Your father?" he said. There was incredulity in his tone, and in his mind. Vice Admiral Jonathan Satterbee, "Johnny Jump-up," was not an innocent. The word was absurd. He was a man of wide experience, wide knowledge, marked skill at his trade. He had been important in the Pacific – not Halsey, not Spruance, certainly not Nimitz. But his book about the Pacific war, the book on which Jerry had bet an advance which now and then slightly alarmed him, was not the book of an "innocent" man, if by the word his daughter meant a man without experience, without "savvy."

"You don't know," Freddie Haven said. "I know how it sounds. He's a wonderful man. He was a

68

fine officer. He's been everywhere. But –" She shook her head. "He's been sheltered," she said. She almost smiled. "All of them have," she said. "Army men, Navy men. Dad's wonderful, he's special – but he's one of them."

She looked at them, at Jerry, at Pam. She shook her head. She said they didn't understand.

"It's all so – arranged," she said. "Their whole lives are arranged. They live in a place with a wall around it. Look – I've been Navy all my life. All my people, almost all my people, have been Navy. A man like Dad, even a brilliant man – I think he is – gets to feeling that he's different from ordinary people. He's had – oh, security all his life; authority for a long time. He didn't have to do ordinary things. He just – took them for granted. He doesn't really know about people, except other people in the Navy – other officers in the Navy. In the world outside he's – he's innocent." She paused and shook her head. She told them she said it badly.

"He thinks things are simpler than they are," she said. "That – oh, I don't know." She paused, seemed to nerve herself. "He didn't like Bruce," she said. "He didn't want me to marry Bruce. Bruce was a different kind. He – he'd lived outside the wall. And he was a politician. Dad hates politicians."

"Listen," Jerry North said. "My God, Mrs. Haven! Are you trying to tell us –"

"Of course she isn't, Jerry," Pam said. "But — you think he's got involved, somehow? Is that it? That the police won't — understand? That he won't know how to explain?"

Slowly, not quite certainly, Freddie Haven nodded. "Something like that," she said. "I don't know. There was a man —" She stopped. "I'll tell you about it," she said. "Maybe you can tell me what to do."

She told them about going to the morgue, with her father, about identifying Bruce Kirkhill's body. Afterward, for a very few moments, they had been questioned. "A police lieutenant," she said. "A man named Weigand." She looked at them.

"Bill Weigand," Jerry said. "He's the one we know."

"He didn't take long," Freddie said. "He was considerate. He just asked about this evening — when had we expected Bruce, had we heard from him, did we have any idea why —" She broke off again. "You don't know," she said. "It's strange — horrible. He was wearing old clothes, second-hand clothes. He — he died in a doorway down on lower Broadway somewhere. He'd been given chloral hydrate. A lot of it. He just went into this doorway and — and after a while he died."

She put her face down in her hands, hiding it, hiding herself from the world.

She raised her head.

"We didn't have any explanation," she said. "I didn't. Dad said he didn't. Then we went home."

They had put Celia to bed in the apartment and, after a time, given her a sedative. Mrs. Burnley had stayed with her and Curtis Grainger, impotent, angered by his impotence, had been walking the living room, throwing cigarettes, half smoked, one after another, into the fireplace. He had gone after the admiral and Freddie got home; at her request, with dull acceptance, obvious lack of interest, he had agreed to drop Breese Burnley at her apartment. Howard Phipps had gone. Breese said he had telephoned to someone – the police she thought – had sworn in a dazed way at what he had heard and then had gone out. Curt Grainger had added that he thought Phipps had gone to the hotel, to make telephone calls to Washington.

Ten minutes after they came home, the admiral and his daughter were alone in the living room. The numbness Freddie had felt, the dead incredulity that this was happening to her, had begun to wear off.

"I'm sorry, Winifred," the admiral said, standing in front of the fire, looking at her.

Freddie merely nodded, then. There was no point to words. She nodded again when her father said she ought to try to get some sleep.

"That police fellow will be around tomorrow, y'know," Admiral Satterbee said. "Not done with it, I'm afraid."

She shook her head. They weren't done with it. But there was still nothing to say. She turned and started toward the foyer, toward the stairs to the floor above. Her father's voice stopped her.

"Freddie," he said. She turned back, stood, waited. He seemed for a moment not to know how to go on.

"Have to be prepared," he said. "You know that? Things will come out, y'know. Bound to. Have to be ready to stand up to them."

She merely waited for him to go on. The words were distant things, almost meaningless.

"Nasty things," the admiral said. "Things you won't like. About Kirkhill."

That reached her.

"No!" she said. "There wasn't anything like that about Bruce." She moved a step toward her father, looked up at him. "What things?" she demanded.

Again he hesitated. Then, loudly, the door buzzer sounded. The admiral moved quickly into the foyer and opened the door. A man came in.

"Just like that," Freddie Haven told the Norths. "He came in. As if he didn't need to wait to be

72

asked. As if — as if he came in by right."

He had not been a large man; the tall admiral towered over him. He was rather fat, not well dressed; he had kept his hat on until he was well into the foyer. There had been snow on the hat and the man had snapped it off, casually, on the foyer carpet. The man's face was fat, loosely fat. He had not shaved that day, and when he had last shaved it had not been careful. The beard was long in the creases in his cheeks. His eyes, which were light blue — arrestingly light blue — had seemed small in his fat face; small and set incongruously wide apart.

Admiral Satterbee, Freddie told the Norths, did not make any effort to stop the man's entering. Nor did he, for a moment, say anything. The man with the fat face spoke first.

"I figured you'd want to see me," the man said. His voice was soft. ("Buttery," Freddie told the Norths. "Soft and buttery.")

The admiral merely looked at the man; then he turned and looked at his daughter.

"Go up, Freddie," the admiral said. "Go up to bed."

It was a command. She started to obey it, had to move toward the fat man before she could move away from him. He smiled at her; his smile was unpleasant. " 'Evening, miss," he said, in the buttery voice. She did not reply, did not seem to look at him, started up the stairs.

"I told you —" she heard her father say, and heard the fat man interrupt him.

"Told Harry," he said. "Not me. Harry ain't me, Admiral. Harry don't get things." He paused. "Don't add things up," he said.

"Come in here," she heard her father say, as she went on up the stairs. "I don't know what you're after. I'll give you —"

"Take it easy, Admiral," the man said. There was something like amusement in his fat voice. "Nobody said anything about giving."

She had stopped on the stairs, listening. Her father was taking the fat man through the living room toward the library.

"The thing is," the fat man said, "what do you want me to tell the cops? About this —"

Then they went into the library, and the door closed, and the voice was cut off.

She told the Norths how these things had happened, trying to make them as obscure, yet as significant, in the telling as they had seemed to her when they had happened.

But when she had finished, Jerry North looked at Pam, and shook his head.

"I don't," he began. Then Freddie remembered what she had forgotten to tell, interrupted Jerry North, and told of the telephone conversation between her father and — someone. She repeated, as accurately as she could, the words she had overheard: Her father's "circumstances have changed"; the unknown man's, "begins to look like there's something to it" and "it's up to you. He's going to be your son —"

"He must have meant Bruce," Freddie said. "Who else could he have meant?"

Jerry North nodded slowly. He looked at Pam, and saw a shadow on Pam's face.

"That," Freddie said. "Then this — this awful man. He knew about Bruce — about Bruce's being — murdered."

The word was a lonely and awful word, standing apart from other words. It carried terror in its syllables. "Murdered."

"Your father seemed to know him?" Pam said, and Freddie Haven nodded, hating to have to nod.

"On the telephone," Pam said. "Your father said that circumstances had changed. That was all?"

Freddie thought; then she spoke slowly.

" 'As of tonight,' he said," she told them. " 'As of tonight, circumstances have changed.' " Then she looked at them, and waited. There was a kind of desperate hopefulness in her waiting.

"It doesn't have to mean anything," Jerry told her, doing his best. But Pam North shook her head.

"Of course it means something," she said. That's ridiculous, Jerry. Only — it doesn't have

75

to mean the way it sounds. It could be – oh, anything."

They looked at her.

"Well," Pam said, after a moment. "Anything. Not that your father knew the senator had been – was dead. And that because he was dead –" The words trailed off, the sentence lost momentum.

"Dad didn't know." Freddie said. Her voice was low, but there was desperate anxiety in it. She was telling herself that her father did not know; it had to be that he did not know. Because if he had known then all the evening he had been lying, by word, by implication, in his attitude toward her. "He couldn't have known," she said. "But – what did he mean? Who are these men?"

The question was so easy to answer that answer was not needed. Men the admiral had hired for some purpose; men he had dismissed, their task done; men who, perhaps, did not plan to stay dismissed. It had been, Freddie had thought, like a Shakespearian cast. Now she thought again of Shakespeare; thought, "Enter two murderers." She put her head down in her hands.

After a moment she raised her head and looked at the Norths. She looked first at Pam, then at Jerry.

"What can I do?" she said. Her voice was

very low, very strained. "I've got to – to help Dad."

"Go to him," Pam said. "Ask him. Ask him what it's all about. Then –"

The door buzzer was loud in the apartment. The Norths looked at each other, surprise on their faces. "What the –" Jerry began, and Pam went to the door, pulled it open. Freddie turned her head, drew in her breath quickly.

It was a man Freddie had seen once before. He was thin, with a thin face, a soft hat canted a little to one side, partially shielding the face. He took the hat off, shook snow from it to the tiled floor of the outside corridor. He smiled at Pam and started to speak.

"Saw your lights," he said. "Thought I'd –" Then he saw Freddie Haven and stopped speaking. He looked at Pam North and his thin face seemed momentarily puzzled.

"Good evening, Mrs. Haven," he said, then. "I didn't expect –"

"Bill," Pam said. There was a slight constraint in her voice. "We were just – just having a cup of coffee." She looked at the coffee table. "With brandy," she added, paying the bottle tribute. "You're – you're just in time."

The man with the thin face looked at her, smiled fleetingly. He looked across at Jerry North and raised his eyebrows.

"By all means, Bill," Jerry North said. "By all means."

"Right," Bill Weigand said. He came in, removing his overcoat. He was wearing dinner clothes. He looked tired, Freddie Haven thought, irrelevantly. He looked very tired.

Pam North felt the silver coffee pot, shook her head over it.

"Cold," she said. "I'll have to make us some more. If there's one thing that's terrible with cognac it's cold —"

"Pam," Jerry said. "Pam. Sit down, Pam."

"The coffee's cold," Pam said. "Cold as ice. It couldn't be colder if —" She looked at her husband, looked at Bill Weigand. "Oh, all right," she said. "Go ahead, Bill."

"Ahead?" Bill Weigand said. He seemed surprised and puzzled. "Ahead, Pam? I was just going by, saw your lights, thought I'd drop in for a minute since you were still up." He looked at Jerry North. "Right?" he said.

"Bill," Pam said. "We love you. We love seeing you. It's four o'clock in the morning." She paused. "We've danced the whole night through," she said, and then, as if she had surprised herself, "For heaven's sake."

"Anyway, it's three o'clock," Jerry said. "In the song. Go ahead, Bill."

Lieutenant William Weigand's glance at Freddie Haven, a glance for a purpose, was so

78

quick that it was hardly a movement of the eyes. But Pam North said, "Oh!"

I'm in the way, Freddie Haven thought; he came for something, to ask them something. He can't, because I'm here. And again, her breath came in a quick gasp. Then she stood up.

"I'll go," she said. "I — I was just going." She fought for poise, momentarily gained it. "It was so good of you to let me come, Mrs. North," she said. She was almost polite, almost casual. "Now I really must —"

"What are you afraid of, Mrs. Haven?" Weigand said. "What frightens you?"

Freddie looked at the thin man she had seen for the first time that night; had seen in the anteroom of the morgue at Bellevue.

"Frightened?" she said. "I'm — I'm not frightened, Lieutenant Weigand." She wanted to stop there, found herself still talking. "I was upset," she said. "Can't you understand? Terribly upset. Shocked. I — I couldn't sleep, couldn't stay at home. I had to talk to somebody. I thought Pam and Jerry wouldn't mind; that they —"

"No, Mrs. Haven," Bill Weigand said. He shook his head. "I'm sorry," he said. "You just met them tonight, you know. You see, they left your party to join my wife and me. They mentioned having met you." He shook his head again. "Having just met you," he said. "They were hardly acquaintances. Right?"

She merely looked at him, her eyes wide; her eyes a little blank, as her mind whirled, seeking an answer. She saw Weigand shake his head.

"You may as well tell me," he said. "Because – they will, you know." He nodded. "Oh, yes," he said. "They won't want to, but they will, Mrs. Haven. Because, you see, they're on my side, if there have to sides. Because we've known one another a long time. You see how it is, Mrs. Haven? So – what are you afraid of? What brought you here? For advice, wasn't it? Somebody told you the Norths have been involved in things? Have experience?" He paused and still she did not speak. "*You* tell me, Mrs. Haven," he said. "It's the best way."

"I –" she said and found she could not go on. She looked at Pam, her eyes intent, her eyes seeking help.

"Why frightened?" Bill Weigand said, and her eyes went back to him. "Not for yourself. Or is it for yourself?"

She shook her head. "No," she said. "No."

Bill Weigand looked at her for a long moment. Then, she thought, he made up his mind about something, because his manner changed. The intensity, the pressure, went out of his manner; he shrugged slightly and seemed to dismiss something. She tried to guess what had caused the change; tried to understand how his mind was working because, she thought, it might become important to know how his mind worked. But there was too much turmoil in her own mind.

"Then don't be frightened," he said, and his tone was casual. "Go home. Try to get some rest. Leave it to us." He smiled, and the smile changed his thin face. There seemed, she thought, to be sympathy in his smile. "It's hard," he said. "I know that, Mrs. Haven. We'll let it go until – until later. Right?"

She stood up; she forced quiet into her manner.

"It was really true," she said. "I did come because – because I had to talk to someone. Someone who didn't know Bruce, someone outside. I know I only met the Norths tonight. I – I just tried to make it understandable. I felt I could talk to – to Mrs. North."

"Right," Bill Weigand said. He stood up also. His voice seemed to accept what she said. "Mrs. North affects people that way," he added. "Sometimes," he said, and suddenly turned toward Pam North, his expression amused. His smile faded. His tone became more official. "There's a car down stairs, Mrs. Haven," he said. "I'll have you driven home. Get some sleep. I'll have to see you tomorrow – you, your father, the senator's daughter."

Weigand picked up his overcoat, shrugged into it. He waited.

"Thank you," Freddie Haven said to the Norths. "Thank you for letting me — barge in. I — I don't know why I did."

"It's all right," Pam said. She hesitated. "Try not to worry." She paused again. "We're both terribly sorry," she said.

Freddie Haven tried to smile, and made little of it. She went through the door Weigand held open for her, stood with him, without speaking, while he brought up the elevator, stood with him in it while the car took them down. Just before it stopped, Weigand spoke.

"Eventually," he said, "you will have to tell me what you think you know. You realize that, Mrs. Haven." He looked at her, and she made herself meet his eyes. "We have to know," he said. He said nothing more, took her out of the apartment house to a car parked in front of it. He spoke to the man behind the wheel.

"Take Mrs. Haven home, Blake," he said. "Then come back."

"Right," Blake said. Weigand opened the rear door and Freddie Haven got into the car. "Good night," Bill Weigand said. He watched the car start up, for a moment regarded it. Then he went back into the apartment house. His thin face was thoughtful.

He knocked briefly on the door of the

82

North's apartment and then pushed it open. Pam and Jerry were much as he had left them. "Well," Pam said, "the coffee's hot, now."

Bill Weigand took off his coat and, abstractedly said, "Good." He took a cup of coffee, poured a little cognac into it. He sipped and said, "Good," again, in a different tone, and then sat down.

"You're not in a spot," he said, then. "I'm not going to ask you anything."

The North's looked at him

"Yeah?" Jerry said.

"Officially," Bill Weigand said, "I didn't stop in. Why should I? Officially, I have no idea that Mrs. Haven came here to – get you to help her? Get your advice?" He shook his head when Pam started to speak. "Advise her. Help her." He looked at them; tired as he appeared to be, he also appeared to be amused.

"Bill!" Pam said. "You – Bill!"

He merely smiled at her.

"Not on a spot!" Pam said. "What would you call a spot? Run with the hare, hunt with the hounds!"

"Is she the hare?" Bill wanted to know.

"And," Pam said, with bitterness, "I made you fresh coffee! No, I don't think she is."

"Then there's no harm done," Bill told her. "If she's not the – hare – she's not being hunted. What you find out may help. It won't hurt."

"It is a spot," Jerry North said. He was sober. "We didn't ask for confidences but — we got them." He looked at Bill. "Well?" he said.

Bill said he appreciated that. His tone, now, was serious. He realized he could get them to tell; that he would only have to ask. He also realized that they would not be happy, telling. That, he told them, was part of it.

"Also," he said, "you're in it again. Both of you. Officially, you're not, of course. But — officially I'm not here, not here to tell you that, or anything. If you can help her, help her. If, along the way, you find the man who killed Kirkhill, you'll let me know." He paused. "Where's the spot?" he said.

"The whole thing's a spot," Pam North told him. "You're throwing us into it; tying us up and throwing us in. Aren't you?" She looked at him. "Suppose I squeal to O'Malley? Tell the great man you invited us in? Threw us in?"

Bill Weigand laughed. Then he became serious.

"Forget it all if you'd rather," he said. "If — if you really think Mrs. Haven's involved, skip it. Forget she was here; forget I was here."

"You think she could have been?" Jerry asked.

Weigand shook his head.

"Directly, no," he said. "At least, I don't think so. At a guess, a man killed Kirkhill. I don't even know Mrs. Haven or any of the rest — I mean Kirkhill's daughter, his secretary, the people he would have met at the party tonight — had anything to do with it. I'd be inclined to think they didn't, on the whole. Actually, I stopped by to see whether you'd noticed anything at the party that might help. Any — strain? Uneasiness? Somebody not worried at Kirkhill's failure to show when you'd expect them to be? Somebody too worried? That sort of thing."

The North's thought it over. Jerry shook his head first. He said he spent most of his time with, or near, Admiral Satterbee. The admiral seemed to be worried chiefly about the protective storage of warships. "Shop talk." Jerry said. "I don't remember any talk of Kirkhill. I did gather he was expected and hadn't arrived."

"She was worried," Pam said. "Mrs. Haven. About as you'd expect. I mean, I didn't know then because I didn't know why, but now it seems about what I'd have expected if I'd — heavens! Where am I?"

"Right," Bill said. "I didn't suppose you'd have seen anything. I was passing by, did see the lights. It was a coincidence you had been at the party Kirkhill — missed." He grinned. "I got more than I expected," he said. "Unofficially."

There was a long pause.

"Well," Jerry said, "she is worried about someone else. Needlessly, probably. And you're suggesting we look into it? Find out what we can? Tell you what we find out?"

"If you like," Bill said. "Forget it if you like. Or — look the ground over and then make up your minds. If you feel you'd be in an untenable position, drop out."

"Subtle," Pam said. "Very subtle. If we drop out, it's because we've found something to make us suspicious of Mrs. Haven. Then, whatever you say, we have to tell you what it is."

Weigand merely smiled.

"Or," Jerry said, "we tell you now what she told us when she had no reason to think that what she said would go to the police."

Bill Weigand smiled again.

"Of course," he said, "you'd be helping the daughter of an author. An author you've bet money on. Who ought to have peace and quiet for those revisions you were talking about. Right?"

Jerry North said "Damn!"

"Anyway," Bill Weigand said, "I'll tell you what we know so far. It's an odd setup; Mullins will say it's screwy." He smiled. "He'll say, 'Look, Loot, this is one for the Norths.' Your public." He paused again. Then he said here it was, so far as they'd got.

The body was found a little after eleven o'clock that night, the last night of the year. A patrolman, working north on lower Broadway, below Canal, cold and bored on a deserted street, flashed his light in a doorway, as he had, expecting nothing, finding nothing, in fifty doorways. This one, the doorway of a cheap lunchroom which had been closed for hours, was different. A big man was sitting in the entry, his legs stretched out, his back to the door. He looked like a drunk; the patrolman said he smelled like a drunk. But he was dead. Snow had begun to drift over his outstretched legs.

It looked like a routine thing. A man with no place in the world, except a flop house when his luck was in, a saloon on the Bowery when he had a dollar or two, had had a dollar or two that last night of the year. He had drunk it up; he had had enough to get too much of the stuff they sold across a dirty bar in a dirty room to hopeless men; to men who had not even the pathetic human hope that a new year would be a better year. He had used up his money, gone out of the bar — out of smelly warmth into biting cold, into a harsh wind — and walked in no direction. He had got sleepy, tried to get into the lunchroom, in his muddle not realizing it had closed, gone to sleep as he

87

stood there and slumped down, and then had frozen. That was what it looked like, at first.

The wagon was summoned, came for him. At the morgue, they might well have done nothing about him for hours had not a doctor, starting home after a late post mortem, stopped by the body and looked at it idly. The doctor had thought vaguely that the man had been eating well, for a bum from the Bowery. Then the doctor had noticed the man's hands, looked at them more closely and let out his puzzlement in a statement that he would be damned.

"He'd had a manicure," Weigand said. "Probably yesterday."

It was enough to start things moving. Once they began to look, almost nothing fitted the obvious picture. Even the clothes, which at first seemed part of the picture, did not really fit in.

The overcoat was worn, but had been recently cleaned. It did not fit the man; he had picked it up, presumably, in a second-hand clothing store. He had, at a guess, worn it only a day or so, if even for a day or so.

The suit under the overcoat was even more at variance with the picture. It was a very cheap suit, it fitted very badly. But it appeared to be almost new. But, although almost new, it was noticeably, almost flagrantly, unpressed. It almost seemed, the medical examiner's laboratory reported, that someone had deliberately stretched the shoddy material out of shape, pulling it, crumpling it, possibly using an iron on it to remove the original creases. Both cuffs of the trousers were frayed, although most of the suit showed no signs of wear. Somebody could have frayed the material with a file, even scraped at it with a knife. "Phoney," a lab man said, briefly, unofficially.

The shoes were worn and scuffed — and were too large for the feet. But the socks were silk, and new. The underwear was of medium weight wool and had cost money. It had been washed several times, but there were no laundry marks. The shirt had been worn a long time, washed often and it, too, had no laundry marks. But it fitted perfectly, as if it had been made for the wearer.

The body was that of a large man, weighing a little over two hundred pounds; the man had been an inch over six feet tall; he had eaten well, taken care of himself, once might have been an athlete. When he slumped down in the doorway of the cheap restaurant and began to die, he had been in his middle forties.

It was strange; it required looking into. Appearances apparently had been created which were a variance with facts. So the police machine started; a report of suspicious death went to the Homicide Squad; fingerprints, measurements and description went to the Missing Persons Bureau. A coded description of the fingerprints went on the wires to various cities, including Washington. A check of the prints was made in the department's own records.

An autopsy was begun at once. There were no injuries discernible. The man had been drinking before he died; he had eaten some hours before. And he had died, not of exposure, but of an overdose of chloral hydrate.

"Knockout drops," Weigand said. "Very tricky stuff. They use it sometimes to put a man out while they rob him. It's too uncertain to be used often in homicides; I don't know that I remember a case. But — if a man has a weak heart, even a normal dose may kill him."

"That happened this time?" Jerry said.

Bill Weigand nodded. He said the doctors thought so. The heart was impaired. Not seriously; with normal care, the man need not have died of the impairment. He would merely have had to be careful.

"Of course," Bill said, "on a night like this, there was a good chance he'd die anyway. If you could get him out of doors, follow him, maybe, to see that he didn't find shelter — he'd have been dazed and sleepy within a short time; probably out within half an hour — the cold would finish your job for you."

A preliminary report of the post mortem was

ready by a little after one o'clock that morning. "Three and half hours ago," Jerry said, rather morosely, looking at his watch. Bill said he knew; said that he wouldn't be long. At almost the same time, identification had come through from Washington.

The man about whom PD, NY was enquiring had been a lieutenant colonel in the Army during the war. His name was Bruce Kirkhill. And — he was presently the junior senator from a western State. They woke Deputy Chief Inspector Artemus O'Malley up, then; they notified the commissioner.

"And," Bill said, "they got me. They showed up at the Plaza just after we'd all left; they caught me at home. Got me down to the morgue to talk to Mrs. Haven and her father. They'd already sent Blake up to the Satterbee apartment."

The Washington police had cooperated efficiently, which accounted for Blake's early appearance at the apartment. They had found Kirkhill's secretary — "his typing secretary," Weigand said. "A girl. His official secretary, if that's what you'd call him — is a man named Phipps." The "typing secretary" had been able to tell the Washington police that the senator had gone to New York, that he was planning to attend a New Year's Eve party there at the home of his prospective father-in-law, Admiral

91

Satterbee; that his nearest relative, his daughter, would be at the same party. So, in Weigand's absence, Sergeant Blake had been sent to the Satterbee apartment to tet someone to make the identification.

"Where's Mullins?" Pam North wanted to know.

"On his way in," Bill told her. "He lives out on Long Island. He was — having an evening out." He closed tired eyes and reopened them. "As weren't we all," he said.

There was a pause, then.

"And there we stand," Bill Weigand said. His voice was suddenly dull. "A United States senator dresses up like a bum, drinks chloral hydrate in rotten liquor in a cheap bar, dies in the doorway of a fourth rate lunchroom while his fiancée is waiting for him to come to a party on Park Avenue." He sighed. "The papers will be very, very happy," he said. "And the inspector will spin."

"Tomorrow," Pam North said sleepily, "we'll talk to the ad —" She paused and then went on — "miral's daughter," she said. "Won't we, Jerry?"

There was a very long pause indeed.

"I guess so," Jerry North said, finally.

IV

Saturday, 4:30 A.M. to 2:20 P.M.

The police sedan moved slowly northward in a world tunning white. The air had the misty whiteness of a snow at night; snow was accumulating on the pavement. The car stopped for lights, skidded a little, started again with the lights, the rear wheels spinning before they caught. In the light from street lamps, the snow blew like a curtain; in the headlights of the car it danced and swirled, its pattern as confused, its moment as dizzying, as were the pattern and movement of Freddie Haven's thoughts.

The car moved through a city which had grown empty. The most dogged of those who welcome a New Year on a city's streets, taking confidence from their own multitude, roaring down their own doubts, had sought shelter now, had sought the warm safety of bed or the fantasy life of late-open bars. Up Fifth Avenue,

93

an occasional taxicab, an occasional private car, went shuttered through the storm, boring into it, swept by it. A Department of Sanitation truck, a monster in the luminous darkness, trundled ahead of them for a block, its plow lifted, like some great reptile from pre-history looking for a place to graze. Around a fire on a corner a group of men, bulky in heavy clothing, clustered, their long-handled shovels momentarily idle, waiting for something – some perfect moment, some direction, the arrival of something or somebody.

The car turned east in Twenty-third Street. It went around a bus which moved slowly, hesitantly, into the northeasterly wind. The bus seemed to be full of people, some of them standing; passing it, looking into the lighted bus, Freddie Haven felt that the people were frozen there, or dead there. She shivered, momentarily, in the warm car. It had all gone wrong; everything had gone wrong.

It had been wrong to go to the North's, to seek from strangers some contact, some reassurance, in a world which had become obscure and baffling. It had been an impulse, a movement made without consideration. Her father and the man with the fat face, the fat voice, had gone into the library and, even after the door closed behind them, she had continued to go up the stairs toward the second floor of the duplex. Then, almost without knowing it, she found herself going down the stairs again, finding a coat in the foyer closet, going out into the outer foyer, ringing for the elevator. It came, after a little. Ben, the operator, had looked at her (she thought now, had not thought then) strangely. "It's snowing, Mrs. Haven" he said. "Snowing hard." He had meant it, she thought now, as a warning, as a caution. But she had only nodded. When the car stopped at the ground floor, and the door opened, Ben had started to speak, had said, "Well, Hap —" and had stopped and seemed embarrassed. "Happy New Year, Ben," she had said, and tried to smile and gone across the lobby and nodded again when the doorman had asked if he could get her a taxi. "Try to," he had said.

She had been lucky, if being expedited in error could be considered luck. He had got a cab almost immediately and then, only when she was in it, had she realized that she did not even know where these strangers lived. It had been precisely that unplanned, that meaningless. A slight woman with wide eyes, with a kind of interested eagerness in her manner, had conveyed — by the movement of her lips? by the expression around her eyes? — that she knew something to be wrong, that she felt sympathy. And because of that, because of that nothing,

Freddie Haven was in a taxicab, not knowing where she was going, seeking a contact which could not help in a world suddenly shaking around her.

She had had the cab driver stop at a drug store; she had had him wait while she looked in a telephone book. Against all probability, she had found Gerald North listed, and an address near Washington Square. She had still been lucky, thought herself lucky at the moment. She had gone on in the cab.

And it had not been lucky. She could not think, now, what she had expected, had hoped for, what kind of help she had thought Mrs. North, Pamela North, could give her. Whatever she had hoped for, that, certainly, she had not got. She had, she thought, given herself away, and was surprised by the shape the thought took, by the implication that she had something to conceal. To conceal from whom? The answer was evident — from Lieutenant Weigand, the Norths' friend; the detective who way trying to find out who had killed Bruce.

The police car stopped for another light. It waited there, in the storm, its lights falling on swirling flakes, isolated. The man at the wheel, a tall man, now hatless, did not turn or move. She saw only the back of his head, but suddenly she remembered his face. It had been thin and sensitive, troubled by the message he had brought them. Remembering his face, she found that he became, in some curious fashion, a companion in the car, a sharer of this isolated small area of warmth.

"It's bad night," she said. She had not thought she was about to speak. She realized that the meaningless words were, must sound like, an appeal. "Speak to me," she was saying. "I am lonely, afraid. Speak to me. I am confused."

"Yes," the man said. He did not turn, and he started the car.

"You're Sergeant Blake," she said. "The one who came to tell us."

"Yes," Blake said. It was odd, she thought, how seldom anyone said, fully, the word "yes." There was a sound for "yes," a sound varied by the speakers, sometimes "yeah" or "yeh" or something like "yuh." But almost never "yes."

Blake did not continue, but his word did not, as it might have done, break the tenuous communication. It left him alive in the car, sharing the car with her, sharing with her the mood of this momentary seclusion from the world, from the storm.

"Mr. Weigand," she said. "Lieutenant Weigand?"

"Yes," Blake said again. "Lieutenant. Acting captain, actually. We all seem to forget, most of the time."

"Captain Weigand," she said. "He's — in charge of the investigation? Of — of Bruce's death."

Blake hesitated. He stopped the car for a light, and this time turned. She could hardly see his face, could see it only dimly in the light from a street lamp.

"Technically," he said, "Inspector O'Malley's in charge. Or the commissioner, actually. But the lieutenant will handle most of it."

"With you?" she said.

He smiled. She could see that in the half light. His sensitive face was attractive when he smiled.

"People like me," he said. "A sergeant named Mullins. A sergeant named Stein. A lot of people."

"You'll find out?" she said.

"I expect so," he said. "ᴊooner or later. One time or another." His smile faded. "Don't worry so, Mrs. Haven," he said. "Don't —" He paused, gave up that line. "I suppose there's nothing to say," he told her. "I know there isn't. It's — it's a shocking thing to face. But, try not to worry so."

He chose a strange word, she thought, and then thought that the word was right. It was not, as it seemed, a substitute for "grieve," for the formality of "grieve." He meant that she was not to worry; the word was chosen precisely. It must be in her manner, then — worry, rather than grief. Worry or — fright. "Don't be frightened." Now this man with a sensitive face, this other policeman, said almost the same thing.

She was silent for a time, and Blake turned back, started the car again. They were in Park Avenue, now; now they were circling the Grand Central Station. Am I worried, frightened, instead of - grieving? she wondered. Is that the way I feel? Is it the strangeness, first, the strangeness of people still alive, of Dad, and Bruce's death only after that? But then — but then it would have been wrong. Oh Bruce, she thought, would it have been wrong? Forgive me, Bruce.

"I was going to marry him," she said, to the back of Sergeant Blake's head. "I was going to marry him. Now he's been — killed. You say, don't worry. Why do you say that?"

He shook his head, not turning, watching the snow swirl in the beam of the headlights.

"It was the wrong word," he said. "I know there's nothing to say. I was trying to say I was sorry. But there's nothing to say."

She did not answer for along minutes. They were far up Park, nearing the apartment.

"I'm not worried," she said, finally. "Not — frightened. Just unhappy."

"Of course," he said. "I used the wrong word.

I'm sorry, Mrs. Haven." He turned the car in toward the curb. He stopped and got out and came around the car. But by then she had opened the door, stood on the sidewalk. The snow began to whiten the fur of her coat.

"Anyway," she said to him. "Thank you."

He misunderstood, or pretended to misunderstand. His answer assumed she was thanking him for driving her home.

" 'S all right," he said. "Would you like me to go up with you?"

"No," she said. "Oh no."

He went with her across the sidewalk, stopped at the entrance to the apartment house. She said "Good night" and went in, not waiting to hear if he replied.

The elevator was standing at the floor, the door open, but there was nobody near it. She pressed the signal button, and there was a loud buzzing from within the car. After a few minutes, Ben came up, apparently from the basement. He was chewing something. She smiled and said she was sorry and he told her, a little thickly, that it was all right. "Grabbing a sandwich," he said. He took her up.

Having watched her go into the apartment house, Sergeant Blake turned back to the car. He opened the front door on the right, found a man sitting behind the wheel and did not appear to be surprised. He said, "Hello, Smitty." He slid into the car beside the man.

"It's a hell of a night," Smitty said. "You've got it nice, Sergeant. Driving dames around in a warm car."

It was without rancor.

"Yes," Blake said. "Very cushy. Spill it, Smitty."

"You know Smiley?" Smitty said. "Private op.? Fat face? They were after his license a while back?"

"Yes," Sergeant Blake said.

"Well, he was around," Smitty said. "First everybody goes away. Anyway, a couple goes away, then a short guy goes away, then a tall guy. You want descriptions?"

"Not now," Blake said. "Give it to the lieutenant."

"O.K.," Smitty said. "Then Smiley comes, looks at the street number like he's not been here before and goes in."

"Into the building," Blake said. "Or did you check?"

"To the apartment," Smitty said. "Sure I checked. Then the girl comes out — the girl you just brought back."

"Mrs. Haven," Blake told him. "Go ahead."

"Half an hour or so, Smiley comes out," Smitty said. "Looks around for a cab and then starts walking downtown. At the corner, he crossed over and walks on the other side. About half a block down, he gets a cab, going downtown."

"All right," Blake said. "I'll pass it along. Anything else?"

"It's cold as hell," Smitty said. "You've got it soft."

"Yes," Blake said.

Smitty sighed. He opened the door on his left, got out into the snow. Almost at once he seemed to disappear. Blake slid under the wheel, started the car, drove north for a block and circled and went back downtown. He thought it was funny about Smiley; that it had been a good idea to stake Smitty where he was staked.

Freddie stood before the door of her apartment and, with the key in her hand, hesitated. She was oddly unwilling to unlock the door, open the door, walk into the apartment. But after only a moment, she did go in. She shook her coat in the foyer and hung it in the foyer closet. There was a light on only there, and she thought everyone was asleep. She started up the stairs and the door of the library opened. From the open door a shaft of light, spreading, fell obliquely across the living room. Then her father stood in the door of the library and said, "Freddie?"

She said, "Yes, Dad?"

"Thought you were in bed," the admiral said.

She was surprised, for a moment. Then she realized that, unless he had gone to her room and found it empty, her father would not need to have known that she had gone out. When last he had seen her, she had been going up the stairs, on the way to her room. She was conscious of a feeling of relief. It would have been hard to explain; since Lieutenant Weigand had found her at the North's, since now, in effect, she had told the police about her father's visitor, it would have been impossible to explain. In the end, presumably, the impossible would have to be faced, since Weigand would question her father about the visitor. But now she had a little time.

"I couldn't sleep," she said, and walked toward him.

The admiral nodded. He said he knew. As she came up to him, he touched her consolingly, touched her red hair, her cheek. "You're cold," he said. "Cold, child."

She stood beside him for a moment and then stepped back so she could look up at him.

"Who was he, Dad?" she said. "That man who was here? What did he want?"

"That man?" her father said, and then appeared suddenly to remember. "Oh — another policeman, Freddie. A detective."

She looked at him for a long moment. Then, slowly, she shook her head.

"I overheard a little," she said. "I — I couldn't help it. He wasn't a policeman."

"A detective," her father said. He hesitated momentarily. "All right," he said. . . . "Not a city detective. A man I hired. He — he came for his money."

Oh, Dad! Freddie thought. That isn't good, darling. That isn't nearly good enough. But she did not say anything. She merely waited.

"Nothing of importance," her father said. "I had him checking up on some things. In connection with the book."

It did not even sound like her father, Freddie thought. If it were true, he would not say it so, not explain it so. She waited, giving him a chance to go on yet knowing, from the way in which he had spoken, from the finality of his tone, that he would not go on. He set up a barrier between them; with his words, with the tone he used, he drew a line she was not to cross.

"You should be in bed," he said, making the barrier more complete, scoring heavily the line she was not to cross. "Do you know what time it is?"

The question had no meaning. She merely shook her head.

"Five o'clock," he said. "After five. Try to get

some rest, Winifred." His tone was tender, suddenly. "Child," he said. "I'm sorry, child."

"I know," she said. She looked up at him. "It's hard to believe," she said. "Hard to take in."

"Have to face it," he said. "Your job, Freddie." He looked at her intently. "All of your job," he said.

It was an order; gently spoken, but still an order. He was the admiral, she was a junior officer. She stood a moment longer, looking up at her tall father, not speaking because it was no use to speak when his face was so, set so, the order given, but with her whole mind crying out to speak. Because he is the child, she thought; he is really the child, not I. For all his certainty, his inflexibility, his sureness in command, he is the child; because of all these things, he is a child in this world which has nothing to do with ships, with patterns established and secure, men and women homogeneous in purpose and behavior. He is a child living behind a protecting wall, an older and hence more decisive child, his place won by seniority and secure, not to be challenged. He can look over the wall, see the other children playing strange games, behaving irregularly, believing inacceptable things – contesting, in a sense, for authority such as he holds by right of early selection, rigid training and, in the end, a ring of a certain design on a finger. His has been a way of life and, she thought. a fine way of life. But it is not the common way, and it does not fit you to understand the common way, or the people who follow it. The trouble with the service, she thought, is that in the end it turns you out, retires you, into a world you have never known. The more dedicated you have been, the more perfectly you have fitted yourself into the service, the harder this is, the more confused you are and the less able to admit confusion.

He's innocent, she thought, looking at her father. He's got mixed up with something he doesn't understand, but he is sure he understands it. In that moment she felt much older than her father and felt responsible for him. This fat man, this devious man from outside the wall, he would have ways and purposes which her father could never understand.

But she said none of this, because it was useless. She was baffled and confused herself, and she was unutterably tired and drained. She had done a wrong thing tonight in going to the North's; perhaps, although she could more clearly see the problems, she was no more than her father equipped to solve them.

"I'll try to sleep," she said, instead of all the things she might have said. She turned away from her father and walked, slowly, without resilience, toward the stairs. A kind of numbness now had succeeded anxiety, unhappiness, even fear. The numbness was merciful; she moved in it carefully, as if she were carrying an overfull glass which she must not jiggle. By so moving in her mind, by keeping numbness level, unspilled, in the glass, she undressed almost without knowing it and lay down on her bed — the curtains drawn, the electric ventilator humming its soft night-song — and after a not very long time she slept. She must have been, she thought afterward, too tired, too drained, to dream. . . .

"I'm sorry, miss," Marta said. "It's a shame, it's an awful shame. But the admiral says —"

"All right, Marta," Freddie Haven said, for the moment not moving. "What time is it?"

"Eleven, miss," Marta said. "It's an awful shame, you up so late and — everything." She turned toward Freddie and her eyes filled. "I'm awful sorry, miss," she said. "We all are. Cook and everybody."

"I know," Freddie said. "What did the admiral say, Marta?"

"Everybody's here again," Marta said, and drew the curtains from one of the windows. She looked out. "It's still snowing, too," she said. She turned off the ventilating fan. "Miss Celia and that young man of hers and Mr. Phipps and everybody. Even that Miss Burnley and her mother." She drew back the curtains at the other window. "And policemen," she said. "It's awful."

But she was excited, Freddie realized. It was awful, but it was exciting.

"Some of the policemen aren't wearing uniforms," Marta said. "You wouldn't know, hardly. Should I get your breakfast now?"

Freddie Haven lay a moment longer, looking up at nothing. She felt weighted down; felt that she did not want to get up, to face this day. The numbness was gone. Now, as she lay there, the fear, the anxiety, began to come back.

Then she moved quickly, swinging long legs out of the bed, sitting on it only a moment while she put on slippers, standing almost at once. "Coffee," she told Marta. "Just coffee. Perhaps orange juice." She went across the room and stood for a moment looking out of one of the windows. The snow was still falling heavily. She took the robe Marta offered her, but did not put it on. The room was warm, she should have turned the fan higher. The soft night-gown clung to her body as she went from the window the length of the room to the bath. She certainly is a pretty thing, poor thing, Marta thought. It's an awful shame.

Marta was back with coffee and orange juice – and toast and a poached egg – when Freddie came out of the dressing room which adjoined her bath. While the maid set breakfast on a table by the window, Freddie dressed, quickly. She put on a dark woolen dress, a dress as deeply green as her hair was deeply red. She found she could eat breakfast, that she was almost hungry. Physically, she was all right again.

It was a little after eleven-thirty when she went into the living room and she went at once to Ceila Kirkhill, from whose young face everything seemed to have washed away. Freddie put her arms around the girl and, as she did so, Celia began to cry. She cried soundlessly, her body shaking. Freddie held the girl; she felt, not tears, but a burning dryness in her own eyes. She looked over Celia's bent head to Curtis Grainger; said to him, with her eyes, "Be good to her." Grainger nodded, but at the same time shrugged slightly. What was there to say to Celia? his movement asked. What was there to say to anyone?

Freddie Haven released Celia to Curt Grainger and looked around the room, and felt that the room, the people in it, had been waiting for her. She smiled, as well as she could smile, at her father, still somehow military in a gray suit; she carried the same smile to the others — to Fay Burnley, correct in black, vitality drained out of her face, leaving there nakedly the years she had lived, for anyone to see; to Howard Phipps, still immaculate but obviously very tired, who had been sitting with his knees spread a little, his elbows on them, his head supported in his hands, until she had entered, who had looked up, then, and who now, as if on some signal, stood up in front of his chair. He stood there a moment, and then came the few steps to Freddie Haven and held out his hand, and shook his head slowly to indicate that there were no words. Since he wanted it, apparently wanted to be kind and gentle, Freddie took his hand, felt it clasp her own. Then he released her hand and shook his head again, and turned away. He started back to his chair, seemed to change his mind and went to another. The chair he chose was near that of Breese Burnley, whose entirely perfect face was, still, entirely perfect. Freddie carried her pale smile to Breese, offered it and received in return an expression of gravity and a slight, sympathetic shaking of the head.

Then, and only then, Freddie Haven looked at the table which had been drawn forward from its place near the big windows which looked down on the street. There were three men there, around the table — one sitting at it, with a notebook open, the other two standing. The man sitting at the table was Sergeant Blake, and his eyes met hers. His lips said "Good morning," without a sound. It seemed to her, oddly, that his face, the way he moved his lips in soundless greeting, were both familiar and, even more strangely, reassuring.

One of the other men was Lieutenant Weigand. The other was a larger man, heavier. He looked, more than either of the others, like a policeman, although he, too, was in civilian clothes.

Lieutenant Weigand's face was tired, as her father's was, as hers was; it was as if he had shared their strain, their anxiety. When Freddie looked at him, he nodded briefly, and said, "Good morning, Mrs. Haven." Then, almost at once, he said, his voice raised a little, "Now that you're all here —"

He paused while attention focussed on him.

"I'm a lieutenant of detectives," he said. "My name is Weigand. I've been assigned, with others, of course, to try to discover the circumstances of Senator Kirkhill's death. The exact circumstances." He paused, and looked around. "I know this is difficult for some of you," he said. "For Miss Kirkhill and Mrs. Haven, probably for all of you. I'm sorry about that, but it can't be avoided. I mean, I can't avoid asking you to help me, to tell me what you know." He paused again. "You see," he said, "the circumstances of the senator's death are very difficult to understand. To make any sort of sense of. I don't know whether you all know what the circumstances were. It was like this —"

He told them, in bare, flat words, of the finding of Bruce Kirkhill's body, of the way the body was dressed, of its identification.

"It appears," he said, "that the senator was engaged in some — masquerade. That he dressed himself, outwardly, for a certain part, presumably that of a man out of work, sleeping in cheap rooming houses, cadging drinks. He was found in, or near, a part of the city in which men like that are — numerous. He had been given a heavy dose of chloral hydrate. Perhaps it would not have killed him except that he had a weak heart."

He looked around at them.

"You all knew his heart wasn't good?" he asked. "Was that fact widely known?"

He paused, to give them a chance to answer. He looked from one to another, and one and then another shook his head. He raised his eyebrows at that, as if he were surprised. But the surprise, Freddie Haven thought, did not go deep; it was professional surprise, leaving the man himself untouched. His confidence was untouched, his assurance. He's very intelligent, Freddie thought and then, belatedly: Was there really something the matter with Bruce's heart?

Freddie looked at Celia, because Lieutenant Weigand's gaze had stopped at Celia. The girl with all but youth washed out of her face looked at Freddie and shook her head, her eyes wide, and then at Weigand and said, "No. I didn't know. He – Dad never –" Her head went down, then, her face in her hands.

"Mrs. Haven?" Weigand said, and Freddie shook her head in turn, and said, "No, Lieutenant, I didn't know."

And the others said they did not know. Fay Burnley, who had kept house for Bruce Kirkhill for years; her daughter, who perhaps once, briefly, had known him very well indeed; Howard Phipps, who had sometimes said that he lived in the chief's pocket; the admiral, who was to have been Bruce's father-in-law and Curt Grainger, who certainly had hoped to be his son-in-law – none of them knew Kirkhill's heart had been (what did they say?) "involved." It must, Freddie thought, seem unlikely to Lieutenant Weigand. It must seem –

"Apparently he was very reticent," Weigand said, his voice without inflection. "However."

Of course, he told them then, Senator Kirkhill might, under circumstances as they were, have died in any case of exposure. But, if his death was intended, the person who intended it could not have been entirely sure of that. The weak heart might have provided the assurance.

He seemed content to leave it at that. He went on. He was succinct, unemotional; he seemed to apply no pressure. He is very sure, Freddie thought; he is very confident. The thought disturbed her; she looked at her father. To her, Admiral Satterbee's face showed nothing. Did it show more to this undisturbed, intelligent man who seemed so sure? Was her father's face, in its very absence of revelation, revealing?

As he understood it, Weigand said, Senator Kirkhill had been expected at the New Year's Eve party about ten o'clock, expected to check in at the Waldorf some two hours earlier. He had not come to the party. He had not checked in at the Waldorf. "Right?" Weigand said, and let silence confirm.

"Apparently," Weigand said, "He came up from Washington on an earlier train. As he had planned?" The question was for Phipps. Phipps looked puzzled, but did not speak. "Where he went then, we don't know," Weigand said. "he went somewhere and changed into this — into this masquerade. He went somewhere and had several drinks, one of them full of chloral hydrate. He walked a while, got sleepy, collapsed in a doorway, died, we think, rather quickly after that. That is all we know — now."

He stopped, and looked at them, looked around at them.

"I hope one of you, perhaps several of you,

know more," he said. "Can help us fill in. Right?"

But nobody offered anything. Freddie looked around at the others, saw their faces blank. But then Phipps spoke.

"It wasn't as he planned," Phipps said. "The time he came, I mean. He planned to take the Congressional. I suppose he found he could get away earlier." He paused, shook his head. "Of course," he said, "he must have planned to get here earlier. To give time for this — what you call this masquerade."

"Whatever I call it," Weigand said, "have you any ideas about it, Mr. Phipps? No hint? He didn't say anything that, now, has a new meaning?"

Phipps seemed to hesitate. Then he shook his head.

If Weigand noticed hesitation, he did not choose to put emphasis on it. He merely nodded, he looked around at the others; at Fay Burnley, at Breese, at Celia, who was looking up, now; who was looking in front of her, at nothing. Will there be something in my face? Freddie wondered. Will he —

"Mrs. Haven?" Weigand said.

She made up her mind.

"I may have seen him," she said, and was surprised that her low voice was steady. She felt the eyes of all the others looking at her, but she looked only at Lieutenant Weigand. "I – I thought it couldn't be. But perhaps it was."

She told of the man she had seen, walking with the wind behind him, on some street far downtown; of the man who had reminded her of Bruce Kirkhill, might have been Bruce Kirkhill. "I don't know," she said. "I knew it couldn't be Bruce but now – now –"

"Right," Weigand said. "It might have been. Probably we'll never know. About what time?"

"I was home a little after six," she said. "It might have been about six."

She could not remember where the car had been when she had seen the man who reminded her of Bruce Kirkhill. She shook her head while Weigand waited. Perhaps on Lafayette Street, she thought; probably on Lafayette Street. But where, where more precisely, she could not remember.

Weigand nodded. He did not seem surprised.

"You got here a little after six," he said. "Here in the apartment. You stayed here after that, Mrs. Haven? Had dinner here?"

The question seemed, somehow, to grow out of what had gone before. But it doesn't, Freddie thought. Not really. Where were you when Senator Kirkhill was fed chloral hydrate? Where were you, Freddie Haven – Mrs. John Haven – when the man you were going to marry was killed?

"I didn't go out again," she said. "Until —"
She broke off. There was no use telling this
quiet, confident man what he already knew. "I
had dinner here, saw that everything was ready,
dressed for — for the party."

Weigand nodded. He said, "Right."

"Dinner alone?" he said. "With your father?"
The question was to both of them. Admiral
Satterbee answered it.

"I dined out," he said. "At my club. Keeping
out of the way, y'know? Got here at nine-five.
Changed. Talked to my daughter a few minutes.
Came down here." He indicated the living
room.

"What is your club, Admiral?" Weigand
asked. Admiral Satterbee looked surprised, almost indignant. Weigand merely waited. The
admiral told him.

"Mean you'll check?" the admiral asked
Weigand.

"We check everything we can," Weigand said,
equably, ignoring the admiral's tone. "Mr.
Phipps?"

"Where was I?" Phipps said.

If he didn't mind, Weigand told him.

"When?" Phipps said.

"In the evening," Weigand said.

"As a matter of fact," Phipps said, "I was one
place most of the day. The public library."

Weigand looked at him, waiting.

"I came up from Washington Thursday night," Phipps said. "On the midnight train. I went to the Waldorf, checked up on the reservations, checked in myself. I had breakfast and went over to the library. Got there a little after ten, probably. I was there most of the rest of the day. Working. Getting together material for a speech the chief's going — was going to make next week. I left the library around nine in the evening, went to the hotel and changed and came here."

"A long day," Weigand said.

"I'm used to it," Phipps told him.

"You went out for food?"

Obviously, Phipps said. For lunch, to an Automat on Sixth Avenue, behind the library. For dinner, to some place on Fifth, just above Forty-second. A big place.

"None of this you can check," he said. "Unless the library slips? Would they show times?"

"Oh, yes," Weigand said. He smiled faintly. "At any rate, we'd know where the books were," he said.

"Fine," Phipps told him. "Wonderful."

Weigand smiled again and went on. "Mrs. Burnley?" he asked.

Mrs. Burnley had been, she said, with her daughter, in her daughter's apartment.

"We had a little dinner," she said. "And talked until it was time to come here. I see Breese *so* seldom, Lieutenant."

Weigand nodded.

"There was a maid?" he said.

Mrs. Burnley shook her head, and earrings swayed.

"Just *us*," she said. "I fixed us a little dinner." She paused. "Lamb chops," she said.

"You were there all afternoon?"

"Oh, *yes*," she said, and then Breese spoke.

"Fay was," she said. "I was working. Modelling bathing suits. Doesn't the very *idea* make you shiver?"

Weigand looked at her and waited.

"I got home about six," she said. "Such an *awful* day. Then we had dinner."

Weigand looked at Curtis Grainger. "Mr. Grainger?" he said.

"Wh-why?" Grainger said. "Not that I give a damn, but why?"

"There are certain things I'm supposed to find out," Weigand said. He was patient, unperturbed. "Meaningless things, most of them. But we're supposed to cover all the ground."

Grainger hesitated, then shrugged. He had gone out the previous afternoon for a late, long lunch with some of the men at the office. He had got to his apartment after four. He had taken a nap. At about six, he had telephoned Celia and suggested dinner, been told she had been out all afternoon and now wanted to rest for the party. He had loafed around the apartment for a time, gone out to dinner, returned and changed. "I picked Miss Kirkhill up at the Chatham and came here," he said. "We planned that when I called her."

He looked at Weigand.

"And," he said, "I was alone, didn't see anybody, pr-probably wasn't seen by anybody, except a waitress who wouldn't remember."

His tone was a little combative, but Weigand did not appear to notice it. He merely said, "Right." He said, generally, to all of them, "Thank you." He recapitulated.

"None of you, then, has any idea why Senator Kirkhill was dressed as he was, was where he was," he said. "None of you knew he had a weak heart. None of you saw him in New York yesterday afternoon or evening." He looked at Freddie and nodded. "Barring the chance you saw him, Mrs. Haven," he said. "None of you saw him to speak to, to get anything which will help now."

He looked around. They looked at him and nobody said anything.

"Then —" Weigand began, and interrupted himself. It was as if, belatedly, he had thought of something of little importance. "By the way," he said, "does any of you know a man named Smiley. Arthur Smiley?" He looked around again, and got no answer. He did not appear to be surprised. "A private detective," Weigand said. "An investigator. He has a partner, a man named Briggs. Harry Briggs?" He seemed to feel that this might prompt a memory. He waited again. He seemed very patient, Freddie thought, very —

Harry, she thought, then. The man who was here said something about "Harry." He had said to her father, in his buttery voice, something like amusement in his buttery voice, that Harry wasn't he — "Harry ain't me." That was what he had said. Then the man who had come to see her father was the man called "Smiley." A private detective, an investigator — a soft, buttery man, with a kind of oily assurance in his voice, a kind of gloating; with a kind of assurance, too, in his manner; a kind of confidence that he could enter an apartment, *this* apartment, when he chose, say what he chose. The turmoil in her mind would show in her face. She tried to pull a shade, an expressionless shade, over her face. But instead she found that she was looking at her father, that her eyes were demanding something of her father, some explanation.

"Mrs. Haven?" Weigand said. "You don't know Smiley?"

There was only one thing to say. She made herself say it "No," she said.

Weigand looked at her for a second,

and then looked away.

"Right," he said. "Probably not important. Somebody thought he'd seen him around in — in the neighborhood." He smiled; he appeared to extend a confidence.

"A very able man, Mr. Smiley," he said. "In his way, that is. In — getting his way. Very odd team, Smiley and Briggs. Briggs might be a lawyer, you see. Very respectable, inspires confidence. None of you has met this Briggs?"

He looked at all of them; he looked at Admiral Satterbee.

"No," Weigand said. "Why should you?"

He turned away, then; he talked to the big man who looked like a policeman in civilian clothes. He turned back and said he thought that was all, for the moment.

"Except," he said, "I'd like to have you talk to Sergeant Mullins, here. Just to fill things in. How long you knew the senator — that sort of thing." He looked at Celia Kirkhill, then. "Not you, of course, Miss Kirkhill," he said, and his voice sounded gentle. "Nor you, Mrs. Haven, naturally. We'll get what we need from Mr. Phipps and Mrs. Burnley, probably." He looked at Admiral Satterbee. "And perhaps the admiral can help," he added, his voice without inflection.

V

Saturday, Noon
to 3:20 P.M.

"Jerry," Pam North said, her voice very wide awake. "The cats want in."

Jerry North said something rather like "Whah?"

"The cats," Pam said. "They —"

Gerald North tried to climb into his pillow. He wrapped it around his head. He said, in a smudged voice, "Tell them —" and did not finish, because he was almost going back to sleep.

"And," Pam said, "besides the cats, there's the admiral." She paused, her voice from the other bed still clear and wide awake. "Your admiral," she said.

It was preposterous that the admiral was outside their bedroom door, trying to get in. That, at least, was clear. Jerry told Pam it was clear. He said, "You're crazy. No admiral. Nobody there but those —" He began to drift off again.

Sherry, the blue-point, had the most pene-
trating voice. It was pitched higher than the
other voices; it was very plaintive. Gin,
the younger seal-point, spoke briefly, more
harshly; it was almost as if she barked. There
was a pause. Martini, her voice soft but still
guttural, spoke in command. It was just as
Jerry thought. Pam's idea was preposterous.

"Just the cats," he said. "The admiral would
say something." He tried to withdraw into the
pillow and, at the same time, under a blanket.
Then he realized, with a kind of cold dread,
that he was awake. He groaned, turned over
and opened one eye toward his wife in the other
bed. Pam was propped up against pillows; she
was entirely wide awake.

"What are you talking about?" Jerry said. "At
this hour?"

"Noon," Pam said. "Don't you remember
about the admiral? Your admiral? And the
senator? Anyway, it was you who didn't want to
lock them up in the kitchen, because it would
be too cold."

"Yowowow?" Sherry enquired, hearing their
voices. "Yah!" Gin said. Martini scratched the
door.

"But go back to sleep, Jerry," Pam said. "I
didn't mean to wake you up."

Jerry opened the other eye. The experience

was trying; a great deal of unwelcome light came in.

"Fine," he said. "Wonderful. I go right back to sleep."

Pam looked at him. She said she was sorry. She did not, Jerry decided, look sorry. Looking at her made him feel much better. Anyway, the worst of it was over. He was awake, now. He had both eyes open. Suddenly he grinned at Pam North.

"I thought you said an admiral was outside the door," he said. "With the cats." Then he remembered. He said, "Oh!"

"For practical purposes," Pam told him, "it's the same thing. I'll feed the cats if you'll turn off the air." She smiled at him. "And you," she added.

Jerry writhed out of bed, shivered, and plunged across the room. He snapped off the ventilator which was pumping cold, damp air into the room. He lifted a venetian blind and looked out and shivered. It was still snowing. He turned on a radiator. He said, "Brrr."

"Well," Pam said, reasonably, "if you wore pyjamas. In the winter, anyway."

Jerry said "Huh!" crossed the room hurriedly and got back into his bed. "Your turn," he said.

Pam North got up as if it were a pleasure. Jerry regarded her with interest.

"Actually," he said, "the difference is technical. I mean, if that — er, garment — is supposed to provide warmth. I mean —"

I know what you mean, darling," Pam said. "Don't you like it?"

"Oh," Jerry said. "As far as that goes —"

Pam found a negligee on a chair. With quick, assured movements she became hopelessly entangled in it. She extricated herself, less quickly, looked at the negligee with irritation, said, "Oh!" and turned the sleeves right side out. This time she went into it cautiously, with evident doubt, and was pleased and a little triumphant when she had it on. She looked at herself in a long mirror and told Jerry that he had good taste. Then she let the cats in. They arched and curved around her; Gin discovered Jerry in bed and went over to lick his face, purring loudly; Martini sharpened her claws briefly on an edge of the blanket, jumped up and said "good morning" with a short emphatic sound which took getting used to.

The cats followed Pam out of the bedroom and followed her back in again. "The papers," Pam said, and presented the *Times* and the *Herald Tribune.* "Scrambled all right?"

"Fine," Jerry said.

Pam went out again, accompanied by the cats.

Both newspapers were, as Bill Weigand had

predicted, happy over the murder. The *Herald Tribune* gave it the right hand column of Page One; the *Times*, more austere, confined it to the left hand column, across the journalistic railroad tracks. But the *Times* gave it more space.

For a column or so, the *Times*, which Jerry dutifully read first, told him little he did not know about Senator Bruce Kirkhill's death. ("Under suspicious circumstances," the *Times* said in its long opening sentence. The understatement, Jerry felt, did the *Times* immense credit.) The *Times* gave the facts; then it began to puzzle over them. The police, the *Times* reported, with a suggestion of disapproval, could not explain why the senator "known for his immaculate dress" had put on such old clothes to be killed in, had found such an inferior doorway to die in. Various explanations had been offered, the *Times* said, not saying by whom. (By various members of the *Times*'s city staff, Jerry suspected.) For one thing, the *Times* told its readers, Senator Kirkhill had long been known for his activity in favor of public housing and slum clearance. It was possible that he had, for reasons of his own, been making a personal investigation of slum conditions and had dressed as he had so as to be able to move in lower East Side areas without attracting undue attention. Presumably, he had been killed, unintentionally, by someone whose purpose was theft. The *Times* seemed, with puzzled reservations, to prefer this theory, but did not limit itself to it.

"Although a liberal," the *Times* said, "Senator Kirkhill was an outspoken opponent of communism and the possibility that communist sympathizers may have been involved is being considered by the police." (The copy desk, Jerry thought, should have cut the "although" with which the sentence began.)

Under a separate headline, the *Times* ran a column and a half of obituary, and Jerry skimmed through it rapidly before he turned to the *Herald Tribute.*

Kirkhill had been wealthy, inheriting a considerable fortune from his father, who had made it in oil; Kirkhill had spent his early maturity making money, also in oil; he seemed to have been precocious at it; he had apparently betrayed no interests less conventional. He had married in 1927, when he was twenty-three, had fathered a son who had died in infancy and a daughter, Celia, who was born in 1930. His wife died in 1939.

Early in 1942, Kirkhill had sought, and obtained, a commission in the Army, going in as a captain – and, apparently, as a specialist in oil. He had spent most of his time in Washington, but he had traveled widely, and hazardously, on missions. (Presumably, although the *Times* did not specify, connected with oil.) He had been in a transport plane which crashed on a Pacific island; he had survived – apparently by tenacity and physical stamina – where a number of other men had died.

He had left the Army, a lieutenant colonel, in the fall of 1945 and, reading between the factual lines, one could guess he came out a different man, with different interests. He did not return to business, to the making of money. He went into politics, and not to defend the concepts normally dear to the interests of a man of wealth. His advocacy of public housing was an example of this variance from the norm. His even more determined support of a vast middle-western flood control and power project was another. "He became, in his few years of public life, widely known as a progressive of the type once so common in the American west," the *Times* biographer remarked, with the air of one writing history. "But he was one of the first to recognize, and to combat, the rising menace of communism." (This time, Jerry took the conjunction in his stride.)

Kirkhill had been appointed to the Senate by the governor of his State to fill out the unexpired term of an elderly and docile gentleman who had succumbed to the pressures of government and the advance of years. Kirkhill had been prominent for a freshman senator; the spring before he had received his party's nomination for the Senate, and, two months before his death, he had been elected. He was survived by a daughter, Celia, and a brother, George.

Already, the *Times* had found many persons of importance, chiefly in politics, to lament this untimely taking off in carefully chosen words. Members of the senator's own party were eloquent, no doubt sincere; members of the opposition party, appropriately more restrained, nevertheless had words of praise. Men associated with him in his business career lamented his passing; even his enemies, now that he could no longer trouble them, were sorrowed by his death. ("He was a determined fighter for what he believed in and a splendid American. Although we many times disagreed, I feel that the whole country is the loser by his death." – Julian Grainger, director of the Utilities Institute.)

The *Herald Tribune,* in a somewhat more sprightly fashion, provided most of the same facts. It, also, said there were many theories to explain the central and most mysterious circumstances of the senator's death – why he was where he was, dressed as he was. Amnesia was always possible, the *Herald Tribune* pointed out. A side story from Washington reported that Senator Kirkhill had, in recent weeks, been under unusual pressure and that he had visited a Washington hospital for a checkup, leaving the reader to find what he liked between the lines. The senator's notorious antipathy to communism was noted, as was also the indignation which his advocacy of the Valley Authority had aroused among "many prominent business men." The *Herald Tribune,* Jerry North noticed, had missed the one about slum clearance.

Jerry North got up, showered in a melancholy fashion, and dressed sufficiently. He went to Pam North and the cats. The cats were spokes in a wheel, their tails high; the hub of the wheel was a paper plate of ground round steak. The Norths also breakfasted. Pam discovered for herself the varied explanations of the two newspapers.

"The *Times* thinks he was killed by a landlord," Pam said. "Because he wanted to clear the slums."

"Look, Pam," Jerry said, "the *Times* says —" He looked at her. "All right," he said. "The *Times* thinks he was killed by a landlord."

The other morning papers, brought in by a bribed doorman, had other theories. The *News,* leaping at the story with unsuppressed delight, told its readers that, in spite of Senator Kirkhill's liberalism, "amounting almost to socialism, in the minds of many qualified ob- servers," he had been "a target for attack by many former New Dealers in his own party." ("I do think," Pam North said, "that even the *News* might admit that President Roosevelt is dead.") The *News* also, by means on which it was hard to put a mental finger, managed to hint that the senator had been on his way to an assignation. "Among relatives and friends ques- tioned was a fashion model, whose lovely face and unforgettable figure are anonymously fa- miliar to millions of readers of advertisements," the *News* reported, licking its lips slightly, but steering wide of libel.

The *Mirror* was more forthright about the possibility of an assignation, and worked in, with no difficulty at all, the suggestion of a "love nest." Its writer, also, had identified Breese Burnley as a model, and noted that she had been "among those questioned." But if it could not have a "love slaying," the *Mirror* indicated its willingness to settle for a rampag- ing Red. "The F.B.I., cooperating with the police, is believed to be concentrating on this possibility," the *Mirror* said, with firm confi- dence and the knowledge that "is believed" covers editorializing like a blanket.

The *Star*, which had been *PM*, openly ad- mitted its inability to guess how the senator had come to be where he was. "The circumstances are macabre," it observed, "and the police have as yet no information to explain them." But the *Star* did not fail to remind its readers of the violent opposition to the Valley Authority, "with which Senator Kirkhill's name had become identified," expressed by the "power interests."

"Particularly violent in his denunciation of the project as 'socialistic' and a menace to private enterprise has been Julian Grainger, director of the Utilities Institute," the *Star* said, and, a safe two paragraphs lower in the story: "Among those questioned by the police, in addition to Miss Celia Kirkhill and Mrs. Haven, was Curtis Grainger, a son of the utilities magnate, who is engaged to the senator's daughter."

There was, as Pam North pointed out, plenty to choose from.

"A landlord," she said. "A communist. A New Dealer. This Mr. Grainger. Miss Burnley."

"And," Jerry pointed out, "just somebody who wanted to roll him and got mixed up on the dosage of chloral hydrate. Or didn't know that the senator had a weak heart."

"Or your admiral," Pam said. "That's what his daughter's afraid of." She poured more coffee. "And it is funny," she said. "This strange man coming at that particular time.

Get down, Sherry. I haven't finished it myself."

Sherry did not get down. She purred, showing that she had heard, showing that she was still waiting for an egg cup, preferably containing egg.

"Get *down*," Jerry said. Sherry, considering this an affectionate greeting, turned quickly, putting her tail in the cream pitcher.

"Well," Pam said, "we've both had enough cream anyway." She pushed Sherry off the table. Sherry landed partly on Gin. Gin bristled and spoke; then she jumped Sherry, who fled in mimic terror. There was the thudding of cat feet and a sound from the bedroom of something falling. Neither North paid particular attention.

"It would be interesting to see the evening papers," Pam said. "Only there aren't any today, are there? They must be furious."

Jerry thought they probably were; a good Friday night murder which they could not touch until the first Monday editions would make any newspaper furious.

"And the radio doesn't really like murder," Pam said. "Real murder, I mean. I mean —"

Jerry said he knew what she meant.

"So," Pam said, finishing her coffee in a decisive manner, "what do we do about your admiral? Do we go see him and — and —" She stopped, looking at Jerry over her cup.

"Tell him to stop?" Jerry suggested. "Tell him he's worrying his daughter?"

"You could always," Pam said, "tell him this sort of thing will be very bad for his book. Tell him he's undermining; that, as his publisher, you think he shouldn't."

But Jerry North shook his head. He thought, he said, that they should do nothing, that there was nothing useful they could do. "Stay out of it," he said. "Let sleeping murders lie."

"Your trouble, darling," Pam said, "is that you've got a hangover. You take a dim view." She, Jerry realized, was taking a bright view. Physiology, he thought, was unfair. "In an hour or two you'll feel much better," Pam told him. "Ready for anything."

"O.K., Mrs. Haven," Mullins said. "I think that's everything. O.K., Willie?" The last was to Blake, who had been taking notes. Freddie Haven looked at him involuntarily.

"Yes, Mrs. Haven," Blake said, "it's William Blake. And – thank you for helping us."

She had been almost the last for this private questioning, and she had been able to tell them little. They had not asked much; probably, she thought, they had got what they wanted most from the others – from Howard Phipps, first; from Mrs. Burnley, who had known Bruce so long, had known him when he was married before, when Celia was a baby; from Breese who had known him – how well? – two years earlier, just before he and Freddie had begun to be so much together; from Curtis Grainger, who had hardly, so far as Freddie knew, really known Bruce Kirkhill at all, save as the father of the girl he wanted to marry. Celia had not been questioned; she had sat, while the others went into the small library off the living room, remained, returned, and had looked at nothing; had sat, Freddie felt, in a kind of shock, trying to understand a life in which her father would not be. They had been close; closer, Freddie thought now, than she had realized. Curtis Grainger had sat beside Celia, except during the brief period when the two sergeants, Mullins and Blake, were questioning him.

Returning from his interrogation, Phipps had looked at her, shaken his head and shrugged. She could not be sure what he meant by that, except that the police were not, he thought, getting anywhere. He seemed, by his shrug, to disapprove of them. But he had not volunteered anything about the questions he had been asked. Fay Burnley had come back, in her turn, and had said, "I can't *think* what they're *getting* at," and had then looked quickly at her daughter and said, "They want you now, darling," Breese had said nothing, had gone, had returned and still said nothing, and had had no expression on her perfect face. Curtis Grainger had come back with his face somewhat reddened, as if he were angry. He had gone to Celia, and put his arm around her, and then, Freddie thought, the girl had seemed to relax a little.

"If we could talk to you a moment now, Mrs. Haven?" Sergeant Blake said then, from the foyer. He let her pass him and followed her into the library, and closed the door behind him. But the big man named Mullins did most of the actual questioning. It was routine in nature, as routine, so far as she could see, as Sergeant Mullins assured her it was. She had known Bruce Kirkhill casually for several years, during the war, in Washington; she had run into Bruce there, when he was still in the Army. Only for a year and a half had she known him well, only for about six months had they thought of themselves as engaged. She did not know of anyone Bruce had considered his enemy.

"Surely," she said, "it must have been somebody in — in that part of town. Someone who robbed him."

"Could be," Mullins said. "Sure it could be. We just have to consider everything, Mrs. Haven." He smiled at her. "We're just doing what the Loot wants done," he said. "Probably won't come to anything."

Her interview, at least, did not come to anything she could understand. Mullins was very polite; he was, in an odd way, almost consoling. And Blake had let sympathy appear openly in his sensitive face. It had been very tactful, and, long before she expected it, Mullins had said he thought that was everything. She had got up and started to leave the room.

"Oh," Mullins said. "Almost forgot. Something the lieutenant wanted me to ask. About this man Smiley."

She turned and shook her head.

"O.K.," Mullins said. "You don't know him by name. The lieutenant realizes that. But he thought you might just have seen him around — in the building somewhere, maybe. He's a kinduva soft, fat man. Fat face. Funny voice, like it was fat too. The lieutenant thought maybe —"

She was ready, by then. She shook her head quickly. At once she wondered whether she had been too ready, had shaken her head too quickly. Should she have seemed to consider?

But Mullins did not indicate that she had spoken with suspicious quickness, suspicious lack of consideration. He merely nodded, as to the expected thing, and said, again, "O.K., Mrs. Haven. The lieutenant just wanted to know." He smiled then, candor apparent on his face, in his voice. "Between us," he said, "the lieutenant would like to get something on Smiley, I guess. Get him off base." Then Mullins looked at her more intently. "He's not a man you'd want to know, Mrs. Haven," he said. "This man Smiley isn't."

"I don't know him," she said.

Mullins said, "Sure." He said, "O.K." He went to open the door for her. He said, "Would you ask your father to come in for a couple of minutes, Mrs. Haven?"

They had all still been in the living room when she returned, or afterward she remembered that they had. She had sought out her father with her eyes and had found that he was already looking at her. She told him "they" would like to talk to him, and watched him get up, tall and straight. Sometimes, she thought he seemed to be growing taller, straighter, as he grew older. She thought so now. He passed close to her. His face was abstracted. But he patted her shoulder as he passed her, and the touch seemed to be to reassure her. But why, unless he was himself uneasy, should he think she needed reassurance?

Apparently the others had been asked to wait until all had been questioned. And perhaps she should remain with them, as hostess. But they had gone beyond that, she thought, and she did not want to sit with the others, to be reminded by Celia's drained face of the loss they shared, to be conscious of Fay Burnley's so bright eyes. She wanted to get by herself so that she could try to understand what frightened her.

She went to her own room. She tried to think things straight. Was she afraid her father had killed Bruce Kirkhill, or arranged for his murder? I'm not afraid of that, she told herself; I could never be afraid of that. He could never do that, and he had no reason. She corrected herself. I cannot think of any reason, she thought. He did not really like Bruce, did not want me to marry Bruce. But the dislike was impersonal; the admiral did not like, did not understand, "people like" Bruce. That could never have been a motive for murder. To protect her, to protect her from any man who might, in some fashion, appear to her father to endanger her, her father might do almost anything. Except hire murderers, she thought. "Enter two murderers." Enter one — a private detective named Smiley. But his generalized disapproval of "people like" Bruce Kirkhill would not seem, even to her father, a basis for regarding them as dangerous.

And yet — her father was involved in some fashion with Smiley, and he had denied it. That involvement concerned Bruce Kirkhill. It did not — it must not! — concern the murder of Bruce Kirkhill.

And her father would not understand such

people, but he would be sure he did understand him. People like Smiley were to be instructed, they were to do what they were told; when they had done what they were told they, as entities, disappeared. Things had been so all of Admiral Satterbee's mature life. But things were not that way. He would not instruct Sergeant Mullins, Sergeant William Blake. Certainly, he would not be able to instruct Lieutenant Weigand. They would do what they thought appropriate, question or not question, reveal what they had discovered or keep it hidden, as they elected, or as their own superiors elected.

But they would move within certain limits, toward a predictable end. Smiley was different; one had only to look at him, to listen to him, to know that he was different. Her father might understand Weigand and Mullins and William Blake, at least in some measure. They were men with a duty to perform. It made them a little less civilian, a little more comprehensible. (He would never be able, inwardly, to understand that they were not under his authority; that they thought of *him* as a "civilian.")

But with men like Smiley the admiral had had no contact at any time. If Smiley was up to something, out to get something, he would have little trouble with her father, Freddie thought. Why, Freddie thought, I know things that Father –

Her own thought came somehow as an interruption and at the same time as an illumination. For an instant, it seemed that the way she must go was revealed like a path suddenly floodlighted in the darkness. (She had experienced a somewhat similar illumination when she had thought of going to the Norths, but now she did not remember that.) Her father would not be equal to this Smiley, to handling him, to knowing whether to give him what he wanted — since certainly he wanted something — or to fight him. But she herself might be. At the least, she could find out what all this was about, find out how her father was involved, what she could do to help him.

Briggs and Smiley — or would it be Smiley and Briggs? She got the Manhattan telephone book and began to look. There were a great many people named Briggs; she looked first under Smiley. Not Smiley and Briggs, that was quickly determined. She went back to the "B's" and down long columns. Briggs — Briggs — "Briggs and Smiley, b.," with an address on Seventh Avenue in the Forties.

She did not think, as, calmer, she would have thought, that no office would be open at one-thirty on the afternoon of New Year's Day. She lifted the receiver of the telephone on her desk, heard the dial tone, spun the dial quickly. She was not surprised, as she might have been surprised, to receive an answer.

"Briggs and Smiley," a woman's voice said.

Freddie asked for Mr. Smiley.

"He is not in his office at the moment," the impersonal voice told her. "I expect to be in touch with him. May I have him call you?"

"I —" Freddie said, hesitating. To have him telephone the apartment might make difficulties. But she could see no alternative. "Yes," she said. "Please do." She gave her name and the telephone number. She replaced the receiver and sat at her desk, looking at the telephone. She would need to answer it first, and quickly.

She waited for more than an hour; she thought of Bruce, probed the emptiness his death left in her life. It was that — an emptiness. It was not as it had been the other time, when she heard of Jack's death. Then, for a time, it was as if she had fallen over the edge of something, had fallen twisting down, pain twisting with her. But now it was an emptiness, a blank space where her emotions had been, her plans had been. Now it was a question of starting all over, of somehow filling that empty place. When Jack was killed, there had been no such thought, because there had seemed to be so such possibility. She had been younger then, known less then. But that was only a partial explanation. This was a different thing and, except for the circumstances, a lesser thing.

And, she realized, for the moment other things
– uneasiness which was a kind of fear, a feeling
of responsibility which nagged at her – partly
filled the emptiness, as the piled up details of
an elaborate funeral might diminish the pain
of loss, quite simply by lessening the time
which might be devoted to feeling pain.

She thought about Bruce, as if he had been
dead longer than he had, and about her father.
She did not, at first, try to imagine who had
killed Bruce. It was not her father, although he
had involved himself in something, had be-
haved suspiciously and now needed her help. It
was, then, someone unknown; someone who
had met Bruce in a bar, thought he had money,
drugged him to get money. She set this up and
did not analyze it, did not try to find flaws in
it.

At some time in the hour, Marta came in,
after knocking. Freddie did not want food but,
in part because Marta seemed disturbed, let the
maid bring her coffee. Little sandwiches came
with the coffee, and in the end she ate them,
hardly knowing she did so.

The police had gone, Marta told her. But
Sergeant Mullins – "the big one" – had said
they probably would be back. He had told
Marta that, when she showed him out.

Miss Celia had gone to one of the guest
rooms and was lying down and Mrs. Burnley,

Marta thought, was with her. The others, she thought, were still in the apartment, but she was not certain. They had been half an hour or so earlier when, at the admiral's instructions, she had taken coffee and sandwiches into the living room and left them available on a table.

It was about two-thirty that the telephone rang. Freddie lifted the receiver, said "yes?" into it, before the first ring had finished.

"Let me talk to Mrs. Haven," a voice said. It was the expected voice, the buttery voice. "Tell her Mr. Smiley is calling."

"This is Mrs. Haven," Freddie said. "I —"

"What can I do for you, beautiful?" the voice asked her. There was amusement in Smiley's voice.

"I want to see you," she said. "About — about the work you were doing for Father."

"Yeah?" Smiley said. "Why you?"

"I'll explain," she said, and realized that part of it had come off; that, tacitly, he had accepted her statement that he was working for her father. So she had been right to be afraid, anxious. "I'll explain when I see you."

He did not answer at once. He seemed to be considering. She could hear his breathing.

"If you want I should come there," he said, then, "it's no dice, beautiful. I'm not sticking my neck out." He paused. "Not right now,

145

anyway," he said.

"Not here," Freddie agreed. "Wherever you say."

He paused again.

"O.K.," he said, finally. "If this is the way the old man wants it. My office. About half an hour." He paused again, evidently looking at his watch. "Make it three o'clock," he said.

He disconnected, and at once she put the receiver back in its cradle. She felt relief that the waiting was over; relief that the telephone conversation had come off, that no one had, as she had feared someone would, answered the call before she could lift the telephone. If her father had picked up the call on the library extension, for example, he would have put his foot down, he would have given orders. And then, for a moment, she became afraid that he had heard the conversation and learned of the plan. Had there been that faint soundless sound, that echo in hollowness, one heard on a multiple extension telephone line when two of the telephones were in use? She tried to remember, realized that she could not; that if there had been she had not, consciously, noticed it.

But still, as she sat briefly in front of her dressing table mirror, she was conscious of hurrying, of racing to be ready, be out of the room, before a knock at the door announced that her father had come to stop her. When she was ready, save for her coat and galoshes, she opened the door fearfully. But the hall was empty, and the stairs were empty.

If her father had not overheard, did not intend to stop her, he would almost certainly not be in the living room, she thought as she went down the stairs toward the foyer. He would have gone into the library, and from the library he could not see the foyer. If the others were still there, if they saw, it did not matter. None of them would ask an explanation.

But she took her coat hurriedly from the hanger in the closet off the foyer, grabbed up her galoshes and carried them, feeling as if she were pursued. She did not put her galoshes on until she was going down in the elevator. She stood first on one foot and then on the other, pulling on the galoshes. Ben told her she would sure need them, but that it had stopped snowing.

A taxicab was waiting at the corner. It came when the doorman beckoned. It slithered through the snow, twisting as it stopped. She gave the number on Seventh Avenue after she was inside, so that the doorman would not hear. That sense of being pursued still was with her.

It was only ten minutes of three when the taxicab stopped in front of the building on Seventh Avenue. It was a narrow building, an old one, pinched between, dwarfed by, two larger, newer buildings. She looked at her watch. She did not want to be early.

"I'm early," she said. "Can you wait here a few minutes? It's warm in here."

The taxicab driver seemed about to refuse; then he shrugged and tipped his flag to put the meter on waiting time. "God knows why I'm out at all," he said, morosely, and lighted a cigarette. She waited in the cab until her watch told her it was two minutes of three. Then she paid the driver, tipped him with money and a smile, and went along a path shoveled across the snowy sidewalk to the entrance of the building.

The building had a narrow entrance and a narrow hall running back from the street. At the end of the hall a man was sitting on a wooden chair, tilting it back against the wall. He did not get up as he watched her coming toward him. When she was quite near he said, "Yeah?"

"Mr. Smiley's office," she said. "He's expecting me."

"Yeah?" the man said. He did not seem convinced. But he tilted the chair down and the legs hit the floor sharply, with a gritty sharpness.

"O.K.," he said. "You want to see Smiley." He jerked his head toward the elevator.

It was a small elevator. She stood against the back wall of the car, looking at the back of the elevator operator. He was an elderly man with dirty, thin gray hair. He did not say anything as the car went up. At the fourth floor he stopped the car and opened the doors. They opened noisily.

"End of the hall," he said, and jerked his head toward the rear of the building. He stood partly in front of the door of the elevator and did not move aside, so that she had to brush against him as she passed. She felt him watching her as she went down the narrow, dirty hall in the direction he had indicated.

There was a door at the end of the hall with the words "Briggs and Smiley, Investigations," painted on it. There was a pane of obscure glass in the door, and light came through it dimly. She knocked and waited. The knock was unanswered, so she pushed at the door, and it opened in front of her.

It opened into a small room. There was a dusty desk on her right and a hooded typewriter. Beyond were two doors and one of them was open. It was from that room that the light came.

At a desk facing the door, facing her, the man named Smiley was sitting. He seemed to be grinning at her; he seemed to be resting his head on the back of the chair and grinning across the room at her. His teeth were white under parted lips. But he did not speak.

She went across the small outer room and started to enter the office with the open door, and still Smiley did not move and did not speak. He merely sat there, with his lips drawn back from his teeth, so that he seemed to be grinning. She was quite close to him before she realized that he was dead.

There was a bloody red hole in his forehead, and the blood was oozing out of it.

Freddie Haven put her gloved right hand against her mouth, the knuckles bruising her lips. She did not scream. For what seemed a long time she did not move. She merely stood in the doorway, looking at the grinning dead man. She put out her left hand and steadied herself by holding to the door jamb. Nausea began, and she fought it down. Steadying her body by the hand held against the door frame, she tried to steady her mind.

She stood there for what seemed to be a long time, her eyes wide, her gloved right hand pressing against her lips. *If only the mouth would close*, she thought. *If only it wouldn't grin!*

But, she thought, Dad wouldn't shoot a man sitting at a desk, unarmed, unready, without a chance. (He would give an order which, if an infinite series of calculations was correct, would snuff out the lives of a thousand men, invisible to him, unwarned, but that would be different. That would be, that had been, war; that had been his trade. But never one man, sitting at a desk.)

She clung to that knowledge, that certainty. Then, taking a deep breath as if she were about to dive, she released the door jamb and forced herself to move toward the desk. She had to know.

She stood, without touching anything, almost against the desk, and looked down at the grinning face. Now, with the head tilted against the headrest on the chair, the face grinned up at her. Again she felt, again fought to quell, the rising nausea.

The left hand of the body was resting on the desk, the fist clenched. The right hand she could not see. It was below the level of the desk top. She moved to one side of the desk and then she could see the right hand. It was in the partly open center drawer of the desk. It seemed to be reaching for something, clutching for something.

She moved again, forced herself to bend down so that she could see over the right shoulder, follow along the arm, see what the hand had clutched for. Not much light fell into the drawer, onto the hand, but there was enough. The hand — a big hand, soft looking, fat — clutched the butt of a black automatic.

Not unarmed, then. Not unready. Merely – slow. Too slow. He had had time before he died, died grinning, to pull open the drawer, get his hand on his gun. To anyone standing in front of the desk, standing near, the motion would have been evident, the purpose clear. A finger must have been ready on a trigger; pressure, as the movement of the man at the desk was seen, would have been – must have been – instinctive and inevitable. Anyone, trained to emergencies, would have acted when Smiley reached for his gun. There was an instant of time; there had been ready decision in utilizing that instant.

That would have been like the admiral. That decision his training had given him, that readiness to grasp the instant. If there was shooting, you shot first. That was the rule. "Seek out and destroy." Seek out and destroy, seek out and destroy. The words beat a senseless, horribly sensible, rhythm in her mind. Seek out and destroy. Seek out the enemy and destroy him. The man with the grin, with the bared white teeth, had been an enemy. He had been destroyed.

It was hideously clear in her mind. This man, this fat man dead with a grin fixed on his lips, had visited her father a few hours after Bruce Kirkhill had been killed. He had been confident, then; there had been assured insolence in his manner, in the inflections of his voice. He had had no doubt that her father would see him; his attitude had implied that her father had no choice but to see him. *That her father would be afraid not to see him.* And — he had been right. Her father had not been surprised at this attitude, had not protested it.

Her mind stopped there, shrinking away from a clear presentation of what this meant; what, if the premises were true, it must inevitably mean. Her mind, caught in its own logic, fled in a circle, as if within a wall, seeking escape from this inevitability. Dad *must* not have done this; it *must* not be this way. He could not have come here —

That was it! He had *not* come here. He was at home, in the library; probably he had not even been alone. Probably Howard Phipps — somebody, anybody — had been with him from — when was it? At about two-thirty Smiley had been alive. He had telephoned her, made the appointment she had kept, was now, horribly, keeping. Was it only half an hour ago, forty minutes ago, that she had heard that buttery voice? During that forty minutes her father had been in the library, talking to somebody, perhaps eating a lunch which Watkins had brought him. That would be the way it had been.

She saw the telephone, then. For a moment

it seemed to grin at her as Smiley had grinned; seemed to challenge her, to dare her. It is obvious what you have to do, the telephone told her. It is perfectly obvious. You can't get out of it.

She reached a gloved hand for the telephone; with the gloved finger of the other hand she spun the dial. She waited, and Watkins said, "Admiral Satterbee's residence."

"Watkins," she said. He got in a quick "Yes, madam?"

"Can I speak to the admiral, Watkins?" she said. This would be it, the answer would be it.

"Certainly, madam," Watkins said. "I'll tell him you're calling."

She felt as if she had held that first deep breath, taken as if for a dive, from the moment she had released her hold on the door frame until this moment, as if only now could she let the breath go. It came out in a sigh.

Then she heard an indrawn breath at the other end of the telephone line and, eagerly, spoke first.

"Dad," she said. "I just —"

"I'm sorry, madam," Watkins said. "I believed the Admiral was in the library. But Marta tells me he has gone out. Is there any —"

The muscles of Freddie Haven's throat seemed to stiffen.

"Has he — has he been gone long, Watkins?"

154

she managed to say.

"About three-quarters of an hour, I believe," Watkins said. "At least Marta —"

"Yes," Freddie said. Her voice sounded dulled, numbed, to herself. "I see, Watkins."

"Is there any message, madam?"

"No," she said. "It isn't important. Thank you."

"Thank you, madam," Watkins said, as she was replacing the telephone.

She stood, her hand still on the telephone, looking at the top of the desk, looking at nothing. Then the telephone seemed again to be challenging her, issuing its dare.

Call the police, the telephone seemed to say. You know you have to call the police. Tell them what you have found. The challenge — which was the challenge of all her training, all its acceptance of authority — was so overpowering that she started to lift the receiver again, even reached out to dial. She knew the number; everyone in New York knew the number. Spring 7-3100. Or you dialed the operator and said that you wanted a policeman.

She drew back her hand. She stood, looking down at the telephone, her mind racing.

If I telephone the police, she thought, they will make me tell them all I know; I will have to tell them what I know. I know when this man was killed, and they will find out that Dad was not at home, that he had gone out – in time. I know that Smiley saw Dad last night. The police can only suspect, even if the Norths have told them what I said when I went there. But only I can say the man was Smiley. The police cannot disprove it if I say it was another man – a man who looked a little like this man, but was not this man. But if I do not telephone now it may be hours before they find Smiley, and then they will not be able to tell exactly when he died and that will help Dad. And then she thought – if they do not even find me, they will not be able to prove that Smiley was the man who visited Dad, unless he tells them. They will only be able to guess. If they do not find me, I will not have to tell anything I know – not about the time he was killed, or anything.

If I can get out of here quickly, quietly, she thought, if I can keep out of the way until I can talk to Dad, that will be the best way. That is what I have to try to do. She looked at her gloved hands and thought that she would have left no fingerprints, so that they need not even know, need not ever know, that she had been there. But then she remembered the man who had brought her up in the elevator.

He would probably be able to describe her; probably if it came to that, he would be able to identify her. That could not be helped. If it came to the point, she would merely deny it, putting her word against his. The police could choose; they might believe the man, but they would find it hard to prove.

This thing was to get out of the office, away from the grinning dead man. She forced herself to remember everything. She had not at any time removed her gloves; she was carrying only her bag. She did not see that she was leaving anything behind which would help them prove she had been there.

She went out of the office and up the shabby corridor toward the elevator. But before she came to the elevator, she came to a door marked "Fire Stairs" and hesitated a moment. There was a chance that the man on the elevator had not looked at her carefully, would not be able to describe her well. In any case, his description would almost certainly be less precise if he saw her only once than if he saw her twice. She went down the stairs, which were lighted by dim bulbs in the ceiling, which were very dirty.

She had thought the stairs would go to the basement of the building, and that from there she would find a way out unnoticed. But the stairs seemed to end on the first floor. As she came out, she thought, she would be in sight of the man if he was sitting on the wooden chair. She thought of climbing back to the floor she had left, ringing for the elevator, since to be seen again openly would be less damaging than to be seen leaving the building surreptitiously. But she decided to chance it. The man might be in the elevator, taking somebody else up. He might merely be somewhere else, about some other business. He might have gone out for a drink.

She pushed open the door quickly and found herself in the ground floor corridor, near the elevator. The wooden chair was there. It was empty. The door of the elevator stood open, but the man was not in the car.

She walked quickly toward the street door, her heels tapping on the corridor floor, tapping loudly, seeming to her to pound like gunfire in the corridor. But that could not be helped, and it might not be important. If she encountered the man now, she could insist she had rung for the elevator, had reluctantly walked down when it did not come.

She was out of the building, however, before she saw the man, and then his back was to her. He was pushing a snow shovel, unhurriedly, shoveling snow from the sidewalk into the street. Apparently he had not heard her, and she turned away quickly. There were more people around now than there had been; in front of a good many of the buildings men were cleaning the sidewalks. The snow had stopped; the sun was trying to come out.

She had gone perhaps a quarter of a block, and was beginning to feel momentarily safe, when she heard the sound of a siren behind her. She turned, involuntarily. A small police car skidded to a stop in front of the building she had just left. There was a policeman getting out, the man with the snow shovel was leaning on it, looking at him, other people were turning, beginning to move toward the car.

She forced herself to turn back. She forced herself to go on. She walked several blocks south before she allowed herself to hail a taxicab. Then she discovered that she had no idea where she could safely go.

VI

Saturday, 3:30 P.M.
to 5:10 P.M.

Pamela North had left the bathroom door slightly open so that, if necessary, the discussion could be continued while she bathed. Jerry, somewhat the better for aspirin and coffee, lay on one of the beds and blew cigarette smoke at the ceiling. He said, not for the first time, that he failed to see how their intervention would help anybody. He said, also not for the first time, that Admiral Satterbee was not, to that extent, "his" admiral.

"You'll be sorry if you do," Pam said, in reply to this. "I'm just telling you. You know how you hate to get your feet wet. I suppose I'm thinking more of the admiral's daughter, really."

This presented no difficulties to Jerry North. One of the cats, probably Gin, was standing with forepaws on the edge of the bathtub, speculating on whether to join Pam in it. It was probably Gin, because Sherry had, on one

160

rather exciting occasion, decided the same point in the affirmative, and Martini had not, since she was a very young cat, even considered anything so preposterous. Martini observed bathing from a distance, with rather haughty disapproval. Sherry now shuddered and closed her eyes to the horrid sight.

Jerry sorted this out, effortlessly, and replied to the remark addressed to him. He said that the admiral's daughter was even less "his" than the admiral.

"But very pretty," Pam said. "And don't eat the rug."

"Still not mine," Jerry said, and was told not to sound so wistful."

"Seriously," Pam said, splashing, "she wants us to help. Bill wants us to help. I think we ought to help."

That, Jerry told her, was the point. Freddie Haven wanted them to help her; Bill Weigand wanted them to help him. "A conflict of interests," Jerry said.

"Not if —" Pam said. "I'm sorry, Teeney. I didn't mean to. I splashed her. Unless the admiral really did do it, or hired the fat man."

Pam splashed again and the telephone rang. Jerry said, "Hell!" and went into his study to answer it. "If it's for me, I'm in the tub," Pam said, raising her voice. "And don't eat the towel, either." Jerry heard this faintly, from a

161

distance. He said "Yes?" into the telephone.

"This is the admiral," he was told and, in spite of the remnants of his headache, Jerry North grinned. Momentarily, he was tempted to reply, "What admiral?" He said, "Yes, Admiral?"

"There's hell to pay," the admiral said. "This man Kirkhill's got himself killed. One was going to marry Freddie." He paused. "My daughter," he said, amplifying.

Jerry North said he knew. He said it was a very shocking thing.

"Damned nuisance," the admiral told him. "Freddie's upset. Hear you've had experience in such things."

"I suppose you mean murder," Jerry North said. "I suppose you think we're detectives, too. We're not."

"Too?" the admiral said.

"Your daughter does," Jerry told him. "Did, anyway."

There was a brief pause.

"That where she is?" the admiral said. "Your place?"

"Not now," Jerry said. "She was. Early this morning. As you say, she's upset."

"What did she tell you?"

Jerry hesitated a moment, made his decision.

"That you had a visitor last night," he said. "Early this morning. After Senator Kirkhill's body had been found. A visitor she didn't like. She's afraid —"

"No reason to be," the admiral said, cutting in. "But —"

Jerry waited. Admiral Satterbee seemed suddenly to have run down. Then the admiral said, "Wumph."

"Something needs straightening out," he said, and spoke rather rapidly, as if he wanted to get through with it. He made a slight sound, almost a gulp. "Tell you, North," he said. "Appreciate your advice. You and that wife of yours. Know you've had experience."

"We'll do anything we can," Pam North said. Her voice was loud in Jerry's ear. She was on the living room extension.

"What?" Admiral Satterbee said. "North, you there? Who —"

"This is Pamela North, Admiral," she said. "*You're* upsetting your daughter, more than anything. You and this fat man."

"Wumph," the admiral said. "Good afternoon, Mrs. North. Your husband seems to feel —"

"He's got a headache," Pam said. "It's nothing. Champagne, mostly. And hating being mixed up in murder."

"I —" Jerry said.

"Like you to come up, then," the admiral said. "Matter of fact, Freddie's — gone away somewhere. Worried about her." He paused. "Worried about the whole business," he said. "I – I may have made a –" He paused, taking a deep breath before a difficult word. "Mistake," he said. "Can't deny it."

"We'll come," Pam North said. "Won't we, Jerry?"

"I –" Jerry said.

"In – oh, half an hour," Pam said. "If we can get a cab."

"North?" the admiral said.

"All right," Jerry North said. He replaced the receiver. In a moment he was joined by his wife. She was wearing a towel and an expression of animated interest.

"The poor man," she said. "What could we do?"

Jerry looked at her and was pleased with what he saw. He stood up, took her shoulders in his hands, and kissed her.

"All right?" she said.

"Sure," Jerry North said. His head no longer seemed to ache. "Sure," he repeated.

"Innocent admiral," Pam said. "Case of the. Get dressed, Jerry."

He looked at her and grinned.

"Heavens," she said. "I'm practically dressed. All I have to do is put on my clothes."

Dressing took neither of them long. Nor were they long in finding a taxicab. But the trip uptown was a slow slither through snow already dirty, churned by wheels. A maid answered the door of the Satterbee apartment, said the admiral was expecting them, took them through the living room to the library which opened off it. Admiral Satterbee, tall, erect, military in a gray suit, came around a broad, mahogany desk. There were two piles of manuscript pages on the desk, one taller than the other.

"Working on your book, North," he said. "Occupying my time. Freddie's not back yet."

He stood looking at them, and his eyes were worried.

"Good of you to come," he said. He looked at them, looked down at them. "I'm worried," he said. "I'm afraid my daughter is — misunderstanding something." He seemed to seek words. When he found them, they were not clarifying. "Didn't want her to make a mistake," he said. "About Kirkhill. But I may have fouled things up." He looked at them, as if this were illuminating. "Didn't know he'd get himself killed, of course," the admiral said. "Couldn't anticipate that. Wumph?"

He seemed to blame Kirkhill, whose action had been irregular.

"But sit down," he said. "Get you a drink?"

"Yes," Jerry said. "That would be fine."

"Scotch," the admiral said, not as a question.

He opened a cabinet, took out a bottle, glasses, a thermos jug of ice, soda. He mixed three drinks. He handed them around. He sat down behind the big desk.

"Two things," he said. "Where's Freddie? What do I tell the police?"

"I don't know," Jerry said. "As for the police, tell them everything."

Admiral Satterbee shook his head doubtfully.

"Fact is," he said. "Freddie misunderstood. That's why she went to you. Won't the police?"

"Not in the end," Pam said. "But we can't advise unless we know what you're talking about."

The admiral said, "Wumph." He nodded.

"Got something there," he said. "See that, North?"

Jerry nodded to indicate he saw it.

"But first," he said, "what experience we've had has been because Lieutenant Weigand is a friend of ours. We don't keep anything from him."

"Permanently," Pam said. "Or except to keep him from making a mistake, of course."

Admiral Satterbee looked at Jerry North, then at Pam.

"We use our judgment," Pam told him. "About when."

Jerry looked at her and seemed about to speak, but the admiral spoke first.

He said, "Fair enough."

"It was this way," he said. "The man who came here last night was a detective. Private investigator, whatever you call them. I'd hired him. His firm, that is. Made the arrangements with another man. Man named Briggs." He paused. "Have to admit Briggs made a better impression. This was a man named Smiley. This friend of yours, Weigand, asked about him."

"You denied knowing him?" Jerry said.

"Wanted to get a course first," the admiral said. "But I may have been wrong."

"You were."

"Go on, Admiral," Pam said. "Water under the dam."

They both looked at her and she seemed to be, at the same time, looking at herself.

"It's something else," she said. "Under the dam isn't right. Bridge?"

"Or over the dam," Jerry said, And, to Admiral Satterbee, "She's right, of course. Go ahead."

The admiral went ahead, using his short sentences, pausing now and then, leaving a good deal half said. It had started, he told them, with an anonymous letter. The letter was about Bruce Kirkhill.

The writer of the letter had said that he (or she) felt there was something about Bruce

Kirkhill that the admiral, as his prospective father-in-law, ought to know, since it might affect his attitude toward the senator's marriage with Mrs. Haven. Kirkhill was not the upright man he appeared to be. "Used the word upright," the admiral said. "Meant honest." Kirkhill was preparing to sell out to the interests opposing the Valley Authority; to sell out, in the most literal fashion, for money. He had been in contact with the Utilities Institute, with its chairman, Grainger. He had accepted money and was to get more. In return, he would change sides. He was preparing a speech in which he would, carefully – arguing that conditions had changed, not his views; that the present was not the time for so great a public expenditure; saving himself as he chose – come out against the project he had so ardently sponsored.

"Not for that sort of thing myself, you understand," the admiral interjected. "Damned socialism, as I see it. But – makes the man a cheat. An – an outsider. Nobody for Freddie to marry. See my point?"

They saw his point.

"But," Jerry said, "was there anything to prove this? To make you believe it was true?"

There had, the admiral admitted, been nothing you could call proof. There had merely been accusation.

"Then?" Jerry said, making obvious what he meant by the inflection of his voice. The admiral seemed, for a moment, almost embarrassed.

"I didn't like the man," he said. "May as well admit it. All right in his way. Not our way. Couldn't see what Winifred saw in him; thought she was making a mistake." He paused, seemed to make an effort. "Didn't think she'd be happy with him," he said, uneasily, as if he were speaking in an unfamiliar language. "Want her to be happy."

"Of course," Pam North said. "Still?"

"You think I'm an interfering old man," the admiral said. "Got too old for my job; turned out to grass. Nothing to do but try to change my daughter's course." There was bitterness in his voice, and challenge, and a desire to be contradicted. "Girl's got no mother," he said.

"It's not that," Pam North said. "It's —" She paused, uncertain. They waited a long moment, but she did not go on.

"Anyway," the admiral said, "this letter. Suppose I grabbed at it. Thought it gave me something to work on. Admit that, if you like. Probably have thrown it away if I hadn't had this — doubt about Kirkhill. Should have done, naturally." He paused momentarily. "Wish I had," he admitted.

But he had not thrown the letter away, forgotten it. He had hired detectives in an effort to find out whether there was any truth in the letter's accusations.

"You what?" Jerry North said.

"Hired these men," the admiral said. He spoke defensively.

"How did you pick them?" Jerry asked. "Somebody recommend them?"

The admiral looked more than ever embarrassed.

"Advertisement," he said. "Public notice thing, in the *Times*. Investigations. Confidential."

"Good God!" Jerry North said. "You mean you just picked these people at random? Showed them the letter? Asked them to find you proof?"

"About that," the admiral said. "Not the way you'd have gone about it, North?"

"Good —" Jerry began and abandoned it. "No," he said, carefully without emphasis. "But go on, Admiral."

The admiral went on. He explained as he went, defensively. He had seen the man named Briggs, and had been favorably impressed. Briggs had seemed to accept the proffered employment as a matter of course, as something they did all the time, and this had encouraged Admiral Satterbee, had made the whole matter seem one of business routine.

Briggs, it appeared, had, by his appearance and manner, overcome the admiral's hesitancy, and the doubts which the "hole-in-a-corner" office had aroused.

Smiley had not been present during the interview, but Briggs had called him in to meet their new client just as the admiral was about to leave. "Didn't pay much attention to him," the admiral told the Norths. "Figured he was just a man working for this Briggs. See what I mean?"

They saw. He continued. This had happened a couple of weeks earlier. The letter had arrived; the admiral had thought it over for a day or so, then gone to Briggs and Smiley. For these two weeks, or a little less, he had been receiving reports. They were at first vague and inconclusive, seeming to get nowhere.

"What were they doing?" Jerry asked. "How were they going about it?"

The admiral shook his head. That had never emerged, apparently. "Don't know how they do these things," he said. "Follow people around, eh? Put in these microphones? Listen in on telephone conversations? I don't know."

Jerry North shrugged, letting it go.

About ten days ago, the admiral said, Briggs had said they seemed to be getting on to something. He had still not been specific. He had merely said they were making progress, that he thought they were getting somewhere.

But at about the same time, the admiral indicated, he had begun to have doubts about what he was doing. "Began to seem like an underhanded thing," he said. "Realized I ought to go to Kirkhill himself, put it up to him, if I was going to do anything. Nasty, snoopy business, this way."

He looked at Pam North, then at Jerry.

"Realized I'd made a mistake," he said. "Not fair to Kirkhill. Not the sort of thing I wanted Winifred mixed up in." He shook his head. "Didn't see it clearly before," he admitted. "Too concerned about the girl. See what I mean?"

"Of course," Pam North said. "We all do things and wish we hadn't."

The admiral had debated the matter, become increasingly dissatisfied with what he was doing. Apparently what had decided him to terminate the investigation was a conversation he had had with his daughter the evening before.

"Asked her if she was sure she was right," he said. "Said she was. Something about her, way she looked, made me feel I was a meddling old fool. So I called these people and ordered them to send me a bill and call it off. Talked to this man Briggs. He wanted to argue, kept saying they were really getting places. Didn't want to argue, so I just told him circumstances had changed. No use telling him I'd changed my mind, you see. Gave him the idea something new had turned up."

"And this," Jerry North said, "was just before — just about the time, really — that Kirkhill was killed?"

"That's it," the admiral said. "That's it, North."

"But really," Pam said, "nothing had turned up. It was just something you said?"

"Yes," Admiral Satterbee said. "But —"

They waited and, now obviously concerned, unhappy, he went on. He had thought it ended there. It had not. "This man Smiley," he said. "Came around, you know. It was Smiley Winifred told you about. Worried her."

"It did," Jerry agreed. "Go ahead, Admiral."

It had been entirely unexpected; it had been alarming. Smiley had come, and had come confidently, with a kind of gloating assurance. When he saw Smiley, the admiral had realized — apparently for the first time — that his position would be unsatisfactory, even uncomfortable, if the whole matter came out. "Might be misunderstood," he said. "By Winifred. Even by the police." He had realized that, little as he wanted to, he would have to talk to Smiley. He had taken him into the library.

Smiley had done most of the talking, the admiral said. There had been a kind of obscurity, a kind of indirection, about what Smiley

173

had said. Smiley had made a good deal of his duty to work with the police; had talked about his license as a private operative, which the police might suspend or cancel if he did not cooperate. But his first duty, he said, was always to his client. He would have to tell the police that he had been investigating Senator Kirkhill. They might think that, in view of Kirkhill's death, the investigation was important.

"But," Smiley had said, "we always try to protect clients. Briggs and I want to get your point of view on this affair."

"I told him to tell the police everything," the admiral said. "None of it had anything to do with Kirkhill's death; that he knew that. He said he understood that; that I understood that. But he wondered if the police would. He said we had to look at all the angles. Said I didn't realize how the police worked. Said, 'You want to think it over, Admiral. Maybe the police'd think it looked funny. Here you've been trying to get something on this guy. This senator. Hiring us to smell around. Then you say, "Forget it, boys. Something new's come up." Like you said to Harry. "Circumstances have changed." Then it turns out somebody's rubbed this guy out. See what I mean?'"

The admiral had not, he said, been ready for this — for the words, for the tone in which they were spoken. The tone, he gave the Norths to understand, had been more important. "He's an oily sort of man," the admiral said. "Not trustworthy. The kind you get rid of if he turns up in a ship. As a reserve, naturally."

"Naturally," Jerry agreed, without inflection.

Smiley had spoken this piece of his, and then had sat smiling at the admiral. "Lot of teeth," the admiral said. "Showed them all." He had apparently been waiting for the admiral to say something; had spoken as if there were an answer to this. The admiral had not at once got the point. Smiley had waited, had shaken his head at the admiral's slowness and then had said, promptingly, that he and Briggs would hate to have to tell the police "about all this." He had said that they hated to get a client in a bad spot. But there, he had said, it was.

"Still didn't get what he was after," the admiral said. "Not used to men like Smiley. He sounded as if he were thinking of my interests, but I could tell he wasn't. Sounded like a man after something."

"Yes," Jerry North said. The admiral's daughter had said her father was inexperienced. "Innocent," she had said. Could he really be as "innocent" as he now indicated?

"Then," the admiral went on, "he began to talk about his license again. Said that his livelihood depended on it. Said he'd be on a

175

spot if he didn't go to the police with what he knew. Said he'd be taking a big chance. That —"

"In the end," Pam North said, "how much did he want? Not to go to the police?"

The admiral looked at Pam.

"Get it, do you?" he said. "Obvious all along, I suppose." He shook his head. "I got it, finally," he said.

Smiley had not, the admiral told them, said how much he wanted. He had said that he would have to think the matter over; he had made a point that he had not asked for anything. He had even pretended to be surprised at the admiral's interpretation. He had said he would have to talk it over with his partner. He had, in short, avoided putting in words anything which, repeated, would convict him. But the admiral, by then, had had no doubt what Smiley meant. And he had agreed that he would see Smiley again, after Smiley had talked to his partner.

"Going to call me up," the admiral said. "Arrange a place to meet. 'Talk the whole matter over,' he said." He paused. "Well?" he said.

"Go to the police," Jerry told him, at once. "Tell them the whole story. If — they'll understand."

" 'If it's true,' you were going to say," the

176

admiral told Jerry North. "There it is, North. Who's going to believe it? Do you?"

"Yes," Pam said. "Anyway, weren't you here, in the apartment, when Senator Kirkhill was — when somebody poisoned him?"

The admiral shook his head. He was unhappy about it. But he had not been in the apartment. He had gone out to dinner, alone. "There was this party coming up," he said. "Lot to do in the galley. Went out to my club and had dinner. Already told the police that."

"If you can prove it, you're all right," Jerry pointed out.

"North," Admiral Satterbee said, and his tone was suddenly peremptory. "I didn't kill Kirkhill."

"I'm not talking about that," Jerry said. "I'm talking about — if this man, this Smiley, goes to the police, can he make you any trouble? Any real trouble? Beyond embarrassment? Can you prove where you were from — say about six o'clock last evening until the party started? The police will want to know, after they hear this story. As a matter of routine."

They already wanted to know, the admiral told the Norths. He had already told them that he had had dinner at the club. That, presumably, he could prove. But — he had gone out early, walked — it had not begun to snow, then — found he was not yet hungry, stopped in a newsreel theater, stayed perhaps half an hour, then walked on. He had dined quickly, alone. Probably the waiter would remember that. But then he had gone into the club's library and read the afternoon newspapers for, possibly, an hour. The library had been almost empty; he was not sure he had been seen. He had picked up a taxicab in front of the club at a few minutes before nine o'clock, and got home at five after. He had noted the last time; he was vague about the others.

"Not satisfactory," he said. "I see that. You still say go to the police? Tell them the whole thing?"

"Yes," Jerry North said. "If it comes down to that, it will be your word against Smiley's, assuming he tries to go beyond the — what you tell us. Your word ought to be good."

The admiral said he supposed so. He did not appear confident.

"As to where your daughter is," Pam said, "didn't she tell anybody?"

Admiral Satterbee looked at her a moment, apparently arranging ideas. Then he shook his head.

"Watkins says she telephoned me earlier this afternoon," he said. "Says she sounded — excited. I was out. Try to get a walk in when I can. Like to keep in shape."

"But she didn't say where she was calling

from?" Pam asked.

Admiral Satterbee shook his head.

"The anonymous letter," Jerry said. "Have you got it?"

Again the admiral shook his head.

"Tore it up last night," he said. "After I decided not – not to meddle. Burned it in the fireplace." He indicated the library fireplace with a movement of his head. "Anyway," he said, "it was typed. You couldn't tell anything from it."

There was no use going into that, Jerry North thought. Nor did there seem to be anywhere else to go. Admiral Satterbee continued to look at the Norths, first at one and then at the other, as if there were more to be said, or more to be done. But it was not clear to Jerry what the admiral wanted them to say or do.

"Tell the police," Jerry said. "Tell them the whole story. Before this man Smiley does, if you can. As for your daughter –"

But the door of the library opened and Watkins stood in it. He seemed perturbed. He begged pardon.

"Lieutenant Weigand wants to see you, sir," he said. "He insists it's important."

The admiral half rose; he looked at the Norths, and there was, it seemed to Jerry, suspicion in his face. But before he could speak, Bill Weigand had replaced the butler at the door.

Bill looked at the three, and did not seem surprised that two of them were the Norths. His face was grave; he nodded briefly to Pam, to Jerry, and turned to the admiral.

"This man Smiley," Bill Weigand said. "The man you say you didn't see, Admiral Satterbee. He's been shot. Killed." He paused a moment, his eyes on the admiral. "Or did you know?" he said. His voice was level and very quiet.

Admiral Satterbee, standing tall behind his desk, standing straight, merely looked at Weigand. His eyes seemed to go blank.

"About three o'clock," Bill Weigand said, in the same tone. "A little before, a little after. In his office. While he was trying to get at his gun. Or did you know, Admiral?"

He waited, this time.

"No," Admiral Satterbee said. "I didn't know. I —"

"But Smiley was here last night?"

Admiral Satterbee looked at the Norths. Momentarily, he hesitated. Pam North nodded her head.

"Yes," Admiral Satterbee said. "He was here last night. I had —"

"Employed him," Bill Weigand said. He turned, spoke into the living room. "All right, Sergeant," he said. "Bring him in." Weigand moved into the room, leaving the doorway free.

A square man in his middle forties came into the doorway. Sergeant Mullins was behind him. The man, who looked like any business man, looked clean, well dressed, confident, nodded to the admiral.

"Good afternoon, sir," he said.

"Good afternoon, Mr. Briggs," Admiral Satterbee said.

VII

Saturday, 3:40 P.M.
to 6:15 P.M.

After she had got into the taxicab a few blocks down Broadway from the building in which she had left a man who grinned at death, Freddie Haven merely sat for a moment. The taxicab, warm, redolent of cigar smoke, was for that moment less a vehicle than a refuge. But then the driver had turned and looked at her and had said, "Where to, lady?" and she had had to find an answer.

Apparently the police had already been told that the man Smiley had been murdered. Presumably, arriving so soon, they could tell within half an hour or so when he had been shot. Therefore, her reasons for avoiding the police became less exigent. But they did not cease to exist. She did not know how precisely a physician could set the time of death; she assumed that final precision remained contingent on circumstances, even if the body was quickly found. A physician might be able to say, for example, that Smiley had died between two and three o'clock. Then if her father had been in the apartment until two-thirty –

"Lady," the driver said, his voice intentionally patient. "You want to go some place, lady?"

"The Waldorf, please," she said.

She did not know why she had, so suddenly, thought of Howard Phipps. She did not really know him well, although she had seen a great deal of him. It was only that now, as in the early hours of morning when she had made that ill-advised visit to the Gerald Norths, she felt an almost desperate need to share with someone, someone responsible and skilled, the anxieties which obsessed her. It must be, she thought as the taxicab started up, because I suddenly feel lonely. It is as if Dad weren't around any more.

It was not so much – surely, she told herself, it is not so much – that she was by nature dependent. It was rather that, since she had been grown, she had always had someone with whom to share things: share happiness and sorrow, and the little fears of life, and the perplexities. There had been her father, after her mother had died. Then there had been Jack, for so desperately short a time; then her father again. Now, for the moment, with her father thus involved, and thus surrounded and cut off from her, there was no one. She had thought of the Norths, so now she thought of Howard Phipps.

Bruce had trusted Phipps, and relied on him. Bruce would not so have trusted anyone who was not competent, able to meet situations, what her father would call "savvy." And, except for Celia, except for herself, Phipps had been closer to Bruce than anyone, would thus be more involved in these circumstances which, vaguely and inconclusively, appertained to Bruce's death.

The cab went up Seventh Avenue and past the narrow building, hemmed between big neighbors. There were three small police cars in front of it, now, and a large sedan which, presumably, had brought other men from the police. The taxi driver slowed and looked at the cars.

"Something's going on there," he told her. "That's a squad car." His head indicated the big sedan.

She said, "Yes," in a voice which carefully revealed no interest. The driver, she felt, was disappointed; he speeded up, she thought, reluctantly. But he did drive on, drive past the building, and at the next east-bound street he turned to the right. He peered down the avenue as he turned, clearly hating to leave the scene of excitement.

184

It was about four o'clock when she reached the hotel and paid off the cab. She walked down the long lobby, strangely feeling herself conspicuous, feeling that people were looking at her. This is the way a fugitive must feel, she thought; a person who is running away must feel this exposure, this uneasiness.

She found a house telephone and asked to be connected with Phipps's room. There was a wait, and the sound of the telephone ringing. Then Howard Phipps came on. His clipped tones, his controlled voice, were immediately recognizable.

"Howard," she said. "This is Freddie Haven. I'm downstairs. I — can I see you?"

There was the briefest hesitation. Then Howard Phipps said, "Of course, Freddie."

"Shall I come up?" she said.

She had hardly finished the question when he said "no." He would come down, he said; he would meet her by the house telephones; he would buy her a drink. "Wait there," he said. "Won't be a minute."

He was more than a minute, but he was quick. She stood near the telephones, waiting as he had asked. In three or four minutes he came toward her. He moved with familiar quick confidence; he smiled when he saw her, but the smile gave way quickly to an expression of gravity. He held out both his hands in greeting and she, responsive to cordiality, to sympathy, took them both. And then, surprisingly, she thought, why, he smells of perfume! The scent of perfume was, momentarily, very sharp. Then she could not detect it any longer; then she thought, it was one of those odd tricks of the senses. Some woman is near us, wearing a good deal of scent; there was some movement of the air, some eddy of the air.

"You need a drink," Howard Phipps told her. "We both do."

He took her to one of the cocktail lounges, ordered for both of them, did not let her speak of anything, stopped her by a shake of the head, until the drinks were in front of them.

"You need this," he told her, again. "You look done in, poor kid." It was strange to be called a "kid"; curiously it was consoling. "A dreadful thing," he said then, his voice low. "An awful thing. I haven't had a chance —" He broke off. He smiled with a kind of hopelessness. "There isn't anything to say, is there?" he said.

"Nothing," she said. "About Bruce — nothing. Howard, I want you —"

And then, again, the fragrance came, as Howard Phipps bent toward her. It was a low-pitched scent, faintly musky; so feminine that, emanating from a man's clothing, it was improper, unnatural. And now there was no woman near them.

Emotionally she recoiled, even before her mind straightened out this oddity. Then her mind found a solution, made, at the same time, two discoveries. Within a few minutes, Howard Phipps had been holding some woman in his arms; holding her close, so that scent from her clothing had clung to his. That was the first thing; the second was that, without conscious thought, the name of the woman came into her mind. Within a few minutes of the time she telephoned Howard Phipps, he had had his arms around Breese Burnley. He had been holding her close to him. The low-pitched scent, the musky scent, was hers.

The conviction was so absolute that she did not further analyze it; did not tell herself, as she might have, that hundreds of women in New York used that scent, that any one of them might, after an embrace, have left this revealing fragrance on Howard Phipps's clothes. She thought: It was Breese Burnley. She must have been with him when I called. But – why didn't he have her join us? That would have been the ordinary thing to do. There was nothing between them, had never been anything between them, which would make him hesitate to say that Breese was with him, nothing in the fact to prove embarrassing to anyone. Yet —

"Anything I can do," Howard Phipps said, answering her unfinished request. He shook his head. "It's an awful thing," he said. "A horrible, unnecessary thing." For a moment he seemed lost in the thought of Bruce Kirkhill's death. He returned. "What is it, Freddie?" he said. "What can I do?"

But now she did not say what she had planned, tell him what had happened, ask his help. Now Howard Phipps was someone else; now he had become, for the first time since she had known him, a person existing in his own right, complicated in himself. Before, she thought, he was merely a kind of projection of Bruce.

She made herself smile; she made the smile deprecating, a little embarrassed.

"I'm silly," she said. "I — I just had to talk to somebody. Somebody who knew Bruce." She paused. "Howard," she said, "what's it all about? Don't you know — anything? It's so — so mixed up. So strange."

"I know," he said. "I've been trying to think. Why was he *there?* That's the strangest thing. I —"

"Was he meeting someone?" she said. "It — it doesn't matter now, Howdie. Was there some other — somebody else? Somebody he was meeting?"

188

"Down there?" he said, and his voice was surprised. "Some woman, you mean? But why, Freddie? It wouldn't make sense." He drank. "Anyway," he said, "there wasn't anyone else. You know that sort of thing about other men." He smiled faintly. "Usually," he said, "they tell you. One way or another."

"There used to be Breese Burnley," Freddie said. "I know that. But it was a long time ago. Wasn't it?"

He looked at her quickly; apparently he saw nothing in her face.

"There was never anything that mattered," he said. "What there was was years ago." His voice was casual; the casualness, she thought, was studied.

"Breese is lovely, of course," she said. "Don't you think so?" Now she was very casual; she spoke as if abstractedly, as if she were hardly aware of what she was saying. He looked at her again. Her expression was abstracted.

"Sure," he said. "Very lovely." His tone, in turn, displayed lack of interest. He was filling with words a gap in thought. "About this other," he said. "I've been trying to think of something. Some explanation." He seemed to be thinking as he spoke. "There's only one thing," he said, and turned toward her. "You knew about his brother? George?"

She shook her head.

"I knew he had a brother," she said. "A year or two older, wasn't he? But I thought he was dead."

Now Howard Phipps shook his head.

"No," he said. "Unfortunately. So far as I know, so far as the chief knew, I think, George is alive all right. Alive and probably in trouble. Probably making trouble. He always did, from what the chief used to let drop. Always in jams." He narrowed his eyes slightly, as if he were concentrating. "His being there may have had something to do with George," he said. "I'm just guessing but —"

He ordered them more drinks. He went ahead.

Bruce's older brother, he said, had always been a good deal of a problem. Phipps didn't know the details, only the general picture. Inheriting jointly with Bruce at their father's death, he had used up his money fast. He had drunk it up, gambled it up, played it up. When it was gone, he had turned to Bruce for help, and had got it. "Got a lot of it, I imagine," Phipps said. But help had never put George Kirkhill on his feet. It had never kept him out of trouble — financial trouble, once or twice (Phipps said he guessed, rather than knew) trouble with the law, a good deal of trouble with women. "A no-good," Phipps said. "All around, no good."

In recent years, Phipps thought, George Kirkhill had been in the east, still going down-hill.

"For the past couple of years," Phipps said, "I don't think the chief knew where George was, or what he was up to. I guess the chief didn't much want to know; that he figured there wasn't anything he could do for him. Then about a week, ten days ago — well, here I'm guessing."

A week or ten days ago, Phipps said, Bruce Kirkhill had received a letter marked: "Personal. Confidential." Normally, Phipps opened such letters, assuming the inscription to be a device. But this one he had not opened. "Looked as if it might *be* personal and confidential," he said. "Hand addressed, no return address, postmarked New York." He had passed it, unopened, to Senator Kirkhill. He had been in the office when Kirkhill opened it and read it.

"Whatever it was, it made the chief sore," Phipps said. "Upset him. He read it, went back and read part of it again and then he said, 'Damn George!' He sounded pretty sore. Then he tore the letter up and threw the scraps in the wastebasket, and after a bit we went on with the stuff we had to do. But he was upset the rest of the day."

She waited.

Phipps shook his head. He said that was all he knew. He said if he went on from there, he'd be guessing.

He went on from there.

"But," he said, "this brother of his may have ended up on the Bowery. It would have been like him. Maybe he wrote the letter, asking the chief to meet him. Maybe there was some reason the chief thought he had to meet him. Maybe George had got mixed up with crooks of some sort, and maybe somehow he had given them a hold on the chief. Maybe the chief went down to — well, to bail his brother out of something. Maybe the chief didn't like the setup and got tough and —" He finished with a shrug. "I don't know if any of this is true," he said. "I'm guessing. But I do think he heard from his brother, or about his brother. It's the only think I can think of."

Phipps finished his drink. He said, again, that this was all he could think of.

"All you can say for it," he said, "is that it's possible. It's — well, I guess it's just better than nothing; than no explanation at all."

Freddie sat looking at her almost full glass. If it could only be this, only something this simple, this far from all of them! If all of it could only be pushed away, like this; laid on someone anonymous, faceless, a brother of whom none of them had ever heard. The air would be breathable again; her mind clear again. Then it would be simple — a sense of loss, only; grief only. Not this anxiety, this turmoil of inchoate fear, this dark uneasiness. She found she was grasping at the proffered explanation, trying to stretch it, make it cover everything. But how did it cover the man with his teeth bared in death?

"Have you told the police this — this theory?" she said, finally. "Given them this to work on?"

Thrown them this — distraction, she thought? Tried this legerdemain?

Phipps shook his head. He said he supposed he should. He pointed out how small the factual basis was, how spreading the theory built on it.

"But it's something," she said. "Anything is better than nothing. If they knew why Bruce went there —" She broke off. If they knew that it would be enough? She thought: Nothing but all of it will be enough; they won't stop until they have all of it. She wanted to explain that to Howard Phipps, as she had first planned to do; to tell him all of it, about her father, about the man named Smiley, to have him share the problem with her. It was ridiculous, it was meaningless, that she now could not, merely because a man who was nothing to her had, by an inadvertent revelation of emotions she had

193

not expected, or thought about, become a person to be considered as — as what? An individual complexity. No longer, as she had thought of him before, a mind functioning efficiently and abstractly, but a mind like her own, involved. Involved, in short, in all of this, because in part of this his emotions apparently were involved.

"We must tell them," she said. "Tell this Weigand, this lieutenant. Or Sergeant Blake." She was surprised that she thought of Blake. "It's William Blake," she said, and was vaguely surprised to hear the words, to realize that she thought of him as William Blake.

"Funny name for a cop," Phipps said. "All right. Probably I ought to tell them about it, for what it's worth."

Harry Briggs had spoken concisely. You felt that he planned his sentences in advance, was sure before he spoke not only of the content, but of the form of what he was about to say. His recital had been bare, uninflected.

"About two weeks ago," he said, "Admiral Satterbee came to the office. It was the eighteenth of last month, of December. He said he had seen an advertisement we run in the *Times*. He wanted to employ us. He wanted us to check up on something he had heard about Senator Bruce Kirkhill."

He looked at the admiral, then. The admiral nodded.

"From information which had come to him," Briggs said, his words precise, his tone precise, his face square and without expression, "the admiral believed that Senator Kirkhill was accepting bribes to alter his position on the Valley Authority. He wanted to verify this fact."

"Did you ask him why?" Bill Weigand said.

"No sir," Briggs said. "I did not feel that that concerned us."

"But you felt competent to conduct this investigation?" Weigand asked him.

"We accepted — I accepted — his retainer," Briggs said. "Five hundred dollars. If I had not —"

"Right," Weigand said. "Go ahead."

"I personally was concerned with another investigation," Briggs said. "My partner was not in the office at first, although he came in before the admiral left. After the admiral had gone, I conferred with Mr. Smiley and we decided that he would handle it. I believe he continued the investigation until — until today."

"You believe?" Weigand said.

"To the best of my knowledge," Briggs said. "Mr. Smiley was a member of the firm. He did not, as an employed operative would have, make regular reports. He was entirely in charge of the enquiry."

"In other words," Weigand said, "you stepped out of it. You washed your hands of it. Right?"

Briggs looked at the lieutenant for a moment.

"It was Mr. Smiley's investigation," he said, after that moment. "My own time was occupied with another matter."

He was told to go ahead.

"I presumed," Briggs said, "that Mr. Smiley reported at intervals to Admiral Satterbee."

He looked at the admiral.

"Telephoned two or three times," the admiral said. "Never was specific. Just said he wanted to report progress. But didn't say what the progress was."

Bill Weigand's face betrayed no satisfaction with this, but he did not press Admiral Satterbee. He turned back to Briggs.

"You're saying you knew nothing about it?" he asked.

Briggs shook his head, then.

"I did not say that, precisely," he pointed out. "Mr. Smiley spoke to me about it, of course. When Admiral Satterbee telephoned yesterday evening to terminate the investigation, I was able to tell him that our investigation appeared likely to substantiate the allegations against —"

"You said, 'seems like there's maybe something to it,' " the admiral cut in. "Something like that."

"I may have," Briggs said.

"You based that on something?" Weigand asked. "Something you'd got from Smiley?"

Briggs hesitated.

"Or were you just stringing a client along?" Weigand asked him.

"Certainly not, Lieutenant," Briggs said. "You are aware that our agency —"

"Skip it," Bill Weigand said. His voice sounded weary. "What did you base it on?"

"Mr. Smiley was satisfied with his progress," Briggs said. "He had indicated as much."

Weigand looked at him and waited.

"Very well," Briggs said. "Mr. Smiley had come to believe that the senator's secretary, Mr. Phipps, was making contact with the Julian Grainger office. Mr. Grainger is director of —"

"I know," Weigand said.

"I put two and two together," Briggs said. "That is all. If Mr. Smiley had more specific information, he did not disclose it to me."

"And that is all you know?" Weigand asked.

"Except that Mr. Smiley was shot and killed this afternoon, yes," Briggs said.

Bill Weigand looked at the admiral. "Well?" he said.

"Perfectly true, far as it goes," Admiral Satterbee said. "That is, you say this man Smiley was killed. Don't know about that."

"Then," Bill Weigand said, "what did Smiley

want to see you about?"

Admiral Satterbee looked at Jerry North, at Pam North. They nodded together.

"Well," the admiral said, "it began with this letter. Anonymous letter, typewritten. Then –"

The admiral told Weigand what he had told the Norths, ending with Smiley's visit.

"Wanted to get money from me," the admiral said. "Realize I should have filled you in at once. But –"

"But you didn't," Weigand said. "Did you plan to pay him?"

"Don't know," Admiral Satterbee said. "Thinking it over. Don't think I would have."

"But you would have seen him again?"

"Probably."

"Admiral, *did* you see him again? This afternoon. Say at about quarter of three? Did you –"

"No!" the admiral stood up. "You have no authority –"

"I have," Weigand said. "You deny seeing him this afternoon?"

"Certainly."

"You were here, in the apartment?"

"Yes, I – No. Matter of fact, went for a walk. About half an hour. Left some time around two-thirty, quarter of three. Gone three-quarters of an hour."

"Walking?"

198

"Walk every day."

"In snow? And slush?"

"Well," the admiral said, "doesn't snow every day, you know. Eh? If it snows, yes. In the Navy learn —"

"Right," Bill Weigand said. "You went for a walk. You had no communication with Smiley after you talked to him last night, or early this morning? You never found out how much he wanted to — keep you out of this?"

"I didn't talk to Smiley again," the admiral said.

"And you called off the investigation merely because you had changed your mind? Thought you were meddling, decided against it?"

"Yes."

"Bill," Pam said. "Can I ask Mr. Briggs something?"

"In a moment, Pam," Bill said. "Sergeant."

Sergeant Mullins came farther into the room. He said, "O.K., Loot?"

"Get in touch with Mr. Grainger," Bill said. "The son — what's his name — Curtis. And ask him to come over here."

"Ask him?" Mullins said.

Bill Weigand smiled faintly.

"Urge him, Mullins," he said. "Urge him."

"O.K., Loot," Mullins said. He looked at the Norths. Slowly he shook his head.

"All right, Pam," Bill said. "Go ahead."

"Only," Pam said, "was Mr. Smiley following?" She looked at Briggs. "Tailing?" she said. "Would that be a way of doing it?"

Briggs looked at her. He blinked momentarily.

"The senator," Pam said. "Would Mr. Smiley follow him around? Last night, say? Because, if he did, he might – might have found out something."

Briggs considered this. He spoke slowly. He said, "Possibly."

"That," Pam North said, "seems to me much more likely than the admiral. That's what I mean."

She looked around at the men. "Of course," she said, "I realize it's perfectly obvious. Still, nobody *asked* it. I mean –"

Bill Weigand nodded slowly.

"Suppose," Pam North said, "Mr. Smiley was waiting for the senator when he got off the train. And followed him and saw him – saw this landlord give him the knockout drops. Or –"

"This what?" Jerry North said. Then he said, "Oh!" "She reads the *Times*," he told the others. "Landlord is just a figure of speech."

"Of course," Pam said. "Or communist. Or whatever it was. Then, of course, Mr. Smiley decided to blackmail whoever it was, the way he did the admiral and – oh!" She looked at the admiral. Weigand looked at the admiral. Weigand said, "Well, Admiral Satterbee?"

"Told you," the admiral said. His voice was resolute, possibly the resolution was a little exaggerated. "Didn't make any such — such idiotic claim. Would have kicked him out."

"I mean," Pam said, "if we consider the admiral a side-issue." Admiral Satterbee looked at her. He seemed, Jerry thought, faintly puzzled, even resentful. "Two birds with one stone," Pam said. "Both ends against the middle. Sauce for the goose —" She paused and said, "Goodness!"

"Anchor to windward," Admiral Satterbee said, unexpectedly. Everybody looked at him. Then Bill Weigand looked at Pam North. He narrowed his eyes a little; his expression was quizzical.

"Two strings to his bow," Pam said. "The real murderer, because he saw him. The admiral, because he thought he might turn a pretty penny." She shook her head. "The trouble is," she said, in a different tone, "once you start them you can't stop."

"Pam!" Jerry North said. "Listen, Pam."

"Anyway," Pam said, after a moment of appearing to ready to listen, "the real murderer killed him. Mr. Smiley, I mean. Mr. Smiley called him up, or something, and arranged to meet him and — you said his office, Bill?"

Bill Weigand said, "Right." He said, further, that Pam was presumably right about the appointment with — somebody. Otherwise, Mr. Smiley hardly would have been in his office late in the afternoon of New Year's Day.

"Look," Pam said. "How did you happen to go there, Bill? I mean, did you just drop in as a matter of routine and find — find he had been killed?"

Bill shook his head. He was riding it, Jerry North thought; he was letting Pam set the pace, he was content to watch, to take up such points as he chose. Not for the first time, Jerry North had a feeling of interplay between Pam and Bill Weigand, a kind of *rapprochement* in these matters. He found himself wondering, abstractedly, whether Dorian Weigand ever had that feeling about her husband and Pam North. He recalled himself.

"We got a squeal," Bill said. "That is, somebody called us up. Said that there had been a murder and gave the address, and the room number, of Smiley's office. The boys went around."

"And," Pam said, "of course you couldn't trace the call, because it was from a dial telephone and —"

"We didn't," Bill said. "Actually, it's possible to trace a call from a dial 'phone. If you can keep the person talking for forty minutes to an hour. Usually, you can't."

"Man or woman?" Pam asked.

Bill shrugged. "Whisperer," he said. "In and out very fast. The switchboard man isn't sure."

"But," Pam said, "why? To fix the time?"

Bill Weigand shrugged again. He said they didn't know, yet. His tone set a period to this interlude. He turned back to Admiral Satterbee.

"You want to stand on what you've told us?" he asked. "You don't want to say anything more?"

Admiral Satterbee shook his head. He was decisive. But then he hesitated, and did speak, and there was a little triumph in his voice.

"Reason for reporting the murder was to fix the time," he said. "If it was. Notice fixes a time when I was out taking a walk? What do you think of that, Lieutenant?"

That, Bill told him, was a point. It could also be a coincidence. "Further," he said, "who knew you were taking a walk?"

"Watkins," the admiral said. "My dau —" He broke off. But he realized, showed the realization of his expression, that he had broken off too late. He grew suddenly red, angry. "Won't have —" he began, and someone knocked at the door.

Bill Weigand did not seem disturbed at the interruption. He said "Right" to the closed door, and Mullins opened it.

"This Grainger'll be over," he said. "And Mr. Phipps is here, now. The red — Mrs. Haven's with him. They want to see you."

He was told to bring them in.

Freddie Haven came first. She had changed since the party, Pam thought; she had changed ever since the strange interview in the North apartment after the party. Her face seemed to have been hollowed out. She's afraid, Pam thought. She's even more afraid.

Freddie went to her father, holding out her hands.

"Dad," she said. "You're all right? Everything's —"

Possibly, Pam thought, watching the two, there was warning in the admiral's expression as he looked at his daughter. He took her hands. He nodded and smiled, looking into her eyes. Only then, only after a long moment, did Freddie seem to become conscious of the others. She looked at Pam, at Jerry North. By the faintest movement, her eyebrows lifted.

"Your father has," Pam said. "Just now." She wanted to add, "Don't be afraid," but she did not.

Freddie looked at her father again, looked away, looked at Lieutenant Weigand. There was no expression she could fathom in his face; he seemed merely to be withdrawn, waiting. He said, "Good afternoon, Mrs. Haven," and there was no emphasis in his tone.

Phipps had been standing at the door, waiting. He came in, then. He said, "Good afternoon, sir," to the admiral, looked at the Norths and paused for an instant, and then turned to Weigand.

"Yes?" Bill Weigand said. "You have something to tell us?"

Howard Phipps, standing, speaking slowly, a little deprecating by tone, by expression, the information he was giving, told Weigand about Bruce Kirkhill's brother, about the letter which might have been from the brother, or about him. Freddie found herself looking at Lieutenant Weigand, studying his thin face, trying to listen to this with his ears, his mind. But Weigand's face told her nothing. He listened, he was courteous, he seemed interested. But his face changed little.

"You think this might have explained Senator Kirkhill's going where he went, dressing as he did?" Bill Weigand said when Phipps seemed to have finished.

Phipps shrugged.

"It seems possible," he said. He looked at Weigand. "I realize you may have other information," he said. "May know things that makes this of no importance. Still —"

"Right," Bill Weigand said. "We'll look into

it. It may be important." Then he asked a few questions, crisply.

The answers were not, Freddie Haven thought, illuminating. Phipps did not know more about George Kirkhill than his name. He did not know anyone who could give more, could give a description for the police to work on. He hesitated, then. "Unless Fay Burnley," he said. "She knew the chief in the old days. Before the war."

Freddie could not tell how the thin-faced detective took this. He merely nodded; said, "Right," again. Then he went to the door and talked to someone outside it for a few minutes and came back. He nodded to Howard Phipps and, now, thanked him. He said they'd find out what they could.

Freddie thought Lieutenant Weigand was dismissing Phipps, and Phipps seemed also to think that. He said, "Well —" and started to turn away, and Weigand seemed about to let him. Freddie heard, from Pam North, the faint sound of an indrawn breath and then she saw Lieutenant Weigand's long fingers flutter at Mrs. North, although he did not turn his head toward her. "Oh," Pam said, softly, using up the breath she had got ready.

Possibly, Lieutenant Weigand said, his voice still level, almost expressionless, Mr. Phipps could help them further. "Since you're here,"

Weigand said, and Phipps looked interested, nodded, turned back into the room. At a gesture from Weigand, he sat down.

"Someone wrote a letter about the senator," Bill Weigand said. "To the admiral, here. Anonymously. Charging that the senator was selling out, or was about to sell out, to a group which opposed this hydro-electric project. The Valley Authority. Since you were close to the senator —"

Phipps did not let him finish. Phipps leaned forward in his chair, and began to shake his head. He seemed indignant. He feels as I feel, Freddie thought. He feels it's absurd — cruel — a rotten, cruel thing.

"Not the chief," Phipps said. "I'd as soon believe —" He paused, seemed to get control of himself. "It's a lousy lie," he said.

The swirling blackness was back in Freddie Haven's mind. A letter — what wat this letter? She grasped, through the blackness, as this thing Lieutenant Weigand said so flatly, so casually. She looked at her father, and her eyes were wide, puzzled, frightened. He had got his letter, he had believed it, he had hired these men —

"Oh," she said. "Oh!"

"You didn't know about that, Mrs. Haven?" Weigand said. His voice seemed to come from a long way off. "You didn't know about the letter?"

She shook her head, slowly. She looked at her father.

"Made a mistake," he said. His voice was gruff, strained. "Should have torn it up, paid no attention. But —" He broke off. "Made a mistake," he said. "Sorry about it."

"Your father employed a man named Smiley," Weigand said. "And Mr. Briggs, here." He indicated Briggs. "You saw Smiley last night? That was what upset you, Mrs. Haven?"

She nodded, slowly, toward the distant, unemphatic voice; nodded out of the swirling confusion in her mind. She felt that Lieutenant Weigand was waiting for her to say something, make some comment. But she merely nodded again.

Weigand turned back to Howard Phipps. Answering Phipps's assertion, he said that the letter — the allegation in the letter — were things that had to be looked into.

"It's — preposterous!" Phipps said. "You couldn't bribe the chief, get him to sell out. Some crack-pot — it must have been one of those people." He looked at Weigand. "Hell," he said. "You know how those things are. Someone's prominent, a lot of people believe in him, something comes out from under a rock and —"

"Right," Bill said. "I know. Probably you're

right." He paused for a moment. "There's only one thing," he said. "Did you ever hear of a man named Smiley?"

They were all looking at Howard Phipps. They were all looking at him, waiting. Freddie Haven found herself wanting to speak, to break the moment, to tell Phipps that the man named Smiley was dead.

Phipps shook his head. The only expression in his face was one of bewilderment.

"No," Lieutenant Weigand said. "Why should you, Mr. Phipps? But – he was investigating this letter. For Admiral Satterbee. And – he's dead. Somebody killed him."

They all looked at Phipps's face. It was suddenly blank, incredulous.

"But –" he said. "I tell you the chief –" Phipps shook his head slowly, shaking off an impossible thought. "I tell you," he said. "It couldn't be that. It's a coincidence. This Smiley – he was a detective?"

"Right," Weigand said. "Private."

"Then it was something else," Phipps said. He leaned forward; he was intense. "It must have been! He was killed because – because of something else he was doing. It's – it's just one of those things. It's *got* to be."

"Of course," Weigand said, in the same uninflected voice, "the senator might have been approached without your knowledge, Mr.

Phipps. You have only — what would you call it? — a moral certainty. You're very sure, I'm sure Mrs. Haven here is equally sure. But —" He finished with a just perceptible lifting of his shoulders. He seemed to wait.

Howard Phipps began to shake his head, slowly, unwillingly. But then he lifted his head quickly and spoke quickly.

"More than that," he said. "The chief was making a speech in a couple of weeks — a big speech. I was getting material for it, starting a rough draft. He was coming out stronger than ever for the project. You see? If there was anything to this charge, he'd have begun to hedge, to —"

"Yes," Bill Weigand said. "Right. It's a point, Mr. Phipps. As you say, the letter may merely have been the work of a crank." Weigand looked at the admiral, briefly. "Probably was," he said. "Unless — have you any idea who the crank might have been, Mr. Phipps?"

Phipps shook his head.

"You, Mrs. Haven?" Lieutenant Weigand said. "Admiral?" Freddie shook her head. The admiral said, "No."

"Right," Weigand said, without inflection. "Now — for the record. You were walking this afternoon, Admiral? From two-thirty or a quarter of three until three-fifteen or three-thirty.

That's all you can tell us?"

"Yes."

"And you, Mrs. Haven?"

She made her voice steady, tried to make it casual.

"I guess it runs in the family," she said. "Walking in the snow. That's what I was doing."

It sounded false to her own ears; her voice sounded brittle. But Weigand only nodded, said "Right," and turned to Howard Phipps.

"Here until — oh, about two-thirty," Phipps said. "Then in my room at the Waldorf. On the telephone, most of the time. Going through papers. It's — it's all a hell of a mess, you know."

"I," Harry Briggs said, without being asked, "was in my apartment, where your man found me. Listening to the radio."

Weigand thanked him.

"Now, Mr. Phipps —" he began, and interrupted himself and said, "Yes?" in response to a knock on the door. The door opened; it was Sergeant Blake, this time. They all looked at him. Fleetingly, his eyes caught Freddie's, momentarily held them. Why, Freddie thought, I could talk to him! It would be safe, it would be all right. But, as quickly, she realized this was not true. He was one of "them" — one of those who could not be told she had made an appointment with Smiley, talked to him a little before he was killed. And then, for the first time, she realized fully, consciously, why they could never be told. She had talked from an extension here, in the apartment. *In her father's apartment!*

She had begun, unconsciously, to smile toward Sergeant Blake. The smile faded away.

VIII

Saturday, 6:15 P.M. to 11:10 P.M.

Sergeant William Blake had brought Curtis Grainger, and Grainger was angry. His face reddened when he saw Lieutenant Weigand, and he said, "Listen!" Then he looked around at the others, hesitated a moment, and looked again at Weigand.

"All this st-stuff about my father," he said. "In the newspapers. If you th-think —"

"I don't edit newspapers, Mr. Grainger," Bill Weigand said. His voice was mild.

"Libels!" Curtis Grainger said. "I'll —"

"I doubt it," Weigand said, interrupting. "But if you like, if your lawyers like, sue them." His voice was easy. "In any case, don't yell at me," he added. He smiled faintly.

"Dad hasn't anything to do with this," Curtis Grainger said. "You're crazy. You —"

"Sit down," Bill Weigand said. "Sit down, Mr. Grainger."

213

Grainger continued to stand for a moment. His anger seemed slowly to fade. "M-make anybody sore," he said. But then he sat down. He looked at Freddie Haven. "S-sorry, Freddie," he said. "Make anybody sore." He looked at Weigand. "Well?" he said. "You asked me — told me — to come over here?"

"Right," Weigand said. "Take it easy, Mr. Grainger. About these hints in the newspapers. Your father did oppose this project Senator Kirkhill favored? The Valley Authority?"

"You're damned right he did," Grainger said. "So?"

"Please, Mr. Grainger," Bill Weigand said. His voice was patient, obviously patient. "I realize you're upset. Realize your — loyalty. But just let me ask a few questions. Right?"

There was a kind of boyishness about Curtis Grainger. He fumed like a boy. But now he seemed to regain control.

"One thing first," he said, and turned to Freddie. "Celia all right?" he said. She nodded. He turned back to Weigand. "Sh-shoot," he said.

"It has been charged," Weigand said, "that there was an effort to bribe Senator Kirkhill to abandon his advocacy of this hydro-electric project. That your father, or his associates, tried to bribe him — or succeeded in bribing him."

Grainger started to speak.

"Wait," Weigand said. "This charge was made in an anonymous letter. To Admiral Satterbee. Admiral Satterbee started an investigation. Hired private detectives."

Grainger looked at the admiral. Anger crept back into his expression.

"So?" he said. "What lies did they —"

"Young man," Briggs began. "I want you to know —"

"No," Weigand said. He did not seem to raise his voice. But Briggs stopped speaking.

"This is Mr. Briggs, Mr. Grainger," Weigand said. "He is connected with the firm the admiral employed. A man named Smiley was doing the actual work." Again Grainger started to speak. "This afternoon," Bill Weigand said, ignoring him, "Smiley was killed. Shot through the head."

Weigand stopped them. He looked at Grainger and waited. Now Grainger did not speak.

"Well?" Weigand said.

"That's too bad," Curtis Grainger said.

For the first time Freddie Haven saw Lieutenant Weigand appear irritated. He did not speak for a moment. Then he said, "How old are you, Mr. Grainger?" Grainger looked at him in surprise for a moment. Then he flushed. He said he was twenty-six. "Act it,"

Weigand told him. Grainger swallowed, grew more flushed.

"If you mean this man found out something involving my father and got shot for it, it isn't true," Grainger said. "Is that what you mean?"

Bill Weigand's irritation seemed to have passed. He said merely that it was something to be considered.

"No," Curtis Grainger said. "We wouldn't — F-Father wouldn't —"

"According to a report Mr. Smiley made to Mr. Briggs here," Weigand said, "he thought he had established that Senator Kirkhill was in contact with your office." Weigand paused. He looked at Howard Phipps. "Indirectly," he said. "Through you, Mr. Phipps."

Freddie Haven heard her own breath drawn in. It made an odd, small, fluttering sound. She looked at Howard Phipps, saw his orderly face change, his eyes widen. Phipps leaned forward in his chair.

"That," he said, "is a damned lie. Whoever said it. It's —" He broke off. "Also," he said, "it's second hand. Smiley isn't here to —" He broke off again.

"Right," Bill Weigand said. "Smiley isn't here."

(The picture came back to Freddie Haven's mind; the horrid picture of teeth bared at death. Involuntarily, she put fingertips to her forehead, as if to push the picture away.)

"Winifred," she heard her father say, and his voice came from far off. "Winifred. What is it?"

She shook her head. She lifted it and managed to smile at her father. "It's all right, Dad," she said. Then she looked at the thin-faced detective, and found he was looking at her. There was a considering expression in his eyes.

"Third hand," Pam North said. "Mr. Smiley to Mr. Briggs to Bill." She paused. "To us," she said. "Fourth hand."

"Pam!" Jerry North said. "What —"

Pam North said she was sorry. She said it had just come out. She said it hadn't sounded like enough, before, and that she had counted up.

"Pam," Jerry said, and Lieutenant Weigand said, "All right, Jerry," and looked at Pam North and smiled. "Very quick of you, Pam," he said. He did not look displeased.

But it had been opportune, Freddie Haven thought. If Mrs. North had intended to break a building tension, to — she looked at Pam North. Pam North looked back at her. Her eyes were wide and interested, and friendly. Why, Freddie Haven thought, she did intend it.

Howard Phipps still leaned forward in his chair, his eyes still on Lieutenant Weigand, tenseness in his attitude.

"I had no contact with the Grainger office," he said, speaking carefully, making each word heavy. "Curt can tell you that."

"I c-can," Curtis Grainger said. "This man was lying. Or —" He looked at Briggs.

"That is what he told me," Briggs said. "As I told the lieutenant, he did not amplify. But that is what he told me."

"You'll be wasting time, Lieutenant," Phipps said. "This won't get you anywhere. Somebody strings the admiral along, makes it look good. Don't you see that?"

Of course it was that way, Freddie thought. Why can't he see it? And then she thought, Oh Dad. *Dad!*

"We have to go into everything," Lieutenant Weigand said, and his voice was mild. "Even statements which may be baseless. It's part of our job. We have to try to consider every possibility."

"T-try Breese Burnley," Grainger said. "Leave us out of it. S-she was in love with him."

But that is wrong, Freddie thought. That may have been true, but it was long ago.

"Yes?" Weigand said.

"I t-took her home this morning," Grainger said. "After we — after we heard. She broke down. She said things she didn't mean to say. She was in love with Bruce. Still in love with him." He turned to Freddie. "She hated you," he said. "Did you know that?"

218

Freddie shook her head. I didn't know that, she thought; I don't believe that. But at the same time she thought, I wouldn't have known. She's not like most people; she — she's so smooth that things don't show.

"No," she said. "It was a long time ago. Whatever it was."

"It was this morning," Grainger said. "She was broken up." He turned back to Lieutenant Weigand. "She would have tried to keep Bruce and Freddie from marrying," he said. "She might have tried anything. This letter you talk about. Why couldn't Breese have written it? Hoping the admiral would do something to — to stop the marriage?"

He stopped speaking, but he did not seem to have finished. His eyes were narrowed, as if he were working something out.

"Yes?" Weigand said.

"You want a possibility," Grainger said. "You want to consider everything. All right. Breese makes this thing up, writes this letter. How long ago did the letter come?" This last was to Admiral Satterbee. But Weigand answered. "Ten days," he said. "Two weeks."

"She writes the letter," Grainger said. "And, she waits. And, so far as she knows, nothing happens. The letter's a dud. And so —" He spreads his hands, making the implication clear.

"You make quite a jump," Bill Weigand told him.

"Think about it," Grainger said, and Weigand nodded. He said, "Right."

"Meanwhile," he said, "tell me where you were this afternoon between two and four, Mr. Grainger."

"The hell –" Curt Grainger began. Bill Weigand sighed. "Please, Mr. Grainger," he said. His voice was weary.

Grainger flushed again, momentarily. His stammer was somewhat more apparent when he spoke. But he managed to speak quietly; to say he had been in his apartment, to agree he had been alone. "Trying to work things out," he added. When he finished, Bill Weigand merely nodded. He was standing by the admiral's desk, the fingers of his right hand beat a tattoo on the desk. There was a considerable pause.

"Right," he said. "I think that's all, for the time being. Unless someone else has remembered something?"

He gave them time to answer. It appeared that no one had remembered anything. Weigand did not seem surprised.

"It's terribly mixed up," Pam North said, and took, in a perplexed way, a sip from he cocktail glass. "Everything cancels everything."

They were at Charles bar, sitting around the corner. Jerry and Pam sat with their backs to the windows; Dorian Weigand and Bill were at right angles to them. There were not many people at the bar, and those who were looked rather tired, worn by the labor of dragging the New Year in.

"How many do you make?" Pam said, putting her glass down, and addressing Bill Weigand. "I make five, not counting the admiral and Mrs. Haven. Mrs. Burnley and Breese — why Breese, do you suppose? — the brother, if there is any, Mr. Phipps and the Graingers."

Jerry had counted with his fingers. He said that it made six, not five.

"Oh," Pam said, "I count the Graingers as just one. Like father, like son. The sixth would be just a coincidence."

They all looked at her.

"Stray Bowery bum," she said. "An accident. A coincidence." She took another sip. "Although really," she said, "it's all so confused that there's nothing for it to be coincidental with." She considered. "Coincidental to," she said.

Bill Weigand and Jerry North, simultaneously, raised their glasses and drank. They put them down and regarded Pam North, who looked thoughtful.

"Why," Dorian said, "don't you count this

admiral and Mrs. Haven? From what Bill says —" She stopped and looked at her husband.

"Well," Pam said, "for one thing, it makes too many. It would be simply ridiculous. You might as well count Mr. Briggs. Or the senator's daughter. By the way, Bill, is there really a brother?"

Bill Weigand appeared tired; there were lines in his face. He nodded; he said there was a brother; he corrected himself. He said there had, at any rate, been a brother. He had been, apparently, much as Phipps described him. They had been able to find no one who knew him.

"From the outside," Dorian said, "where I seem to be, I'd vote for the brother. He sounds like a man who might be on the Bowery. Probably he inherits something, perhaps a lot." She paused. "You'll have to admit it's neat," she said. "Tidy."

Bill Weigand looked at his empty cocktail glass. His regard was reproachful. Gus moved near and paused, briefly, politely, in front of the four empty glasses. "Please," Pam said. Gus made more martinis. "Bill," Pam said, "where are you getting?"

"We haven't found anyone downtown who remembers seeing the senator last night," he said. "Phipps checked in at the Waldorf early

222

Friday morning, as he said he did. Smiley was shot with a thirty-eight at three o'clock Saturday, give or take fifteen minutes either way. Breese Burnley was still seeing a good deal of the senator as recently as six months ago. Nobody we've been able to get in touch with at the Grainger office remembers seeing Phipps there, or will admit it if he did. Breese saw something of Grainger — the father, not the son — from a little after Thanksgiving until he went back west about a week ago. Mrs. Haven left the apartment this afternoon at eighteen minutes of three. The admiral left three or four minutes before she did. She was perfectly calm when she called and asked for her father a little after three, according to Watkins, who would stand on his head twenty-four hours for either the admiral or his daughter, and may very well be lying. Phipps was in the public library as he says he was most of Friday, consulting reference books on hydro-electric projects — and irrigation projects since Babylon. That is — he was if we believe the times on the withdrawal slips, if we forget he could have been in and out a dozen times without being noticed. Senator Kirkhill telephoned his daughter a little before nine yesterday morning and said he was taking the next train from Washington. He took the nine o'clock, which put him into Penn Station at one in the afternoon. Most of what we're getting from most of these people is only half the truth, if that."

"Goodness," Pam North said. "How thorough!"

Bill Weigand grinned at her. Even his grin was tired. He told her to think nothing of it; he said he had merely scratched the surface.

"That's true enough," Pam said. "But I meant Mr. Phipps, not the police. Why Babylon?"

Bill Weigand shrugged.

"The touch of erudition which adds the *je ne sais quoi*," Jerry North said. "Pass the peanuts, will you, Bill?"

"You'd think," Pam said, "that he'd have Babylon at his fingertips by now. Because Senator Kirkhill had been talking about dams for years. Did Phipps write the speeches, do you suppose?"

Bill Weigand said that Phipps talked about rough drafts. Dorian said, abstractedly, that she would bet. Pam said it certainly was mixed up. Jerry North ate peanuts with crunching sound.

"What I don't see," Pam said, "is how nobody knew the senator had a weak heart. Take Jerry, now." She paused. Jerry stopped crunching.

"There's nothing the matter with my heart," Jerry said. He sounded aggrieved. "Barring that touch of neuritis in —"

"That's what I mean," Pam North said. "It isn't human not to talk about ailments. Particularly if it's a man. Jerry's got this touch of neuritis and everybody knows about it. Once I was waiting in his office late and the cleaning woman came around and asked about it. The cleaning woman for the whole floor. And the senator was a man, of course."

"I don't," Jerry said, "see what being a man's got to do with it." He took a drink, "But she has something," he said.

Bill Weigand nodded.

"Right," he said. "You'd expect most of them to know — his daughter, his fiancée, his secretary, his housekeeper. And Miss Burnley, if he — if they saw as much of each other as they seem to have."

"How much," Pam said. "For innocent ears?"

"Plenty, apparently," Bill said.

"What's she like?" Pam said. "Otherwise, I mean."

"Otherwise?" Bill repeated, and then said, "Oh." "Very polished young woman," he said. "Covered with the best grade enamel."

"But seething underneath?" Pam said. "A hidden volcano?"

"For heaven's sake!" Jerry said.

Bill Weigand said he hadn't been underneath. For all he knew —

"She sounds dreadful," Pam said. "So — so dishonest."

They all looked at her. Jerry North ran the

fingers of his right hand through his hair. He said, "Listen, Pam."

"Calculating," Pam said. "Banking her fires." She looked puzzled. "Just what is a banked fire?" she asked, of the others in general. But when Jerry, in a bemused tone, actually started to tell her, she said, "Rhetorical, Jerry. Some other time." She turned to Bill.

"Would Dorian like her?" she asked. "Would I like her?"

Bill Weigand shook his head.

"Would Jerry?"

"Er," Bill said. "She's a very attractive wench."

"Listen," Jerry said, but Pam shook her head at him.

"Otherwise?" she asked Bill.

Again Bill shook his head.

"Calculating," Pam said, "Conniving. Not letting her face show what her right hand's doing." She stopped and seemed to regard this remark. "Anyway," she said, "not dishonest. Not — candid. Is she?"

"I shouldn't think so," Bill said. "But listen —"

"But suppose to have been in love with the senator," Pam said, not listening. "Really volcanic underneath when he decided to marry Mrs. Haven instead. And then — what are you waiting for?"

"Pamela," Bill Weigand said. "I admit she isn't a person either you or Dorian would particularly like. Now, if I follow you, you decide she killed Kirkhill." He looked at her. "Really," he said.

"Not because of that," Pam North said. "Because she's dishonest. Who else is? Not Mrs. Haven. Not the admiral. Imagine a dishonest admiral!" She paused to give them the opportunity. "Not Mr. Grainger, because people who stammer never are."

"What?" Jerry said.

"Dishonest," Pam said. "It would be much too difficult. Not the secretary, I shouldn't think, although it *is* funny about Babylon. And, of course, we're looking for someone dishonest. A dishonest murderer." She looked around at others. "You all see that," she said. Jerry and Bill Weigand looked at each other, but Dorian looked at Pam North and nodded slowly.

"The old clothes," she said. "The part of town. The whole bizarre setup."

"Of course," Pam said. "To mislead. Dust in our eyes. In other words, a kind of sleight of hand. So that we'd look in the wrong place. *Fundamentally dishonest.* And what did you say once, Bill? 'Make the character fit the crime'?"

"Not I," Bill said. "That is, I quoted. It was Heimrich. But really, Pam! Are you arguing that it's that easy?"

Pamela North looked, for a moment, a little hurt. Then she said she didn't see what was so easy about it. When you looked at it, she said, it was perfectly logical. "Step by step," she assured them.

There seemed nothing to add to this. They welcomed Hugo, coming to proffer a table in the café.

He seemed so certain, Freddie Haven thought, thinking of Lieutenant William Weigand. It was as if, in what was to her only the confusion of an eddying fog, he was moving along clear paths, toward a destination already apparent. There would be no way of stopping him, no way of changing his course. There was not even any way of telling how much he already knew, because he did not seem surprised at anything which was said. It was as if he expected certain things to be said, planned to have them said. She felt that it was hopeless to try concealment; that any move toward concealment she, or any of them, might make would be counted on in advance, planned against, even used.

Freddie, lying on the chaise longue in her room, the lights low, tried to fight against this conviction. This man with a thin face, with a level voice, was not, could not be, what she was thinking him. He had certain methods; by doing certain things, asking certain questions, he achieved calculated results. He was trained for that, professional in that. But under this there was merely another human mind, sometimes baffled – as hers was now; sometimes, from incomplete observations, reaching conclusions which were incomplete, or even inaccurate. He was like anyone else – like William Blake. She thought of Blake with no surprise, as an example which came naturally to her mind. Blake, too, was intelligent, was trained. But things which were not really essential would distract him – the expression in eyes, the shapes of faces, his own sympathy, his own emotions. She had hardly talked with Blake, but she accepted these things about him as obviously true. She did not try to understand why this was so.

She felt, lying there, her eyes closed, very tired and, now, dispirited, rather than frightened. Her thoughts no longer ran, around and around, in the squirrel cage of her mind. All fleetness seemed to have left her mind; it seemed difficult to understand even simple things. She felt that each thought came with a slow effort; it was as if she were moving, heavily, draggingly, through deep sand, each step to be made only by a conscious, wearying attempt.

She had begun to feel this way after Weigand

and the Norths had gone. Briggs had gone at once, after them. Howard Phipps had stayed a few minutes, saying little; seeming let down, puzzled. Then he had said, in a tired voice, that he would have to get back to it; had said, vaguely, that it was all a mess, and had gone, she supposed, back to the Waldorf and whatever he was doing there to knot up the straying ends of a public career hacked through. Celia had come down, hearing Curtis Grainger's voice; had smiled with effort, the same smile strange on her drained face, and Grainger had gone to her quickly, taken her to a corner of the big living room. They had sat there talking, his arm around her. Was that before Phipps had left, or after? It was an effort to remember.

Her father had walked out of the library with the others, but then had stopped just beyond the door and shaken his head with an effort at a smile, and had gone back into the smaller room, closing the door behind him. It was then that Freddie had gone up to her room. Marta had followed her, tried to persuade her to eat something and, failing in this, had gone away with shaking head.

It was hardly thought, this plodding effort which had ensued in Freddie Haven's mind. She had tried, for a while, to determine where Weigand's search was taking him; tried to follow, through this mud, in this fog, the path on which he seemed, to her, to be moving with such assurance. She tried to put together what she now knew, what she had heard. But she could not concentrate. She could only hear voices – the voices of her father, of Phipps, of the man named Briggs. (When she thought of Briggs, she thought inescapably of the man who was dead, and who still grinned at her across his desk. She tried to close her mind to the thought, force the image away.) She heard Pamela North's light, quick voice, intervening when, with the picture of Smiley too vivid in her mind, Freddie had almost given herself away. But most of all she heard the voice, level, unsurprised, of Lieutenant Weigand.

The heavy, plodding wakefulness merged, after a time, imperceptibly, with heavy, plodding sleep. But her mind did not sleep. It toiled on in dreams. She was in a room and, all around her, were voices, sometimes recognizable but without source. The voices were making her play a kind of arduous, exhausting game. She had, within a certain time – the time vague, undefined, yet limited – to put together into a coherent whole what these voices were saying. The words she heard were part of a story, and to win the game, the losing of which would bring some dreaded, but also undefined, catastrophe, she had to put what the voices said together in a certain order. "Circumstances have changed," a voice said, and it was her father's voice. "I just changed Bruce into a man with grinning teeth and you must not call the police." The last started in her father's voice, but then the voice changed into one she could not identify, and another voice broke in saying, "But *darling* I hate you, darling" and then there was a voice which smelled of scent (and this was entirely reasonable and to be expected), saying, "You killed him in the public library, because it was on page three o'clock and where were you, Admiral, because there was so much snow?"

These words, meaningless, full of meaning, became pieces of paper, and she had to pick up the pieces of paper from the floor of the room and put them together, matching the torn edges, but as soon as she found pieces which matched the pieces changed shape in her hands. You have to hurry, hurry, hurry something said, and she hurried so that she could hardly breathe. But then she was in a small room and a hand reached into the room holding a glass and a voice said, "You have to drink this, you know, and you have to hurry if you want to help your father," and she reached out toward the glass but the glass fell between her hand and the other hand, and papers spilled out of it. There were words on the papers and they were at first in a language she could not understand, and then they seemed to be written backward and then, as she looked at them, the words were the names of people. One of the names was Aunt Flo, and another Fay Burnley's, and the third was that of William Blake. There were many other names, some of which she did not recognize, and now she knew that she had to pick the right name — that there was one name which was right, and all the others were wrong, and that if she made a mistake, or even if she waited too long, the walls of the room would close in and —

Then she was awake; quite wide awake. Celia Kirkhill was standing beside the chaise longue, looking down at her. Celia's eyes seemed unnaturally wide open and the skin of her face looked drawn, flattened against the bones of the eye sockets. Celia was dressed in a wool frock; why, Freddie thought, she has changed since the others went.

"I didn't know you were asleep," Celia said. She sat down on the edge of the chaise longue. "Curt told me he thought Breese was in love with Dad. Why did he say that?"

It was oddly as if they were continuing a conversation already begun, as if they had previously been talking about this.

"Something she said when he was taking her home," Freddie said. "Something she did." She reached out a hand, took the girl's slender wrist. "It doesn't mater now, Ce," she said.

"Don't worry about it, dear."

"Dad didn't feel anything about her," Celia said. "Not anything. Not for a long time. She was pretending. If it was anybody —" She paused. Freddie waited. "If it was anybody, it was Howdie," Celia said. "I — I saw them once."

It didn't matter, Freddie told her. It didn't matter any more.

"It's all mixed up," Celia said. "Terribly mixed up." She began to cry. She did not sob, but tears formed in her eyes and began to creep down her face. "Freddie," she said. "It's so awful. So awful."

"I know," Freddie Haven said. She pressed the girl's wrist. "I know, Ce."

"He sounded so — so happy," Celia said. "When he called me in the morning. Just to talk to me. So happy to be coming up. He said, 'Give my love to Freddie, baby.' He said —"

"Don't, dear," Freddie said. "I know."

Celia did not appear to hear her.

"He was getting away earlier than he had expected," Celia said. "He thought he might get here earlier. There was something they had to do and he didn't know how long it would take. But he thought it might not take long and he would —"

"I know, Ce," Freddie said. It is so hard the first time, Freddie thought; so hard when things change, when you first find out that things change. "You just have to try to start over," she said, but it was more to herself than to the girl beside her.

"It was all *planned*," Celia said. There was a kind of incredulity in her voice. It could not be the way it was, because it had been planned another way. "It was all planned, Freddie." She paused a moment. "Freddie," she said. "Dad loved you. He — he was so happy. Underneath this — he was worried a little about Uncle George, but underneath he was so — looking forward to things so."

"Uncle George?" Freddie said. "His brother?"

"Dad worried about him," Celia said. "Things weren't ever right about him. Dad had to —"

"Celia," Freddie said. She was suddenly wide awake. "You said Bruce had something to do. In New York? Was it about your uncle? You said —" she tried to remember the words. "Didn't you say *they* had something to do? That that was why he was coming earlier than he planned? Was it about your uncle?"

She was conscious of a new quickness in her own voice. She saw Celia become conscious of it.

"Why," she said, "I don't know, Freddie. I — I think it was something he said made me think it might be about Uncle George. But I don't think —"

"Try to remember," Freddie said. She sat up, manoeuvred to sit beside Celia, put an arm around the girl's slim shoulders. "Try to remember, Celia. Bruce was coming up early for some special reason. Was it because of your uncle?"

"I thought it was," Celia said. "I can't remember why. I don't think Dad — Dad said that. Wait a minute. He said something about 'the same old thing' or 'the same old trouble.' He was always having to help Uncle George, get him out of some sort of trouble. That's why I thought —"

"He said 'they' had something to do," Freddie said. "Who did he mean, Celia? What did he say?"

Celia shook her head.

"Just that there was something to do in New York," she said. "I think he said 'we,' meaning himself and — well, and Howdie, wouldn't it be? It was almost always Howdie in — in things like that."

"But Howdie didn't meet him," Freddie said. "Howard was in the library, working on this speech." She paused. "Could it have been Breese?" she said. "Or Mrs. Burnley?"

"I don't know," Celia said. "I suppose — but I don't think he had seen Breese for months.

Really, Freddie." She turned to look into Freddie's eyes. "It was just you, Freddie," Celia said.

The poor baby, Freddie thought. She's trying to – to comfort me. She came to do that. But now that is so far off; it matters, but not the way she thinks it matters. Freddie said, "I know, dear," and tightened her arm about Celia's shoulders. But she spoke abstractedly.

It was a little as it had been in the dream, but now the pieces were stable; now they did not dissolve as she touched them, change shape and texture, alter from words written to words spoken. What Celia remembered was vague, inconclusive. But it was still tangible. Bruce had changed his plans. Either he had changed them at the last moment or he had, at the last moment, mentioned the change to his daughter. He had planned, with someone else, to do something in New York during the afternoon or early evening. It as at least possible that it was while doing that something, perhaps as a result of it, he had been killed. And, someone was associated with him. If it was one of them, one of "ourselves," whoever it was had not admitted, had concealed it. But that meant –

Celia was wrong in thinking her father had meant Howard Phipps when he said "we." Phipps had been at the library; he had, she gathered, been able to prove it. Then it was one of the others – Breese Burnley or her mother,

Curtis or – not Father, she thought. *Not Father!* But possibly Celia's Uncle George himself; perhaps that was all Bruce had meant.

"Breese and Howdie," Celia said. "The last few months it's been Breese and Howdie. I don't think it was important, but I used to see them together. Dad knew and – he didn't care, Freddie. So you see –"

Breese in Howard Phipps's arms, leaving the memory of her perfume on his clothing. Breese and Howard; Breese and Bruce Kirkhill; Breese and – Breese and Curtis Grainger, in a taxicab after the news of Bruce's death, and Breese sobbing because the man she loved was dead. Or was that true? Had Curtis invented it, used an invention for his own purposes? To – to lead away from the anonymous letter, and the things it had charged against Bruce and, at the same time, against Curtis's father, or, perhaps, Curtis himself?

"Have you told them about what your father said?" Freddie asked. "Told the police?"

Celia shook her head. "I don't think so," she said. "It's – it's been hard to remember." She had stopped crying, now she began again. Freddie Haven tightened her arm, held the girl, said, "I know, Ce. It's awful, Ce."

"But you ought," she began, and stopped. For what was there, really, to tell the police? That Bruce Kirkhill had planned to be in New York for most of the afternoon and early evening of the day he was killed; that he and someone had planned to do – something. What could the police make of that? It shrank almost to nothingness as she thought of it. It was not worth telling; it was nothing to tell. Then she realized, and was puzzled, realizing, that out of intangible substance of this repeated conversation, she had built something which had almost the solidity of a conviction.

"It must have been Breese," she said. "I think it must have been Breese he was going to see." Celia started to speak, but Freddie shook her head. "Not because there was anything between them," Freddie said. "I don't mean that. But – perhaps there was something left over. Or, from what there had been, something new developed."

Celia shook her head. Her eyes were puzzled.

"I know," Freddie said, and smiled faintly. "It doesn't make much sense, does it?" Even with the background of my own thoughts, it doesn't make much sense, Freddie thought. To Celia – her mind did not finish the thought. If I went to Breese, she thought, asked her whether she saw Bruce, whether he had come to New York to see her, perhaps I could – could help.

"I don't think it was Breese," Celia said. "I'm sure it wasn't."

But she was not sure. Her voice revealed that;

the very shape of her words revealed it.

They looked at each other.

"We could ask her," Celia said. "Why don't we ask her?"

"Not you," Freddie said. "You —"

But the girl began to shake her head. "I have to know too," she said. "Don't you see that, Freddie? Because it was about Dad, I have to know."

Pam North pointed out that she had never said it was the only logical solution. She said it was merely the one which, on what they knew, covered everything. They were back in the North's apartment, after dinner at Charles. They had been talking and sipping drinks; they had had long pauses, in which the silence was companionable. Dorian, curled in a big chair, seemed only half awake.

"But," Pam said, "starting with the character, and with the dishonesty. What else covers both, and everything else? She's calculating, as you said yourself, Bill." Bill Weigand shook his head. "Oh," Pam said, "In other words. I'll give you other words. She was in love with the senator; according to Mr. Grainger, she was still in love with him. She didn't want him to marry Mrs. Haven, so she wrote the admiral this letter. When that didn't seem to be working, she killed him. 'All men kill —' "

"Pam," Jerry said. "No!"

Pam said she was willing to admit it was an exaggeration; she had merely been going to use it because it fitted.

"How did she kill him?" Bill asked. "How did she go about it?"

That, Pam said, she obviously didn't know. She said she could suppose, if they wanted her to. Bill nodded.

"Well," Pam said, "which letter was first?"

They all looked at her.

"The letter the senator got from his brother? Or about his brother," she said. "The letter the admiral got about the senator?"

"According to Phipps," Bill Weigand said, "the George letter was about a week ago. The other was a week before that, apparently. Roughly."

"All right," Pam said. "She writes this letter to the admiral. Nothing happens. Or, she thinks nothing is happening. So she writes this letter about George. Maybe she pretends she *is* George. She says she – George, that is – has to see the senator about something important. Suppose she – that is, George – says she, I mean he, or course, is in a jam which will bring disgrace on the family name and, for his own protection – I mean the senator's own protection – he – I mean George – has to have him –"

241

"You mean the senator?" Jerry said.

"All right," Pam said. "I'm just talking the way I'm thinking. Yes, the senator, bail George out. All right so far?"

"Well –" Jerry North said.

"Good," Pam said. "Now, still pretending to be George, she makes an appointment to meet the senator down on the Bowery, where George is living. I just say the Bowery, of course."

"Right," Bill said. "Of course."

She looked at him. She pointed out that she had been invited to suppose.

"She tells the senator to dress so he won't be recognized, because if he's recognized this gang –"

Jerry North said, "Pam! Darling!" and ran the fingers of his right hand through his hair. "What gang?"

"The gang George is in jam with," Pam said. "Naturally. This gang will recognize him and that will spoil everything. Shall I suppose why?"

"No," Bill said. "Just go ahead."

"Is there anything the matter with it?" Pam asked.

"No," Bill Weigand said. "I don't say there's anything the matter with it."

"All right," Pam said. "She meets him. In disguise?" Pam hesitated. "No," she said, "I don't think that, really. She has some explanation of being there. Wait a minute — this gang has found out about her and the senator, through George, and George has got in touch with her, too, and —"

"All right," Jerry said. He looked at Bill. "You know," he said. "There *isn't* anything wrong with this. At bottom. Prune it a bit and —"

"Right," Bill said.

Pamela thanked them both.

"So while they're waiting," she said, "they have a drink. He is full of knockout drops and they — well, they knock him out. Or partly, because he has to go from wherever they were to this doorway. Then he — then he dies. She's planned it this way, of course — this *oblique* way — so his death won't be connected with anyone in his circle. So the police will think it was a thug. That's what's so dishonest."

"Right," Bill Weigand said. "Go ahead, Pam. Smiley?"

That was easy to suppose, Pam said. Suppose Smiley was following the senator, saw him meet Breese Burnley, guessed what had happened, tried to blackmail Breese, got killed for it. "Anybody could suppose that."

"And then called us up to report his death?" Bill said.

"Why not?"

"Why?"

Pam said she was willing to suppose. To fix the time, for some reason. Presumably, because it was a time for which Breese had established a fictitious alibi. But Bill Weigand shook his head at that. The trouble was, she did not have an alibi. Mullins had checked. She had been in her apartment, alone, taking a nap.

"And," he went on, "this afternoon you thought that Mrs. Haven had found Smiley's body. And, presumably, notified us."

"Bill," Pam said. "You don't think —"

"Oh yes," Bill Weigand said. "I do. So do you. All that nonsense about third of fourth hand."

Pam North said, "Bill," in an aggrieved tone, but he only smiled at her and nodded.

"You're guessing," she said. "Intuition." She paused. "Anyway," she said, "she's just worried about her father, which is ridiculous. Or —" She looked at Bill Weigand.

"Why?" he said. "Why is it ridiculous, Pam?"

The telephone rang, then. Jerry jumped, slightly, as if he had been a considerable distance off. Dorian, curled in a big chair, opened her greenish eyes. Jerry said, "Yes?", said "Yes," again without interrogation, and shook the telephone at Bill. Bill took the telephone and said, "Weigand," and, after a second, "All right, Smitty, go ahead." Then he listened.

His eyes narrowed as he listened. He said,

"Try to get Mullins. And Blake." He listened again. He said, "Right," and replaced the telephone and for a moment looked at it.

"Mrs. Haven has just left the apartment building," he said. "She's got Miss Kirkhill with her. I wonder if —"

He did not finish.

IX

Saturday, 11:30 P.M.
to Sunday, 1:10 A.M.

There had been an increasing tenseness, a
feeling of urgency, of something about to happen, on the way from the apartment building
in Park Avenue to this smaller building in a
side street west of Central Park. Out of the
intangible, something tangible seemed on the
instant of being born. The weariness, the sense
of plodding vainly, had left Freddie Haven; she
had willed the taxicab to go faster, risk the
slippery pavement of the street which ran in a
gorge through the park. Hurry, hurry, she had
thought; if we can only hurry, we will know.

But now all this ended, was snuffed out, in a
small vestibule. Freddie Haven again pressed
the button above the name of Breese Burnley —
pressed it long and hard, and waited. Surely,
now, there would be a responsive clicking
sound in the lock of the door in front of them.
But again, nothing happened.

"It's no use," Celia said. Her young voice was weary; in the dim light of the vestibule, her face was indescribably weary. I shouldn't have let her come, Freddie thought, and said, "I guess there isn't, Ce." Her own voice sounded deadened, muted by disappointment. She had built so much on this and only now realized how much she had built, and on how little. The unresponsiveness of this small inanimate thing, this little push button, mocked her. There's nothing here, it said; there was never anything here.

"She just isn't at home," Celia said. "We should have telephoned."

For an instant, Freddie Haven was almost angry. Didn't Celia realize? You couldn't telephone. You had to go, to see a face, hear a voice, know from the expression in eyes, from the movement in hands, what words did not tell you.

"Yes," Freddie said, "I suppose we should have. She isn't home. We — we may as well go back."

She pushed at the door leading into the building, pushed at it knowing it would be locked. It was locked.

"All right," she said, and turned away from the door toward the other door leading to the street. "Come on, Ce. We'll —"

She stopped. The door was opening. It will

be Breese, Freddie thought, and at almost the same moment saw it was not Breese. Fay Burnley, huddled in her fur coat, came into the vestibule.

"Ouh – h," she said. "It's *so* cold." Then she looked at Celia and Freddie Haven and said, "What's happened? Something *dreadful's* happened." Her voice was excited, and frightened.

"Happened?" Freddie said. "Nothing's happened, Fay. We wanted to see Breese, but she isn't home."

"Then something *has* happened," Fay Burnley said. "Oh – my *baby!*"

It was odd to hear Breese Burnley called a baby, even by her mother. It was, for some reason, rather touching.

"She *must* be here," Fay Burnley said, and moved a step or two so that she could reach out and press the little button above her daughter's name. She pressed it and, as if the identity of the finger would make a difference, all three turned toward the door and waited. But nothing happened.

"What makes you afraid something's happened, Fay?" Freddie Haven said. "She's – she's just out somewhere."

"We'll go in," Fay said. She began to search through her bag, evidently for a key. It took her time, the key seemed to elude her hurrying fingers, to secrete itself in the depths of the bag.

But then she drew it out, and unlocked the inner door. "She was coming to the hotel," Fay said, over her shoulder, going in. "We were going to have dinner together. I waited and − and *waited.*" She started to climb the stairs.

Celia seemed to hesitate, and Freddie said, "Come on, Ce," and they went in after Fay Burnley. They climbed after her, one flight and another flight. The same key unlocked a door with a number on it, opening off a corridor on the third floor.

The apartment was dark and before she went in Fay, evidently knowing its location, reached around the door jamb and flicked a light switch. Light came from a bowl in the ceiling, fell softly on a room which looked like an hotel room, which had two windows at one end, opening on an iron balcony, evidently a disguised fire escape landing. The room was very neat, very empty. No − it was not entirely neat. On a coffee table by the sofa there was a highball glass, emptied, abandoned.

The apartment was small − the living room, a bedroom which was little more than an alcove, a kitchenette which was immaculate and seemed little used. But on the top of the icebox there was a bottle half full of scotch, and a larger bottle, less than half full, of charged water. The bathroom, tiny, seemed more lived in. There were drops of water on the shower curtains, there was tinted bath powder spilled on a dampened bath mat, a big towel on its rack was damp to the touch.

"She isn't *here*," Fay Burnley said, as if her daughter's absence were a new, unanticipated fact. "She isn't *here*, Freddie. Something *has* happened."

"Fay," Freddie said. "Don't get so – so excited. She's just gone out somewhere. You and she misunderstood each other about dinner. She's – she's just out." Freddie looked at her watch. "After all," she said, "it isn't even midnight."

"But don't you *see?*" Fay said. "She was going to have dinner with me. At the Chatham. I waited and *waited*. I kept trying to get her on the 'phone. Where *is* she?"

There was no use answering; there was nothing to answer. Freddie looked at Fay and smiled. The smile was meant to be reassuring. But Fay Burnley looked at her blankly. Why, Freddie thought, she's really upset, terribly upset.

Fay Burnley did not look like her daughter now. The blue eyes were not, now, bright at all; there were lines in her face. She looked very tired. As mustn't we all, Freddie thought, and was glad there was no mirror in which to see herself.

"She would have let me *know*," Fay said,

jumping at the final word in that odd way of hers, almost as if she were a cat pouncing. "Don't you *see?*"

I'm too tired to go on with this, Freddie thought. I'm just too tired. I —

Then a buzzer sounded loud in the apartment. The sound came twice. "Over there," Fay said, and Freddie found and pressed the button which released the downstairs lock.

"It isn't *Breese,*" Fay Burnley said. "She wouldn't —" The sound seemed to have frightened her. After a long minute, there was a knock at the door. It was Freddie who crossed the living room and opened the door.

Sergeant William Blake was standing there. He was very tall, she thought. He was also, at the first moment, surprised.

"Well," he said, "so this is where you are."

He said it only to her; the words were ordinary, but the tone was personal. He seemed pleased, and relieved.

"Why, yes, Mr. Blake," Freddie said. "But why —"

"We've been looking for you," he said, and then, at the expression on her face, went on quickly. "Nothing's happened, Mrs. Haven. We just wanted to find you. You and Miss Kirkhill." He smiled. "The lieutenant got worried about you," he said. "About your — wandering around."

He came into the room. He said, "We just wanted to know where you were." He looked around the room. "Miss Burnley not at home?" he asked.

Freddie shook her head.

"Why?" she said. "Why were you trying to find us? How did you know we weren't — that we'd gone out at all?"

He looked at her. He seemed amused.

"Now Mrs. Haven," he said. "We try to keep an eye on things. We don't — don't want anything to happen to you." He paused, amplified. "To any of you," he said.

"My *daughter*," Fay Burnley said. "Something's happened to *her*."

"Happened to her?" Blake repeated, and the smile left his face. His face seemed to grow tighter. "What do you mean, Mrs. Burnley?"

Fay Burnley told him, pouncing on the words.

"She says it was a misunder*standing*," Fay said, indicating Freddie with a movement of her head. "But it was perfectly *clear*. She was coming to the hotel about seven-thirty and we were going to have dinner and *then* we were coming back here."

"And she didn't get in touch with you?"

"Not a *word*," Fay said. "Not a *word*. And I kept calling and she didn't *answer*."

Blake stood for a moment, looking at her.

Then he turned to Celia, to Freddie.

"You just came over to – to call on Miss Burnley?" he said. "Without telephoning or anything? Or – did you have some reason to think she'd be here?"

Freddie shook her head. "We should have telephoned," Celia said. "We just –" She stopped. Sergeant Blake waited, pointedly, for her to go on. She looked at Freddie Haven.

"We wanted to see her," Freddie said. "To – to talk to her. But she wasn't home. We were in the vestibule downstairs, just about to go and – and Mrs. Burnley came."

Blake looked at her; again there was a kind of insistence about his waiting.

"That's all," she said. "That's really all."

"You didn't come up?" he asked. "Before you met Mrs. Burnley?" His expression was grave, a little worried. He didn't want to ask that, Freddie thought. "I have to ask that," he said.

She shook her head. He looked at her a moment longer, then he nodded. He said, "Right. Of course" and then, "Wait a minute, will you?" He looked around the living room, his eyes intent, as if he were seeing the room so that, if it became necessary, he could sketch it from memory. He went into the kitchen, was gone a moment; came out and went into the little bedroom and the bath which adjoined it. He was gone a longer time. When he returned, there was nothing to be read in his face.

"There's no sign of − anything," he told Fay Burnley. "She bathed, had a drink, went out. Nothing to indicate that anything else happened." He gave her a chance to speak, but she merely looked at him. "It's probably as Mrs. Haven says," he went on. "A mixup about dates. Perhaps she's trying to get you at your hotel."

"You're just going to let it go at *that?*" Fay said. There was incredulity in her tone.

"Yes," he said. "For the moment. Unless you want to make a formal report that she's missing." He smiled. "After all, Mrs. Burnley," he said. "You're worked up, you know. Understandably. But you're magnifying this, don't you think?" His voice was persuasive. Freddie saw doubt in Fay Burnley's eyes.

"Of course, she *could* have misunderstood," Fay said. The admission was reluctant.

"Of course," Blake said. "I'll tell you, Mrs. Burnley. Why not go back to the hotel? As I said, she may be trying to get you there. Leave a note here for her, go on back. Of course, if she doesn't show up in a few hours − but I'm certain she will."

Fay Burnley hesitated. She looked questioningly at the tall detective, and he nodded, slowly.

"Well −" Fay said. "Well, all right." She

turned to Celia. "Dear," she said. "You look so tired. Why don't you come back with me?" She turned to Freddie. *"Shouldn't* she, Freddie?" Fay asked, and nodded quickly. "Anyway," she said, again to Celia, "all your things are there."

Celia hesitated, but more, Freddie thought, from weariness than from indecision.

"She has a room at the Chatham, next to mine," Fay Burnley said to Blake, who said, "Yes, I know." "It was just *simpler* for her to stay at Freddie's last night after —"

"I know," Blake said again.

"All right," Celia said, in a voice too weary to be like her own, almost too weary to be young. "I guess so."

She went with Fay Burnley, after Blake had promised, more than once, that they would find Breese if she were really missing. Blake closed the door behind them. "Give Mrs. Burnley something else to think about," he said. "Having Miss Kirkhill with her, I mean."

"Yes," Freddie said. Her own voice was tired; Blake appeared to notice it. "As a matter of fact," he said, "you ought to be at home yourself. Sleeping." He paused. "What did you want to ask Miss Burnley?" he said.

"Whether —" Freddie said, and stopped. He waited. But this time there was no pressure in his waiting. He smiled down at her. There was, Freddie thought, friendliness in his face.

"Whether she met Bruce," she said. "Yesterday. Celia heard from him yesterday morning. She thinks —"

She told him what Celia thought might have been the implications in what Bruce Kirkhill had said. Repeating it, she felt again that she had built on nothing. But Blake, his face serious now, and interested, nodded as she spoke.

"You thought Miss Burnley might have met the senator?" he said. He hesitated. "Why, Mrs. Haven?"

Now she shook her head slowly.

"You know," she said, "I don't know. I just — just wanted —" She broke off. She looked up at him. "I guess I really don't know," she said. "I was just grasping at something. At — anything. Mr. Blake, do you know what — what it's all about? What's happening?"

He shook his head. For a moment he was not a policeman, for that moment he was merely another person, seemingly as puzzled, at as much of a loss, as she.

"Come," he said, "I'll take you home, Mrs. Haven. There's nothing you can do —"

And then someone knocked quickly on the apartment door. Blake opened it. Howard Phipps looked at them, and blinked.

"Oh," Phipps said. "I — has something happened to Miss Burnley?"

He was as neatly dressed as always, as impeccable as always. The events of the past twenty-four hours seemed to have left little mark on him. Perhaps the small lines in his carefully shaven face were a little deeper than they usually were, perhaps there was weariness around the eyes. And I, Freddie thought, I feel as if I had been pulled through a knot-hole; I must look as if I had been.

Howard Phipps touched his smoothly brushed hair, smoothed it further. But there was anxiety in his face.

"Has something happened?" he repeated, when he was not immediately answered.

"Why no, Mr. Phipps," Blake said. "No. Not that we know of." Blake spoke slowly, almost tentatively. "What makes you think something has happened?"

"Your being here, for one thing," Phipps said. Blake smiled and shook his head. "Her not being."

"After all, Mr. Phipps," Blake said. "It's only a little after midnight. Not late for Miss Burnley. Or, I shouldn't think so." There was interrogation in the last sentence. Did Mr. Phipps think so?

Phipps nodded, but not with conviction. His agreement was to a statement in the abstract. He seemed to think something over, reach a decision.

"She telephoned me," he said. "About – oh, about twenty minutes ago. Asked me to come here. She made it sound urgent. Now, she's not here."

He moved further into the room; he looked around it, as if to verify Breese Burnley's absence.

"I'd worked all evening," he said. "I'd turned in. Just fallen asleep. Naturally, I asked if it wouldn't wait – whatever it was." He looked up at the taller man. "What she wanted to talk about," he amplified, needlessly. "She made me feel it wouldn't wait. So I dressed like a fireman. And – well, rushed over to the fire. And now – now she isn't here."

He was apparently a little annoyed by now; reasonably annoyed, as a man might be who was hauled out of bed for no purpose.

"Was she here when she telephoned?" Blake asked.

Phipps shrugged. He amplified the shrug; said she had not said so, that he had assumed she was.

"Anyway," he said, "she wanted me to come here."

"She had something to tell you?"

Phipps nodded. Then he hesitated.

"Actually," he said, "she didn't say so in so many words. Said she had to talk to me. Said, 'Darling, it's *vital* I talk to you.'" He smiled at his own mimicry. His anxiety seemed to be ebbing slowly. "Actually," he said, "I probably took her too seriously. Things – well, everything sounds more important when you're only half awake. She's just having one last drink with someone. No sense of time." The last was, half humorously, chiding of the absent Breese Burnley.

"Did you assume what she wanted to tell you had to do with the senator's death?" Blake asked.

"Yes," Phipps said. "Naturally, Sergeant."

"Did she say so?"

Phipps shook his head.

"But of course I thought that," he said.

Blake nodded. He said, "Of course." His tone seemed to end the discussion.

"Mrs. Haven and I were just leaving," he said. "Do you plan to –"

The negative shaking of Howard Phipps's head made the rest of the question unnecessary.

"I'm going back to the hotel," he said. "Back to bed. If Bee-Bee wants to talk to me, she can call me again. And wait until morning." He looked at them. "God, I'm tired," he said. "Aren't you, Freddie?"

She nodded.

"Then," Blake said, and moved toward the door. They went out, closing the door. Blake turned the knob, made sure the door had locked itself. He said, halfway down the stairs, "Never mind" to Howard Phipps's suggestion that he would take Freddie home. "I'll take her home," Blake said. "Drop you off, Mr. Phipps?"

Phipps shook his head. "Take you out of your way," he said. "Anyway —" He broke off. He sighed. "God, I'm tired," he said again.

Blake took Freddie to a parked sedan, indistinguishable from any other parked sedan, and Phipps said, "Well," vaguely, and went off down the street. Freddie sat beside the detective in the front seat; Blake pressed the starter and the engine caught, hurried a moment and relapsed to a murmur. It was very cold and still in the street; even in the car, Freddie huddled in her coat. Blake did not put the car in gear immediately; he seemed deep in thought. Then he turned to Freddie as if about to speak, but instead he merely smiled and started the car.

He said little as he went through the transverse road which gashed Central Park, crossed Fifth and Madison and turned up Park. But Freddie did not feel alone; as it grew warmer in the car, she felt almost comforted. Then Sergeant Blake spoke.

"I imagine Miss Burnley'll be all —" he began, and then stopped. They had been driving north along Park, slowly. Now, as if of itself, the car gained speed. Freddie Haven felt a new tenseness in the man beside her. But he did not finish his sentence, or start another. He looked straight ahead; he seemed to have forgotten her.

"What is it?" she said.

He turned with something of a start. He turned enough to smile at her.

"Thought of something," he said. "Want to get hold of the lieutenant." He smiled again. "Nothing for your to worry about," he said. He drove on.

In front of the apartment house, Blake stopped the car, got out on his side and came around to the right hand door and opened it. He held out an assisting hand, but did not actually touch Freddie Haven as she got out. He walked with her across the sidewalk, let her precede him to the building door and then said, "Go on in, do you mind? Wait for me a moment?"

She went into the warmth of the lobby, and she looked back. As Sergeant Blake stepped back onto the sidewalk, another man joined him. She could see them talking, but could hear nothing. The other man, after a time, nodded and shrugged. Then he turned away. Blake came on into the lobby.

"Everything's all right," he said, and walked with her to the elevators.

Jerry North looked at his wrist watch. He

made only formal efforts to conceal this action; he permitted his face to display faint astonishment at what the watch told him. "Well!" he said, as if inadvertently, as if he were very surprised.

That was one way. Usually it worked. But there was nothing to indicate that Bill Weigand noticed anything. Bill sat in the chair by the telephone table to which he had moved to take the call from Smitty. He seemed lost in thought.

"Well," Jerry North said, in a voice artificially brisk. "How about another drink, Dorian?" Dorian opened her greenish eyes. She smiled, shook her head, looked at her husband. Bill Weigand regarded the carpet. "Bill?" Jerry said, very brisk now. "How about —" Bill Weigand shook his head, without looking at Jerry. "Pam?" Pam said, "No, dear." She looked at Bill Weigand.

That almost always worked, Jerry thought. He waited. Sometimes the reaction was delayed. Sometimes you lighted a fuse and had to wait until it burned up to the designated mind and — Jerry North yawned. He covered the yawn belatedly. Nobody paid any attention to it.

"Well," Jerry said again. He took the ashtray from the arm of the chair in which he was sitting and carried it to the fireplace. He emptied it into the fireplace. He looked at Dorian's ashtray, but it was already empty. He advanced toward the ashtray beside Pam.

"Darling," Pam said. "Don't fidget."

He looked at her gloomily, felt the faintest stirrings of animosity. A fine way for Pam to act, he thought. You'd think she never got sleepy; that she wanted —

"Make yourself a drink, Jerry," Pam said. "Eeny, meeny, miney —"

"Oh," Jerry said, quickly, "guess I've had plenty too."

He remained standing. That never failed.

"Moe," Pam said. "Sit down, Jerry."

He looked at her quickly, shook his head quickly. He looked at Bill Weigand. Bill did not look up, but he spoke.

"I know, Jerry," Bill said. He sighed. "We all are," he said.

"Well," Jerry said, continuing to stand.

Bill looked up and grinned at him.

"Sleepy," he said. "Let's go to bed, these people want to go home. I know. But they'll be calling back."

"Oh," Jerry said. "Well, how about a drink?"

"I didn't think it would be so long," Bill said. "It oughtn't to be much longer. Then we will go."

"I wasn't —" Jerry began and stopped.

"Of course you were, darling," Pam said.

263

"Imagine you emptying ashtrays otherwise. Eeny, meeny, miney, moe."

"All right, Pam," Jerry said, and suddenly smiled at her. "I thought you'd already counted out your murderer. Eeny?"

"To be fair," Pam said. "Impartial. Eeny, it had something to do with the attempt to bribe the senator, if there was any. I mean, whoever wrote the letter to the senator, whether it was Breese or someone else, had something. It was because of that something – because he was ready to sell out – that the senator was killed. By somebody who felt very strongly about the hydro-electric project, or the dignity of the Senate, or – or something. Or by Mr. Phipps, who thought the senator's death was better than his dishonor or – well, that's eeny. In brief." She paused and looked around. Nobody said anything. "Meeny, it was the brother, who enticed the senator down there and killed him to get his money. Does he, by the way?"

"No," Bill said, "his daughter does. With a sizable annuity to Mrs. Burnley, in consideration of her long and devoted friendship. Nothing to the brother. Ten thousand to Phipps."

"Well," Pam said, "the brother for some reason we don't know. Or, Mrs. Burnley, to get her annuity."

Dorian opened her greenish eyes. She suggested that meeny was rather heavily loaded.

"Well," Pam said, "miney obviously is Breese. I've explained that. I still like it best."

"Moe?" Jerry said.

"Moe is a spare," Pam said. "For contingencies, like it having been a coincidence. Or for anything else we think of. Which, Bill?"

Bill Weigand looked up at her. He smiled and shook his head.

"Possibly," he said, "a combination."

"Look," Pam told him, "it's already complicated enough. And —"

The telephone rang. Weigand raised his eyebrows at Jerry North, got a nod in exchange, and lifted the receiver. He said, "Yes," and then, "Go ahead, Sergeant." Then he listened. He listened with a quickening interest. The others could hear the voice Bill was hearing, but not the words.

"Right," Bill said. "Right, Blake. You're damned right it's funny." He listened again. "I would have too," he said. "Don't worry." He listened again. "Well," he said, "I'd rather you took over." The other voice resumed briefly. "Right," Bill said, and listened again. "No," he said. "My hosts are sleepy. I'll be at —" He paused, and looked at Dorian. "The office," he said. "In about half an hour. If I'm not, Mullins will know." He hung up, then. The others looked at him. Dorian seemed to have come, instantly, wide awake.

"Blake found Mrs. Haven," he said. "And Miss Kirkhill. They, and Mrs. Burnley, were at Breese Burnley's. Mrs. Haven is home, the girl's at the Chatham with Mrs. Burnley but – *Miss* Burnley's missing. And then a funny thing –"

He broke off, because the telephone rang again. He did not signal Jerry this time. He picked the telephone up and said, "Yes? Weigand." He listened. He said he'd be damned. He said, "Right, Mullins. No, I'll go," and replaced the telephone and, at once, stood up. His face was tense, interested.

"The brother's showed up," he said. "Walked into the East Sixty-seventh Street station and said didn't we want to see him? Just like that. Said, 'Not that I know a damned thing.' "

"But you think he does?" Pam asked, and Bill looked at her.

"You know," he said, "it would be just as interesting if he didn't." He nodded, in agreement with himself. "Even more," he said. Then he looked at Dorian. "Can you get home by yourself?" he said. "Because –"

"Of course," Dorian said. But Bill looked at her doubtfully. "Of *course*," she repeated. "Just because once I –"

"I'll take her, Bill," Jerry said.

"Of all the silly –" Dorian began, coming out of the chair, standing up, in one smooth,

266

unbroken movement. "Just because I let a couple of –" She stopped. "For years before I met *you*, Lieutenant, I was perfectly capable of going home by myself. And –"

She looked at Bill, looked then at Jerry North. She looked at Pam.

"Males," Dorian said. "Oh, all right. I'll be protected." She smiled at all of them, addressed herself to Bill. "Of course," she said, "you've no idea when?"

He shook his head. He said, as soon as he could.

X

Sunday, 1:25 A.M. to 3:05 A.M.

Sergeant Blake had stood for a moment looking down at Freddie Haven. His sensitive face – it was rather a long face, she thought; he was not really a handsome man, as Jack, for example, had been handsome – was somewhat troubled. He looked at her speculatively, his faint smile serious. She waited, but when he did not speak, but merely continued to look at her, she put her key in the lock of her apartment door. Then he spoke.

"Mrs. Haven," he said. "I –" He paused. She looked up at him and waited. "If anything else comes up," he said, "will you – will you not try to handle it alone? Will you call –" he hesitated momentarily – "us?" he finished. "Not try to handle things yourself?"

She thought he was about to continue, as she thought he had been about to say "call me" and had changed it to "call us." But he did not go on. He merely continued to look at her, his expression intent, as if he were trying to see into her mind.

"We only wanted to see Breese," she said, and he shook his head quickly and started to speak and did not. Then, after that instant, he merely said, "All right, Mrs. Haven," and his expression changed slightly, became less personal. He didn't mean about Breese, she thought. He meant — had he been thinking of the man Smiley she had found dead? But that was impossible; no one knew about that. No one could know.

"Anyway," he said, and now his tone was light, "stay put, Mrs. Haven. Leave it to us. Will you do that?"

"Of course," she said, and her tone was like his; her tone pretended that this was not of importance.

She said, "Good night, Mr. Blake," then, and went into the apartment. As she closed the door, Blake had turned to face the elevator gate. He has, she thought inconsequentially, surprisingly square shoulders.

Watkins, looking very tired, met her in the foyer.

"The admiral has retired, Mrs. Haven," he told her.

"Did he take something?" she asked, and Watkins nodded and said, "The usual, Mrs.

Haven." The usual meant one sleeping pill; the admiral believed, on what evidence Freddie had never been able to decide, that he suffered from insomnia. "Go to bed yourself, Watkins," she said. "You must be tired."

He thanked her, admitted he was tired, looked at her with a question in his expression.

"Have they –" he said. "Do they know anything?"

"I don't know," she said. "I don't know what they know, Watkins. It's all – mixed up."

"Yes, Mrs. Haven," Watkins said. "He's worrying. Upset."

Freddie nodded. She said they all were. "We'll just have to wait, I guess," she said.

"Yes, Mrs. Haven," Watkins said. "He's not used to this sort of thing."

"No," Freddie said. "None of us is. Good night, Watkins."

She went up the stairs to her room. Its warmth, its soft lights, made a refuge. Marta was sitting in a chair, asleep. She woke as Freddie came in, and for a moment seemed dazed. Then she got up, and said she was sorry. Freddie shook her head.

"You shouldn't have waited," she said. "Go to bed, Marta." Then she shook her head again. "There isn't anything new," she said. "Nothing different."

"It's a shame," Marta said. "That's what it is,

Miss Freddie. Their making out it has some-thing to do with – with us."

It has, Freddie thought. Oh, it has! But she merely nodded, agreeing. She let Marta help her, declined a "nice hot bath," undressed and got into bed. Marta looked down at her, and Freddie smiled up. "Go to bed yourself," Freddie said. "Everything's all right, Marta."

Marta did not look as if she believed this; she hesitated, as if there were something she should do, as if she did not know what the something was. She looked around the room for it and, not finding it, sighed. "It's a shame," she told Freddie again, and went.

It is a shame, Freddie thought, lying on her back, looking up at the ceiling. It is mixed up – oh God, she thought, what's happening to us? What's happening to Breese? What –

But her mind was too tired. She wanted to look at things calmly, with detachment; she wanted to try, again, to put it all together, to add it all up; to work out something, some frame, which would include all of it – include her father and the grinning dead Smiley, the scent on Howard Phipps neat blue suit, the letter someone had written her father, the brother named George. But her mind was too tired, her eyes were too tired to see the smudged outlines of these things. She felt herself drifting, felt herself asleep. . . .

And then again it was the telephone, ringing loudly, clamoring at her. But she was not surprised; it was as if she had known that this would happen. She reached for the telephone by her bed.

"Yes?" she said and, almost breaking in on the single word, Howard Phipps said, "Thank heaven, Freddie! I was afraid you'd –" He did not finish that. He began again.

"Breese telephoned me again," he said. "Just now. I just hung up. She's back at her apartment. And – there's something terribly wrong. With her, I mean. Can you – can you go there with me?"

"What is it?" Freddie said. "What do you mean? What did she say?"

"She – she was mumbling. Her voice was all fuzzy. I think she's – taken something."

"No!" Freddie said. "Oh, no!"

"She said 'I've got to tell it' – something like that," Howard Phipps said. His voice was tense, excited. " 'Tell someone before –' and then something I couldn't make out. I kept saying 'Breese! Breese!' and then it seemed to get through to her. She said, 'The letter didn't –' and then something else I couldn't make out. Then she said 'Bring Freddie.' She stopped then and I kept talking to her, but it sounded as if she – she'd just dropped the telephone. Not hung up. Just – just put it down somewhere. Dropped it."

"Did you —" Freddie began, but again he cut in.

"I called you first," he said. "Not — not the police. Because — well, because of what she said about the letter. I thought we'd — you and I — if we could see her, hear whatever it is she wants to say. If she can still —"

It swirled in Freddie's mind. It brought fear swirling into her mind. The letter — the letter someone had written her father. That was what Breese had meant; it must be what she had meant. Howard knew it was what she had meant. But then — then —

"I'll come," Freddie said. "I'll — I'll hurry. You'll be there?"

"As soon as I can," Phipps said. "I'm — I'm afraid she wants to — to confess something. To us — you. About — about all of it."

"I'll come," Freddie said again. "I'll come. Don't —"

"No," he said. "Not until we've seen her. But hurry."

"Yes," she said, and heard the click as he hung up. She was out of bed, moving swiftly, fear swirling in her mind. *The letter — her father — the letter —*

She dressed and started for the door. And then, almost as she was opening it, she stopped. She knew then another fear. And

273

quickly then she went back to the telephone on the desk. She looked at a number she had written on the memo pad beside the telephone. She began to dial.

"Then why did you think we'd want to talk to you?" Bill Weigand said. He looked at the man sitting across the desk from him. The unshaded lights of the precinct squad room were harsh on the man's face. He looked like his brother, except that he was a little older than Bruce Kirkhill had been when he died, except that the muscles of his face were softer, sagged a little. He was a big man, too.

"I read the papers," George Kirkhill said.

There was, Bill Weigand pointed out, nothing in the papers about him, about George Kirkhill.

"I'm not a fool," Kirkhill said. "There will be. Anybody could guess that. Bruce was found downtown. I used to live down there." He paused a moment. "Also," he said, "I was fond of Bruce. He was my brother, after all."

"Still?" Bill Weigand said.

"I used to live down — down that way," George Kirkhill said. "In a flop house. When I was drinking. Somebody was going to add things up."

"And you say they don't really add?" Bill asked him.

"To nothing," George Kirkhill said. "It's been

274

two years since — two years ago Bruce made me a loan. I wasn't in contact with him again."

"Yes?" Bill said.

"I was drinking too much," George Kirkhill said. He smiled suddenly, not happily. "Hell, he said, "you've heard. I was a drunk. A Bowery bum. Well, I quit."

"After this last money from your brother?"

The big man nodded.

"Just like that," George Kirkhill said. "Just like that. I — well, I got bored with the other. That's it — just bored with it. No reform. No — moral compunctions. Just bored as hell. I got a place uptown, dried out, looked around for a job. Two years ago. And — I left Bruce alone. Figured he had it coming."

"And since you've been living at this place uptown, working at this cigar store?" Bill said.

The man nodded.

"You didn't write your brother a letter a couple of weeks ago? Or any time within a year?"

"That's right."

"And you were working Friday night? New Year's Eve? From six until two?"

"That's right," George Kirkhill said. "Selling cigarettes to people. Cigars. Most of the people were drunk. A little drunk anyway."

"You realize we can check this?" Bill asked. "About where you were, I mean? Where you've been for the past two years?"

"Sure," George Kirkhill said. "Want you to."

"Actually," Bill said, "that's why you came here, to the station house, isn't it?"

"Sure," Kirkhill said. "Doesn't it make sense?"

"Yes," Bill said. "It makes sense. And that's all you know?"

"I don't know anything."

"Right," Bill said. He hesitated. "You knew your brother, of course. Used to, anyway."

"Sure."

Bill Weigand hesitated, but only momentarily.

"There's been a suggestion," he said. "A charge. That your brother was getting ready to sell out to the people who don't want this hydro-electric development he was interested in. What would you think of that? Between us?"

"I'd think it was a damned lie," George Kirkhill said. "Bruce wouldn't sell out. Anyway – why would he? He's – he was filthy with it."

Bill Weigand nodded.

"He'll leave you some of it," he suggested.

Kirkhill shrugged. He said he could use it.

"But I doubt it," he said. "Anyway – I don't give much of a damn now." He looked at Weigand. "You know," he said, "it's funny, but I don't. Can you believe that?"

276

Bill nodded. He said he could believe a lot of things. Even that. He stood up.

"Thanks for coming in," he said. He read from his notes the address George Kirkhill had given, verified it, watched Kirkhill go. A detective at the door looked at him enquiringly, and Bill shook his head. George Kirkhill could go, without an appendage. George Kirkhill went. After a little, Bill Weigand went out into the cold night, got into his car – which was also cold – and drove downtown to the Homicide Squad office. He hoped things were going to work out from here on in. They'd better, he told himself. Deputy Chief Inspector Artemus O'Malley would be very annoyed if they didn't. Bill thought of O'Malley, who was undoubtedly comfortably asleep, and thought it would be fine to go home and turn in. He thought of Dorian, waiting in their apartment. He sighed deeply, and drove on, in the wrong direction. He stopped in front of the building in West Twentieth street and climbed the stairs to his small office.

Sergeant Mullins was sitting at Weigand's desk. He got up and sat on it; Bill sat in the chair. Mullins looked interested.

"About what I thought," Bill said. "Otherwise, why would he show up so conveniently? Why not make us find him?"

"That's right," Mullins said. "The

boys are checking up?"

"Right," Bill said. "We've got to keep everybody honest. Even if they are."

"You know what, Loot," Mullins said, "sometimes you talk like Mrs. North. You know that?"

Mullins was advised not to let it get him down.

"Speaking of the Norths," Mullins said, "where are they?"

"Safe at home," Bill told him. "At least, Jerry may still be taking my wife home. Don't worry, Mullins."

"Listen," Mullins said. "I *like* them. Only – well, everything gets so screwy. You know that, Loot."

Not this time, Bill told him, smiled and went to business. Yes, the alarm was out; the Missing Persons Bureau was on it.

"Although," Mullins said, and Weigand, not waiting for him to finish, said "Right."

"To keep everybody honest," he said. "In case we're wrong." He tapped his fingers on his desk top, beating out a rhythm. "Blake?" he said.

"Unless something got fouled up," Mullins said, "he's there."

Bill Weigand nodded. He continued with his tapping. He said, more to himself than to Mullins, that it was working out very neatly. Mullins made sounds; the Loot liked to have sounds made, at appropriate intervals, when he was talking to himself.

"Miss Burnley was in love with the senator," Bill said, and counted it off with one finger. "She didn't want him to marry Mrs. Haven. She picked up — probably from the elder Grainger — something she thought would be useful. She wrote the letter to the admiral. Right?"

Mullins accepted the invitation.

"You figure he was selling out?" Mullins said. "Like she said? If she wrote the letter?"

"I figure she thought so," Bill told him. "And that she got it, at least the start of it, from Grainger himself. Not the boy, the old man. I doubt if they'd let young Grainger in on anything so — so touchy. Anyway, say she wrote the letter. The admiral, instead of flying off in all directions, telling the senator to quit darkening his door, hires Briggs and Smiley."

"The poor old guy," Mullins said. "Jeeze."

"Right," Bill said. "She doesn't know about this, thinks the letter was a dud, takes other methods. She, incidentally, would have been almost certain to know about the senator's weak heart. Somehow, she gets him to go downtown, dress up in old clothes, have a drink of chloral. He goes off and dies; so he doesn't marry Mrs. Haven."

"Like Mr. Grainger suggested," Mullins said.

"The one who stutters."

"Right," Bill said. "As was suggested. But Smiley is following the senator, sees Miss Burnley with him, decides there's money in what he knows, tires to collect and —" Bill shrugged.

"Collects lead," Mullins said.

"Right," Bill Weigand said. "That's the picture, Sergeant. You like it?

"Well," Mullins said. "It's neat. And then she runs away?"

"Right," Bill said. "Then she runs away."

"Why?" Mullins asked.

"Because, when the news comes that her plan's really worked, that Kirkhill's dead, she breaks down and lets out she was still in love with him. Lets it out to young Grainger. Remember, it's in the picture she really loved Kirkhill; probably she didn't quite believe, didn't really believe, she'd killed him. She waited all evening, keeping bright and chipper for the party, all sorts of things going on underneath — and then Blake walks in and tells her and the rest of them that the senator's dead. She doesn't have to wait for identification. She knows who it is, all right. She manages to hold in until she gets in the cab with Grainger, then she gives way. Later she gets to thinking about what she's said, realized we'll follow up, decides to run. O.K., Mullins?"

"O.K., Loot," Mullins said. "It's a picture."

"A very nice picture," Bill Weigand said. "Simple, tangible, possibly not covering everything, but it isn't necessary to cover everything. We know that. The extraneous always crops up. Brother George, the letter Mr. Phipps thinks the senator got from George, or about George, and destroyed. Phipps was just guessing, of course. He says so. It remains intangible. Presumably it was from, or about, somebody else named George."

"And Mrs. Haven?"

"Innocent bystander," Bill said. "As, essentially, her father is. And Celia. And Mr. Phipps, of course. It's neat enough, Mullins."

"Who called to tell us Smiley'd got it?" Mullins asked.

"Who but Mrs. Burnley?" Bill asked. "Wanting, for some reason, to establish the time. Something we're to find out when we catch her."

"If," Mullins said.

Bill Weigand looked across the room at the wall, then. His face changed; the tattoo of his fingers grew more rapid. The ringing of the telephone interrupted him. He answered, listened, noted down numbers in two groups of three. He said, "Thanks," hung up, and said to Mullins, "As we thought."

"Smitty?" Mullins said. Bill Weigand nodded. He said, "Right, Sergeant." He was silent for a long moment. "I hope Blake makes out all right," he said, then. "We'll just have to wait."

"He's a good man," Sergeant Mullins said, generously.

Pamela North sat in a deep chair and three cats sat on Pamela North. They had needed resolution to find space on this favorite human, but they did not lack resolution. Martini had come first, speaking softly, but with command, and Pam, who had been curled in the chair, stretched out her legs. Martini flicked up from the floor, advanced up Pamela and approached a masked face to this, at intervals, adored belonging. Pam scratched behind the black-brown ears, rubbed the slender jaw, and made the appropriate remarks. Martini purred, reached out a dark paw and patted Pam's cheek and then, having had enough of sentimentality, turned around, went down Pam, and stretched on Pam's legs, facing out.

Sherry, after watching all this with interest, gave a small sound and jumped up behind her mother. She then advanced and sat on her mother's head. Martini made sounds of great disapproval and pretended to bite her blond daughter. Sherry ignored this. Martini wriggled out from under, backed up, and curled, leaving most of the original spot for Sherry.

Gin, the junior seal-point, trotted briskly around the room, letting out angular cries. This activity seemed to have no bearing on anything, and the remarks baffled translation. The other cats, from security, looked at her with mild interest. Martini then yawned, and put one forepaw over her eyes, apparently to shut out the sight. Gin stopped her circling, scratched behind her right ear without sitting down, which is a trick even for a cat, and then noticed, apparently for the first time, where her mother and sister had gone. She jumped behind Martini, making Pam say "Ouf!", said, "Wah?" herself, and walked over the other two, licking each in passing. She found a tiny freehold on Pam's knees and made the most of it.

"Goodness," Pam said. "Have you three any idea how much you weigh? As a whole?"

Nobody answered this. Pam's leg began to go to sleep. Then Pam began to go to sleep. Then the telephone rang. All three cats leaped away from Pam angrily, then sat in a circle and stared at her. Pam, fighting against an unreasoning conviction that something had happened to Jerry, moved almost as rapidly as the cats, snatched the telephone and said, "Hello?" in a kind of gasp. She went on, unable to stop herself in time, and said "Jer —" and then did stop herself. It as not Jerry, or, seemingly, about Jerry. It was Freddie Haven.

"Go slower," Pam said. "I don't —"

"— someone to know where I am," Freddie Haven said. "I said I wouldn't tell — them. Not yet. But I want someone to know. It's —" She gave a number in the West Sixties. "Breese Burnley's," she said.

Pamela North pursued elusive meaning, captured it, captured part of it.

"No," Pam said. "Not by yourself. Wait a minute."

"I have to," Freddie Haven said. "Anyway —" she added, and stopped. "It's all foolish," she said. "I know it's foolish. I'll be all right. I — I just wanted someone to know. Good —"

"Wait a minute," Pam said. Her voice was anxious, hurried. "You mustn't go there, or anywhere. Tell the police if — if there's something."

"Not yet," Freddie said. "I've got to go now, Mrs. North. It's — I can't wait any longer. Have you got the address?"

"Yes, but —" Pam said. Then she did not say anything more, because she heard the click of the disconnected telephone. She put her own telephone back, looked at it, took it up and dialed.

She got Homicide. She did not get Bill Weigand, whose line was busy, or Mullins. She was invited to hold on or leave a message. She asked for Sergeant Blake. She was invited to leave a message. This time she did. "Tell the lieutenant, tell any of them, that Mrs. Haven has gone to Miss Burnley's apartment," Pam said. "Gone alone, I think. And — and that I couldn't hold on because I've gone too. Mrs. North. Because there isn't anyone else and someone has —" She broke off. "Never mind the last," she said. "Just that about Mrs. Haven and Miss Burnley's apartment."

"O.K.," the man at Homicide said. "Mrs. Haven, Miss Burnley, Mrs. North. O.K."

Pam North replaced the telephone.

Why did I say that? she thought. I didn't know I was going until then. I didn't know I had to go until I said it. I wish Jerry would come.

But Jerry, who had no way of knowing that there was any reason to hurry, might be another half an hour. It just isn't possible to wait another half an hour, Pam thought. I'll leave Jerry a note and he can come and get me.

"Dear Jerry," she wrote. "It really is Breese and she's got Mrs. H to go there so I have to too. Please come but don't let the cats out." She read this over and signed it, "Love, Pam." Then she drew a line under the word "is." With that attended to, Pamela North let herself out.

Sergeant William Blake parked the inconspicuous sedan a block away and walked the remaining distance. The wind had gone to the northwest and blew up the street, steadily, with purpose, harshly cold. The tall detective bent to it, but he did not walk like a man in a hurry. In front of the building he hesitated a moment, the light from a street lamp on his face, and then walked on until the light was behind him. A smaller man appeared out of nowhere and said, "Got a match, buddy?"

"Don't ham it, Smitty," Blake said. "Well?"

"Yeah," Smitty said. "About the five-ten minutes ago."

"Good," Blake said. "Give the lieutenant a buzz. Come back and stick around."

"O.K.," Smitty said. "You'll be?"

"Around, I hope," Blake said. He shivered slightly. "It's cold," he said.

Smitty said that Blake was telling Smitty. He disappeared again. Blake walked on for a few paces, decided he was hamming it himself, and turned back.

Smitty said, "O.K. Loot," and left the warmth of the telephone booth in the all-night drug store at the far end of the block. He decided to chance it, ordered a cup of coffee and drank it quickly. He went to the door, looked out at the street, hesitated unhappily, and then went out into the cold. The wind blew him up the street. He had gone only a hundred feet or so when a taxicab came down the street and passed him, its roof lights on. It sounded as if it were running in second. Smitty noted it, but he had something else to do. He began to check the numbers on the license plates of the few cars parked in the block.

She ran up the steps and then, before she opened the outer vestibule door, she involuntarily paused. She had to make herself open the door; it became, in that second, an act of will against all instinct. She opened the door and said, "Oh!" with an indrawing of the breath.

Phipps stood in front of the mailboxes on the vestibule wall. He was pressing a button over one of them. He turned as she entered and shook his head before he spoke.

"She doesn't answer," he said. "I just got here. I've been ringing. She doesn't answer."

His normally deep, musical voice was higher pitched, excited. He shook his head again. He turned back and pressed the bell push agian; Freddie Haven could see his thumb flatten on the button as he pressed.

"She can't be asleep," Freddie said. "You said —"

"She just called me," Howard Phipps said, his thumb still on the button. "Just before I called you. Of course she can't be asleep, unless —" He did not finish. He released the pressure of his thumb on the button and then pressed it several times, quickly. They both waited. There was no response.

Howard Phipps turned to face Freddie Haven. His brows were drawn together; there was an expression of surprise on his face, and an expression of growing anxiety.

"I'm afraid," he said, and stopped and started again. "I'm afraid something's happened. We'll have to call —"

He interrupted himself. He turned to the door leading into the building and she saw him trying to turn the knob. That's no use, she thought; it was locked before; it's always locked. Phipps did not, she thought, take the knob as if he expected it to turn. It was, she thought, only a gesture; it was the futile thing one did in order to be sure one had done everything. And then she saw the knob turn.

Even as he pushed the door open, Howard Phipps turned back to her.

"I don't —" he began, and then, suddenly, he swore softly. "She must have come down and unlatched it," he said. "So we could get in. So we could — *find her!*" He said the last two words quickly, running them together. He did not wait for her to precede him through the door; he went in and said, "Come on, Freddie," over his shoulder. She went after him. Fear was swirling in her mind again.

It was a long way, seemed a long way, up the two flights of stairs; a long way down the corridor to the door they sought. Phipps, still in the lead, did not hesitate, now. He reached for the knob hurriedly, turned it hard. The door opened.

Lights were on in the living room. Phipps said, *"Look!"* and was across the room as he spoke. He bent over the girl on the sofa. He said, *"Breese! Breese!"* He took her shoulders and began to shake her, gently, twisting her back and forth. He kept calling her name. And then, while Freddie was still crossing the room so quickly had he moved and spoken, he said, "Thank God." He turned to Freddie, then.

"She's taken something," he said. "She's taken something, but she's alive." He paused. "The poor kid," he said. "Whatever she'd done — the poor kid."

By then Freddie was kneeling beside the sofa. Breese moved slightly. Then she lifted one arm as if to put it across her eyes, but the movement faltered, ended, the arm fell back.

"Coffee!" Phipps said. "That's what she needs. We can — maybe we can bring her out of it."

"We'll get help," Freddie said, but Phipps shook his head.

"Not yet," he said. "Let's — let's give her a chance, Freddie. If we can bring her out of it, give her a chance to talk – about – about all of it. The letter, everything. You see?"

Freddie shook her head, but the movement was uncertain. She looked at Breese Burnley again, and saw the girl's eyelids flutter. Breese did not, now that Freddie looked more closely, now she could look more calmly, seem deeply asleep. Perhaps Howard was right.

"The kitchen?" Phipps said and then, at once, "Oh – of course." He started for it. "See if you can do anything," he said. "I'll make coffee. If I can find it."

"Breese," Freddie said. "Breese – wake up!" She began to rub the girl's wrists. "Try to lift her," Phipps said from the kitchen. "Try to get her sitting up. Damn it, where's the – oh." He had found it – the coffee, the percolator. The taut exasperation ebbed from his voice. She could hear water running, then the hiss of a gas jet turned high. After a moment, while she still tried to lift Breese, get her sitting upright on the sofa, Phipps came back. "Got it started," he said. "Is she –"

"I think she's beginning to wake up," Freddie said. "I think –" Then Breese's blue eyes flickered open. They were blank. Freddie did not think the girl saw her. Then the eyes closed again. But now Freddie, her arm around the girl's shoulders, felt Breese's body respond. "She trying to sit up," Freddie said.

"The coffee'll do it," Phipps said. "She must have — have misjudged the dose. Or, subconsciously — well, you know what I mean. I think she's going to be all right."

"What do you suppose she took?" Freddie asked. Phipps looked down at her, with an expression of surprise.

"Don't you see?" he said, and shook his head. He spoke more gently. "Well, I'm afraid she must have had chloral hydrate to — don't you *see*, Freddie?"

She did see. It was all too easy to see. Involuntarily, she withdrew her arm from Breese Burnley's shoulders.

"I know," Phipps said. "It's — I'm afraid that's the way it is. She was going to tell us. She lost her nerve and — well, thought she'd end it. She fixed the doors so we could get in, but she thought we'd come — well, too late. Or, she thought she thought that. I suppose, subconsciously —" He shrugged.

Freddie continued to kneel by the sofa, close to the unconscious girl. She looked at Breese. Even now, she was beautiful, perfect in her orderly beauty — perfectly dressed, perfectly groomed. It was almost as if she had dressed for death, perfumed herself for death. It was hard to believe that Breese had loved so, then hated so. Because, if it had been Breese, love which changed to hatred would have to be the reason.

291

"She's pretty," Howard Phipps said, and Freddie was faintly surprised to discover how his thoughts must have been paralleling her own. He stood looking down at her, his expression abstracted. "What was that scent she always used? Do you know, Freddie?"

Freddie shook her head. "I don't know the name," she said. What did it matter, now? It could not matter to Phipps; probably he did not even realize what he had said. "I don't know," she repeated.

"I'll get the coffee," Phipps said. "It ought to be ready. Then we'll get her sitting up and — and see what we can do."

Freddie did not move. She knelt there, looking at Breese. Did you love him so much? she asked, without words. Did you hate him so much? And then, unconsciously, she shook her head. Was Bruce like that? she asked the sleeping girl. Could he make you feel like that? So that — that you changed when you were with him, so that he was — not like anyone else? Was *Bruce* like that?

"Here," Howard Phipps said. He came out of the kitchen with a cup of coffee in his hand. "Help me. We'll get her to drink this. Well —"

But then he stopped. A buzzer sounded loud in the room. For a moment, meaninglessly, both Phipps and Freddie Haven looked at the door.

"It's somebody downstairs," Phipps said. "I didn't think they'd – it must be the police."

Freddie stood up.

"Wait," Phipps said. "We'll give her the coffee, now it's ready. Help me, Freddie."

But," Freddie started to say. Phipps shook his head at her, commandingly. "Help me," he ordered. "We – we can't seem to have done nothing. Don't you see that? We –"

But she was not listening. *Fragment* – that was what they called the scent Breese wore. She remembered, now, absurdly, incomprehensibly, that she had once before remembered. She had made herself remember before. So that she could be sure. Only –

The apartment door opened.

"Oh!" Pam North said. "You didn't answer. But nothing was locked. Has she – has she killed herself?"

There was a moment of silence. Then Howard Phipps and Freddie Haven spoke at the same time. "What the –?" Phipps began and Freddie said. "No! You shouldn't have –" And then both stopped speaking. Phipps looked at Freddie Haven with an odd intensity.

"I told her," Freddie said, "I wanted somebody to know."

Howard Phipps shook his head as if he were puzzled. He started to speak, said "But" and seemed to abandon the rest.

293

"Anyway," he said. "Help me." He spoke directly to Pam. "She's taken something," he said. "Chloral, probably. We – we just found her."

He picked up the cup of coffee from the table in front of the sofa. "Lift her up," he said to Freddie Haven. But she did not move. "You," he said to Pam North. "Help me."

Pam crossed the room. She sat on the edge of the sofa, got an arm under Breese's shoulders and started to lift her. But the girl, although her eyes were open again, although she seemed to be partly conscious, made no effort to help. She was a dead weight against Pam North's arm. Almost, she seemed to be resisting.

Pam looked up at Howard Phipps.

"Maybe," she said, "maybe it's – maybe we shouldn't. Because this way she'll –"

"No," Phipps said. "We can't decide. Don't you see that? It isn't for us to –"

Pam North nodded. She again began to lift the girl, again felt, imagined, the almost inert resistance. What's the matter with Freddie? Pam thought. Why doesn't she help? Because of course we've got to do what we can. She just – just sits there!

There was something strange about Freddie Haven's expression. It was as if she were listening to something, listening to a faint voice, speaking from far off. Her expression was so strangely intent that Pam North found herself again hesitating.

"Mrs. Haven!" Pam said. "What *is* it!"

And then Freddie Haven spoke. It was as if Pam's question were a signal which she had been expecting.

"Wait," she said. Her voice was strange, tense. She did not move, but she looked up at Howard Phipps. "How did you get in?" she said. "If you didn't have a key, how did you get in?"

XI

Sunday, 2:50 A.M. to 3:55 A.M.

Tomorrow, Jerry North thought, pressing the proper button in the self-operating elevator, I don't get up until the middle of the afternoon. Tomorrow, I don't set foot outside the apartment. Tomorrow – thank God for tomorrow. He shivered slightly, reminiscently. He could still feel the wind on the particularly wind-swept corner where he had waited for a taxicab, waited until a kind of numb hopelessness in his mind had matched the numbness of his body; waited until he begun to tell himself that tomorrow they would find him there, one arm stretched out stiffly but no longer waving; find him a frozen monument to the taxi-hailing American male.

But it was over now. The day was over; if he could manage it, the whole thing was over. If Admiral Satterbee turned out to be a murderer, and hence unsuitable as an author, it would be

296

merely too bad. If he had to kiss the advance goodbye, they would have to count it as – what had Pam said, sometime, long ago? "Water under the dam." If somebody told him (he thought as the elevator stopped) that by going out once more tonight he could exonerate the admiral, save the advance, sell a hundred thousand copies of *Task Force,* he would be too indifferent even to laugh. He walked down the corridor toward the apartment house door. Already, in contended anticipation, he felt himself going to sleep.

He put his key into the lock, remembered with vague puzzlement his mood of some twenty-four hours earlier, and turned the key, so. He opened the door and said, softly, "Pam?" There was no answer, but he had hardly expected an answer. There were three cats, looking at him with sleepy reproach. They were in a pile on the sofa, one lying across the other two. They did not move, but the top one yawned.

Jerry North shed his overcoat. He spoke softly to the cats, who were too sleepy to answer him. He went, still softly, toward the bedroom, loosening his tie as he went. In five minutes, now – three minutes – he would stretch out, look for a moment at his sleeping wife, turn out the light she had left burning for him, feel the warmth creeping –

"Pam!" Jerry North said. *"Pam!"*

She was not in the bed, or in the room. She was not in the bathroom. It was impossible; it was inconceivable. She was not in the study, or in the kitchen. *"Pam!"* Jerry said again, even more loudly. He opened a closet door and closed it instantly. What would Pam be doing in a closet? At three o'clock in the morning?

Anxiety mounted in Jerry's mind. This time she had done it; this time she had really done it. She had got mixed up in something and they had come and carried her away; they had filled her full of chloral hydrate and —

"Pam!" Jerry said. "Pam!"

He was back in the living room by then. The cats were up, now. Something in his voice had excited them. They looked at him, blue eyes round and wakeful. "Where *is* she?" Jerry said. "Why can't you talk?" And then he saw a sheet of paper propped against a lamp. He almost ran for it.

"Thank God!" he said, as he read it. And then he put it down and, still loudly, but in another voice, he again invoked the Deity, not this time in a spirit of thankfulness. This time he sounded a good deal like Father Day.

He tightened his necktie. He picked up his overcoat and got into it, turning the collar up. He put on his hat. He went to the apartment house door.

"God!" Jerry North said, and went out into the corridor. The cats looked for a moment at the door, and then, sleepily, re-piled themselves.

"Right," Bill Weigand said. He spoke quickly, but without surprise. "Blake?" He listened; again he said, "Right."

"Keep the hole stopped," he said. "We'll be along." He put the telephone back in its cradle and stood up behind his desk.

"All right, Mullins," he said. "On our way."

"O.K., Loot," Sergeant Mullins said. "I hope this is it."

"How did you get in?" Freddie Haven repeated. She was still sitting on the floor beside the sofa; she looked up at Howard Phipps. But it did not seem to Pam North that she could be asking the question of Phipps.

"I told you," Pam said. "The door was —"

"Not you," Freddie said. "Howdie. You didn't have a key. How did you get in?"

Howard Phipps shook his head quickly; his eyebrows drew together.

"What do you mean?" he said. "You were with me. The doors were open." He indicated Breese Burnley. "She left them open," he said. "What do you mean?"

Freddie Haven shook her head.

"Not now," she said. "Before. When Breese wasn't here. When Sergeant Blake and I were just leaving. You came in. How?"

Howard Phipps did not say anything. He put down the cup of coffee which he still held. His eyes narrowed. He shook his head again, as if he did not understand.

"One key," Freddie said. "For downstairs and here. You know what I mean. You didn't ring. You just came. You must have had a key."

"Look," he said. "Have you gone crazy, Freddie? What does it matter? What're you getting at?"

"You didn't know where things were," Freddie said, and it was almost as if she were talking to herself. "You even asked where the kitchen was. But – you had to have a key, didn't you, Howdie? To get in downstairs?"

"Oh," Phipps said. He laughed, shortly. "I rang another bell," he said. "Any bell. Somebody released the latch. What on earth, Freddie?"

But Freddie, still abstractedly, still as if she were listening to a voice from a distance, shook her head.

"You didn't know Breese wasn't here," she said. "But you didn't ring this bell. Why didn't you, Howdie? And if you had a key, then – don't you see, Howdie? You would have known about the apartment. But you had to have a key to —" She stopped.

"For God's sake —" Howard Phipps began. But then he stopped speaking. His expression changed, slowly; his eyes grew very narrow.

"So what?" he said, after a long pause. He spoke in a low, level voice. "So what, Freddie?"

She shook her head. She was not looking at Howard Phipps now.

"And the perfume," she said. "The perfume she wears. The one you wanted to know the name of. Was it because — because you wanted to find out if I'd noticed? When it was on your clothes? Was that it, Howard?"

There was a very long silence. It seemed to Pam North, still partly supporting the unconscious girl, that the silence would never end.

"Howard," Freddie said, after the long silence, and now she looked at him again. "Why are you so anxious to have her drink the coffee? Because — *she's coming to without it, you know.* What's — what's in the coffee? *What's in the coffee, Howard?*"

Then Freddie Haven started to get up from the floor. And then Phipps spoke.

"Stay right there, Freddie," he said, and his musical voice was soft again. The tenseness-seemed to have gone out of it. He spoke as if he were inviting her to remain in some place of unusual comfort, urging her not to inconvenience herself for him, for anyone. "Stay right there." He turned to Pam North. "You too," he said. "Stay right where you are." His eyes went back to Freddie Haven.

"Well, my dear," he said, still in the same soft voice, "what makes you think there's anything in the coffee? Don't stop, Freddie. This would be a bad time to stop, don't you think?"

Why, Pam North thought, he talks as if — Why — that makes it all wrong! She looked, involuntarily, at Breese Burnley. Breese's eyes were open — wide open. Why, Pam thought, she's awake. And — she's afraid!

Mullins stopped the sedan against the curb. Smitty came out of a shadow, opened the door and got into the rear seat.

"Down the street," he said. "On the other side. Motor's cold. Forty-six Chevvie, rental plates. Like you said, Lieutenant."

Bill Weigand, sitting beside Mullins in the front seat, said, "Right." He sounded rather pleased.

"Blake was right," he said. "Who walks if he can ride? Nobody in it, of course?"

Smitty said, "Nope."

"No," Bill Weigand said. "The plans got changed, of course. With all the people around."

"A break," Mullins said. "For everybody."

"Well," Bill said. "Almost everybody, Mullins. We hope. Anything else, Smitty?"

"Well," Smitty said, "while I was calling in. I had to go down to the corner. A cab came along here. Sounded like it was just starting up. Ten-fifteen minutes later, another cab and a dame this time. I was down by this car, but it looked like a little dame. She went in."

Bill Weigand said, "Hmmm." Mullins looked at him.

"Listen, Loot," Mullins said. "You wanna bet it wasn't —"

"No," Bill Weigand said. "But how the hell, Sergeant? and — what for? Unless —" he did not finish. A taxicab pulled up in front of the police car and a man got out, hurriedly. He started across the sidewalk.

"Hey," Bill Weigand said, "Wait a minute."

The man stopped, turned toward the car questioningly.

"Well," Mullins said, "I wanted to bet."

"Jerry," Bill Weigand said. "Come here." Jerry North came to the car.

"She got away," Jerry said. He nodded toward the house. "She's in there," he said. His voice was quick, excited. "I'm going —"

"Wait," Bill said. "Pam'll be all right. It's under control. What was it? Just — just a brain wave?"

"I don't think so," Jerry said. "Her note wasn't very clear, of course. I'd guess Mrs.

Haven called her. Is Mrs. Haven in there?" He nodded again toward the house.

"Not that I —" Bill began, and stopped himself. "Damn!" he said, and began to get out of the car. There was surprise in his voice.

"Under control, you said," Jerry North told him, and Jerry's voice sounded angry. "And you didn't know about Mrs. Haven. To say nothing of —"

"Skip it," Bill said. "It's still under control. Only — well, there seem to be complications. Stay here."

He started to move up the street.

"Not me," Jerry said, and went after him. Bill Weigand stopped, started to speak, and shrugged. "Right," he said. "Come on." They went on together; Bill led them into an areaway on the east side of the house. It was narrow, walled by the house on one side, by the blank façade of a towering apartment building on the other. It was like walking into the bottom of a glacier *crevasse*. It was also almost as cold. The wind was not to be outwitted; balked of direct attack, it blew down on them from above. They found a fire escape on their left and began to go up it.

"I don't pretend I know what it means," Freddie Haven said. She still sat on the floor; she looked up at Howard Phipps. Her voice was quiet. "It doesn't prove anything, I guess. Except that you haven't been telling the truth."

"About?" Phipps said. He sounded merely interested.

"You and Breese," Freddie said. "You had a key to this place. You — you had her scent on your clothes. She was with you this afternoon. You pretended — are you in love with her? — is that —"

"No," Pam said. She was surprised to hear her own voice. "That's important. But, what *is* in the coffee, Mr. Phipps. Because that's the really important thing, isn't it? The coffee when she was coming to anyway."

"There's nothing in the coffee," Phipps said.

"Then it's very simple," Pam said. "Simple as anything. Drink it, Mr. Phipps. Just drink it yourself." She paused. "There's nothing hard about drinking a cup of coffee," she said. "Is there, Mr. Phipps?"

He looked at her without speaking. She waited, but he still did not speak.

"Of course," she said, "this other. About the key and everything. That could all just be — well, reticence, couldn't it? And not telling on a lady? So it's all very simple if you just drink the coffee."

"Suppose I don't?" Phipps said. "Then what, Mrs. North?"

"Then it isn't simple," Pam said. "Because

305

then there's something in the coffee. Because nobody dislikes coffee that much. I mean, if it were castor oil, or something, then why should you? Just to prove a point. But there's nothing hard about coffee. You see that."

He looked at her. It came over Pam North, frighteningly, that he did see that. Oh, she thought, I've done it again. I – I should have waited. Because it isn't Breese at all. And, since it isn't Breese it's – oh! It's dangerous, Pam North thought. Because he'll still have a gun. Then –

But he did not seem to have a gun. He merely stood, looking down at the three women. There was nothing apparently dangerous about him. He did not even frown, or look excited.

"Why should there be anything in the coffee?" he asked, as if he wanted to know. "What do you mean? Freddie? Mrs. North?"

He gave them only a momentary chance to answer. They merely looked at him.

"Because," he said, "you've both got yourselves mixed up. First, you bring up all this key business; argue I have a key to Breese's apartment, imply she gave it to me. Then, you say I'm giving her something that will harm her. Poison her, you apparently think." He shook his head. "Freddie," he said. "You came here

306

with me. We both found her – this way. Why would I call you up, ask you to come here, if I'd given her anything? But, if I didn't before, why should I now?"

He looked at Freddie Haven, then at Pamela North. But it's so easy, Pam thought. Doesn't he realize how easy it is? I won't say anything, but –

"To have a witness," Pam said, and was horrified at herself for speaking. "To have someone with you when you found her, some-one see you try to remove her. And right under their noses, you could give her another dose of – oh, of course, chloral hydrate. And they'd think she had taken it herself because she was guilty, because she loved Mr. Kirkhill – oh!"

She stopped herself.

"Go on," he said.

Pam looked at him. I'm doing this all wrong, she thought. I ought to be telling Bill, not him. Because all the time before I was wrong and –

"Go on," he repeated. "You may as well."

"You didn't know she loved Mr. Kirkhill," Pam said, as if the voice of Phipps compelled her. "You – you thought she loved you. But this afternoon – yesterday afternoon – you heard Mr. Grainger tell how she acted in the taxicab. How she broke down. Then – then you got afraid she would tell something she knew. Because why shouldn't she, if she didn't?

307

Love you, I mean. So you decided – decided –"

His eyes stopped her.

"To kill her?" he said, and his voice was no longer low pitched and musical. It was hard, rasping. "To kill her and make it appear she'd killed herself." He looked at her. He looked at Freddie. "You know," he said, "you might get somebody to believe all this. And go on from all this. So I think perhaps – give Miss Burnley her coffee, Freddie. Help her, Mrs. North. And then – then I think I'll have to reward you both for being so bright. So very, very bright."

And now he had a gun. It would be a thirty-eight, Pam North thought.

"Don't be noisy," he said, and then, only then, Pam realized she had been about to cry out, to cry for help. Because surely Bill – Jerry – surely they would not let this happen. "Don't be noisy, Mrs. North. Unless you're in a great hurry."

Pam looked only at the gun. It seemed enormous.

"But –" she said. And then she felt movement in the body she still half supported with one arm; felt muscles tightening; felt Breese moving away from her, slowly, cautiously. Pam did not dare to look, she could only guess. But she had to –

"Sleight of hand," she said. "That's what it was. To make us look in the wrong place. In all the wrong places – at Breese, at the senator's brother; but most of all at some ordinary thug on the Bowery. Wasn't that it, Mr. Phipps? Was it about the bribery, Mr. Phipps? Was that what it was?"

"Give her the coffee," Phipps said. "It wouldn't help you to know."

"About the bribery, then," Pam said. "I can guess. I can –"

There was no pressure at all against her arm, now. But still Phipps did not seem to notice. I've got to talk, Pam thought. It's sleight of hand again. Keep him from –

"Or maybe it was this way," Pam said. "Maybe you and this brother – this George. Maybe you had cooked up something together to – oh, to get money out of the senator. Something dishonest. Maybe George pretended he'd done something he would be arrested for. Stolen some money? But if he restored the money he wouldn't be arrested and of course the senator wouldn't want him to be because he was a senator." She paused, but only momentarily. "I mean the senator was a senator," she said. "And he found out about this and – and was going to do something about it. Prosecute you for fraud or – or –"

I have to think of something else, Pam North

thought. I'm running out of that. In a moment he'll look, he'll see what Breese is doing.

"Or something," she said. "And then you and George enticed him down there and —"

Then it happened. The movement beside her was swift. Breese Burnley was throwing herself forward on the sofa, reaching — reaching for the cup of coffee. And even as Pam threw herself back on the sofa, out of the way, Breese had the cup, hurled it upward, spraying, into Howard Phipps's face.

Breese kept on going, in a kind of falling dive for Phipps's knees. Pam saw the gun start to point downward, yelled, *"Jerry!"* desperately, as loudly as she could, and jumped for the man's arm. She half fell, coming up from the sofa, grabbed something and was conscious of other movement beside her. Phipps kicked and tried to bring his arm down and Pam North frantically dug her fingernails into the wrist, trying to stop the arm. She heard Phipps swear, felt him pulled back from her, realized dimly in a kind of red confusion that Freddie Haven had leaped up, somehow, from the floor and was pushing at Phipps's face.

Then there was a loud noise, almost against her face, and the sound of something crashing and the room was a confused melee of people. I'll bite him, Pam thought and started to, and then all tension went out of the wrist she was holding. She still held on and thought, *I'll bite him, I'll bite him,* and then, finally, realized that Phipps was falling, and pulling her with him. She let go then and thought, Why, I've had my eyes closed all the time, and opened them.

Sergeant William Blake was holding a revolver so that its butt made a club, and Jerry was coming toward her and then she heard Bill Weigand speak.

"All right, ladies," Bill Weigand said. "You can let up on him, now." He sounded excited, but at the same time amused. "Leave us the pieces," he said.

But what surprised her more than anything else was that Sergeant William Blake, still holding the revolver in his right hand, had put both arms around Freddie Haven and was saying, in a hurried, anxious voice, "You're all right. You're all right." Freddie Haven did not, so far as Pam North could tell, seem to mind this. She did not, indeed, seem to be as surprised by it as Blake did himself.

"And," Bill Weigand said, seeming not to notice this, "you've spilled the coffee." He looked down at Howard Phipps who, no longer in the least immaculate, was lying on his back. "But probably," Bill said, "we can get enough out of his shirt." Pam looked at Phipps. She thought they could probably get enough out of his shirt.

"There *was* something in it," she said. "In the coffee. This — these knockout drops."

"Oh yes," Bill said. "I'd suppose so."

"Then," Pam said, "we were right." She nodded at Freddie Haven, who was no longer in William Blake's arms. She looked at Blake, who was putting his gun back in its holster, and who looked very surprised and somewhat bewildered. "All along."

"Well," Bill said and hesitated. "In a manner of speaking," he said. He looked at Breese Burnley, who had gone back to the sofa and was sitting up. Breese had a compact in her hand, she was already making restorations. She did not seem particularly interested in anything else. For heaven's sake! Pam North thought. No wonder I thought —

"Well," she said to Bill, "not all the time. I mean after I got over being wrong. About —" She nodded toward Breese, who continued to restore. "Before you all came in —" She stopped. Her eyes widened. "Where," she said, "did you come from?"

"The fire escape, Pam," Jerry said. "You mean — you didn't notice?"

"Naturally, I had my eyes shut," Pam said. "I was going to bite him and — well, so of course I shut my eyes." She looked now. One window was still open; the venetian blind which had shielded it was tangled on the floor. "You must have come fast," she said. She looked up at Jerry suddenly. "You were there all the time," she told him. She was accusing. "You let —"

Jerry shook his head. He nodded toward Blake.

"He was," Jerry said. "Bill and I were there only a few minutes. Blake was there all the time?" Bill Weigand nodded an answer to the question in Jerry North's voice.

"But then," Pam said, as she looked at Bill, and there was a new accusation in her voice. "Then you knew all the time! And you let me —" She abandoned it. "How?" she said.

Bill Weigand grinned suddenly.

"There were a number of things," he said.

Pam merely waited.

"Well," Bill said, "for one thing — a man doesn't shave just before he goes to bed. What would be the sense of it?"

XII

They had started to eat before Bill Weigand joined them.

"It's practically breakfast," Pam North said and looked at the food on her plate. "How funny to have a broiled lobster for it. Here he comes."

The others had slept; Bill Weigand did not look as if he had slept at all. His face was gray with weariness. But it was also relaxed. A captain came behind him, carrying martinis on a tray. He put them down when Bill was seated and waited. "Anything," Bill said. He looked at Pam's plate. "A lobster," he said.

There were four martinis. Bill drank deeply from one glass, almost finishing it. He waved at the other drinks, at Pam and Jerry North, at Dorian. "Had ours," Jerry said. "Of course —" He watched Bill reach for a second glass. "Nice of you to think of us,

314

though," Jerry said. "Well?"

Bill Weigand shook his head.

"Not yet," he said. "I'm not sure he ever will. What's he to gain?"

"They never have anything," Pam said. "Still, they do. Maybe he will. Do you have to have it?"

Bill Weigand said it would help. He said a confession, duly signed, duly delivered, always helped. He said Phipps could make them trouble if he remained obdurate.

"Too much?" Dorian said.

Bill hesitated a moment. He shook his head. He said he shouldn't think so.

"After all," he said, "there's a weapons charge, which is open and shut. There's assault with intent, which ought to be easy. For the big ones — well, we'll find it." He finished his drink. "Because," he said, "we know where to look, what to look for. And somebody, in the end, always turns out to have seen something. It's a great comfort to the police." He looked at the third glass and looked away. "You know," he said, "I don't think I've eaten all day." He seemed mildly surprised. Nobody said anything for a time.

"You know," Pam said, "I really thought it was Miss Burnley. It was all very — very confusing. I still don't — what *about* men not shaving before they go to bed?"

"A tip off," Bill said. "One of several, actually. Blake noticed that one. When Phipps showed up at Miss Burnley's apartment, said she had called him. He made a great point of how he had rushed over, made quite a picture of it. Spent the evening in his room working, he said; gone to bed, been waked up. Dressed 'like a fireman,' he told Blake. And – he was cleanly shaven. Why? He'd got over from the Waldorf in twenty minutes, he said. Obviously, he hadn't taken time to shave. He'd been working alone all evening. No man shaves for a second time during a day if he's going to stay in his room. No man shaves before he goes to bed. But – Phipps has a very heavy beard. If he hadn't shaved since morning, he'd have had visible stubble. So – he was lying somewhere. He'd shaved a second time; he'd been out somewhere. And, lies aren't purposeless."

"Such a little thing," Pam said. "Was it the same time that he didn't have the key? But really did? The thing that worried Freddie there at – at the end?"

"Right," Bill said. "The same key opened the downstairs door and the apartment door. The usual arrangement. Both doors were locked, locked automatically. Blake himself had to ring from the vestibule before he could get up. But – Phipps didn't. He'd let himself in downstairs, therefore he had a key. He didn't, of

316

course, expect to find anybody in the apartment. When he heard voices, he knocked. He'd obviously planned to let himself in. But, with Mrs. Haven, he'd made a point of not having a key. Another little lie, not purposeless. Blake noticed that, too, and wondered about it."

"A noticing young man," Dorian said. "Are you terribly tired, Bill?"

"His business," Bill said. He smiled at her. "I'm all right," he said.

"Of course," Pam said, "he still might have expected Breese to be in the apartment. Maybe that was his way of — I mean, maybe he just unlocked things and — popped in. Rude, of course, whatever their —" She stopped.

Bill nodded. He said it could have been that way, although he agreed it wasn't the usual way.

"However," he said, "Miss Burnley has filled that in, now. He did have a key. Nevertheless, he always rang downstairs."

"Like the postman," Pam said.

"Not like the postman," Bill said. He took the third drink. "Three times," he said. "Three and a nubbin. But you're right, we didn't know that then. We — well, we just had to guess. From what Blake told me, I guessed Phipps had been sure the apartment was empty. Which meant he was sure Breese wasn't in it. Which might mean —"

"That he knew where she was," Pam said.

"Of course. Where was she?"

"In his car," Bill said. "The car he had rented from drive-yourself outfit. In his car, asleep, moderately full of chloral hydrate. Destined, I imagine, for a park bench – a doorway – any place cold enough to finish her off."

"But why –?" Pam said, and Bill shrugged. There, he said, he would have to guess. There were two possibilities. One – that Phipps, about to drive off, had seen the arrival of Freddie and Celia, then of Mrs. Burnley, finally of Blake. He had got curious, and had figured he could find out what was up and, at the same time, underline his own innocence, if it was in doubt, by the story of having just been telephoned by Breese.

"Foolish," Pam said. "Not to let well enough alone. And, anyway, you said he thought the apartment was empty."

"Right," Bill said. "So I like the other theory better. We found a bottle containing chloral hydrate in the girl's kitchen. With Phipps's prints on it, not hers. That's why I said the assault with intent to charge ought to be easy. The second theory is that Phipps was merely going back for the bottle, which he had forgotten. To put her prints on it. And, possibly, to give her more chloral, if she seemed to be coming out of it. Sitting in the car, he probably checked over the things he had done – washed

318

and put away one of the two glasses they drank from, left the one with her prints, got her out and down as soon as she got drowsy. Then – he remembered he had forgotten to put her prints on the bottle. So – he had to take her back up, or bring the bottle down. Naturally, he chose to bring the bottle down."

"And then couldn't," Jerry said. "Because the place was full of people."

"Right," Bill said. "I'd guess that."

"A confession *would* help," Pam said. "For points like that." She paused. "Not," she said, "that I don't think logic is a fine thing. And then he decided, after all, to take – to take Breese to the bottle? And – make her drink?"

Bill nodded.

"He figured an alarm would go out," he said. "He didn't want to drive her around the streets, try to put her some place. And – the police had already been in the apartment. They knew she wasn't there. So, why not put her back? And then, he improvised. Why not get Mrs. Haven over to help find her unconscious, to see him trying to revive her with black coffee, which is fine for chloral hydrate poisoning – unless the coffee happens to be full of chloral hydrate."

"It was?" Pam said. "From his shirt?"

"Right," Bill said. "We – well, we soaked enough out of the shirt before he came to.

319

Blake hit him rather hard. Plenty of chloral hydrate. His point, of course, being to convince everybody that Miss Burnley had the stuff, had figured we were about to catch up with her, had decided to give the whole thing up in a — well, in a nice, easy way. Phipps hoped we were already suspicious of her and —"

"I was," Pam said. Her voice was rather small. "Weren't you ever, Bill?"

Bill Weigand shook his head. He reminded her he had said from the start that they needed a man, not a woman.

"Also," Bill said, "Mrs. Haven thinks that he had begun to be afraid she knew too much, had become suspicious. Because of something about perfume." He told them about the perfume. "She thinks he may have planned to find out how much she knew and, if she knew too much, well — include her. She may very well be right. He could have shot her, put Breese's prints on the gun and got out, leaving us to assume Breese had killed Freddie, presumably because Freddie had found her out, and then herself."

"In the end," Pam said, "he was going to include us both. Was Blake on the fire escape all the time?"

Bill nodded.

"He waited long enough," Pam said. "You all did."

Bill told her they had wanted to get what they could. He told her that Blake had had his gun ready, and would have used it in time. "But then," he added, "you all three jumped in and he couldn't. So we came in, instead. Blake had unlatched the window beforehand, of course, and lowered it a couple of inches from the top, so that he could listen."

Bill's lobster came. He looked for the fourth martini, and found that Dorian was sipping it. She smiled at him. "Sacrificing myself," she said. "Until you've had food, my dear."

Bill made a face, dug into a claw, dipped lobster into melted butter, and ate. The others had finished. Pam waited until she saw Bill swallow.

"Between bites," she said. "What was it all about? At bottom? Because, so far, we've just got the top. I mean — well, what was it all *about?*"

Bill said he knew what she meant. He said they were still piecing it together. But, at bottom, it was about the effort to bribe the senator to change his position on the hydro-electric project.

"But," Pam North said, and looked puzzled. "I thought — I mean, in addition to everything else, he already *had* so much money. Why —?"

"Right," Bill said. "Precisely right, Pam. Also, I take it he was an honest man. Which is

321

no doubt why Phipps never took it up with him at all."

The other three looked at him. He looked at his lobster, speared the other claw, let them wait.

"Some people," Pam North said, "can't think of anything but eating."

Bill swallowed, smiled at them, and said that it was still bits and pieces. He said they had got a good deal of it from Breese Burnley, who had got the first intimation some time before from Julian Grainger. "I told you she had been seeing him," Bill noted, in parenthesis. "She was a pretty young thing to see when he was in New York, to take to dinner. And so forth. And so forth."

"Delicately put, darling," Dorian said.

Bill Weigand said he was not precisely putting it. He said he didn't know.

"However," he said, "he did tip her off. She says she doesn't remember how, exactly. Senator Kirkhill's name came up and the elder Grainger said something to the effect that she didn't really know him; that he wasn't any knight in shining armor. I don't know whether he thought that would make any particular difference to Breese, or whether he cared. She was just a girl to take to dinner."

"And so forth," Pam said.

"And so forth. Anyway, Breese got enough

from him to make her curious. Enough to make her think she might get something on Kirkhill. Which she wanted – well, because Kirkhill had ditched her. Ditched her, as she figured it, for Freddie Haven. She wanted to get her own back. Maybe get him back. If she could get enough on him to stop the marriage – well, call it love, call it revenge. She would have enjoyed it."

Breese knew better than to try to get anything more from Grainger, Bill told them. But she figured that, if there was anything in it. Phipps would know. So she cultivated Phipps. Bill pointed out that she did not put it so directly, admit it had been so direct. He was summarizing. She had cultivated Phipps and – got him to talk, got him, in the end, to boast.

"Not in specific terms," Bill pointed out. Roundabout – hints. But enough to convince her that Kirkhill was being bribed, with Phipps acting as go-between, and with Phipps making a nice thing out of it for himself. So she took a chance and wrote the anonymous letter."

"She admits that?" Jerry asked.

"Oh yes," Bill said. "She's very annoyed at Phipps for drugging her. She's – well, she's a chastened young woman. The police are her pals. Also, she's not in any trouble herself, which makes her very happy, very cooperative."

"Listen," Pam said. "I thought the senator *wasn't* bribed."

"Right," Bill said. "That's why he got killed." He took the time to finish his lobster. The others looked at him with indignation. He said the lobster was very good, and that he needed coffee.

"With or without chloral hydrate?" Pam enquired, sweetly. Bill grinned at her.

"Right," he said. "These people – the Grainger people – had approached Phipps with a suggestion that the senator could be bribed. Phipps knew he couldn't, but Phipps needed money. He said he would take it up with Kirkhill. He came back and said it was O.K., but the senator couldn't appear personally, of course. He said he would be intermediary. He convinced them. They began to pay off. Phipps just put it in his pocket."

"But he must have known –" Dorian said.

Bill nodded. He said one would think so. But he said that it was undoubtedly one of those things people drifted into, without any idea how serious it would become, without any real idea that, in the end, there would have to be a payoff. Probably Phipps told himself, when he thought about it, that something would turn up – perhaps that the senator would, as senators sometimes do, find another cause to espouse, would lose interest in the Authority project. Or, perhaps,

Phipps figured that, if worse came to the worst, he could merely tell the Grainger people to whistle for their money, realizing that they couldn't do anything about it, having themselves singularly unclean hands.

"Look," Jerry North said, "are you going to be able to prove all this? Or any of it?"

Bill shrugged. He said he hoped so. He admitted it might be difficult. He admitted a confession would help. He said they still might get one. "Because," he said, "of the thirty-eight he had killed Smiley with. And his fingerprints are on the chloral bottle. And — we don't really have to prove motive, you know. We don't have to prove what it was about at bottom. Naturally, it helps if we can. And — we'll get what we want from the Grainger people. We'll have to make a trade. So far, they deny everything. But they've agreed to have the head of their legal bureau talk with the district attorney. They've even — well, they seem almost anxious. They'll come through — to a degree. They won't involve anybody important on their side, naturally. They'll — they'll throw somebody to the wolves. With the understanding that the wolves sniff him, don't eat him. 'Trusted executive — shocked he would enter into any such negotiations — naturally Mr. Grainger knew nothing of all this — would not have countenanced any —' Well, you can figure it. The boy they throw to the wolves gets paid for it. We get what we want."

"You know this is going to happen?"

"I'm morally certain," Bill said. "All of this is a moral certainty. Except the rifling of the thirty-eight, the fingerprints, Miss Burnley's willingness to testify that she had a drink with Phipps, found herself in his automobile three-fourths asleep, remembers being helped back to her apartment; except the chloral in the coffee; except what he said while Blake was listening." Bill nodded as he catalogued. "Oh, we've got him," he said. "A confession would merely be a helpful thing."

"The Grainger people to whistle —" Pam North prompted.

"Right," Bill said. "Well — I imagine he found out that they weren't inclined to whistle. I imagine he found out there were some burly tough people among them. Not Mr. Grainger, of course. Certainly not his son. But — somebody. I imagine he was told to produce, or else. And, at about the same time, Kirkhill told him to get together the data for another speech on the whole issue — a speech that went even further than those he had made previously. So Phipps had to start getting the data — really, writing — this speech which would prove that he'd been engaged in a double-cross — or that the senator had. But he didn't figure he'd be able to convince anybody the senator had. So he had this 'or else' from the bribers on one side and whatever the senator would do to him on the other. Then it ocurred to him that, with Kirkhill dead, it would all come out nicely. He could write another speech, in which Kirkhill did change his stand on the Authority, he could show it to the Grainger people, point out it wasn't his fault if the senator got himself killed before he had the chance to change his coat — presto, everything fine. So he got the senator down on the East Side, filled him with chloral, got him out in the open, probably took him to the doorway — or, at least, followed him, waited around until he was sure the chief, as he called him, was finished. Went to the party. Probably he knew the senator had a bad heart, although it wasn't very bad. Perhaps he didn't, and counted on exposure. Either way, the plan worked."

"How did he get him down there? And — but of course, the why was merely to confuse everybody, to make you look in the wrong place."

"Right," Bill said. "As to how — I think he told us. He used George. George's existence, that is. Probably he went to Kirkhill with some story about George's being in a bad jam, which might involve damaging publicity; went counting on Kirkhill's tendency to go into situations with a kind of violent energy, and to do it personally. Kirkhill may have worked out the rest himself – the old clothes, so he wouldn't be recognized by whoever he was going to meet – thought he was going to meet. I'd assume some plan to pay off whoever had George in this jam, I'd assume that this first meeting was supposed to be merely preliminary, perhaps with the senator posing as a kind of body-guard for Phipps. Maybe Phipps will give us the details, eventually. But it was something like that. The whole thing, as you say, Pam, being to make us look in the wrong place. When we don't – when we don't just write it off as the work of a thug – Phipps throws us a little of the truth. He throws us George. How was he to know that George had reformed? That George had a perfectly sound alibi?"

There was a pause. Bill's coffee arrived.

"And Smiley was following the senator? Saw it?" Pam asked.

Bill shook his head.

"Smiley was following Phipps," he said. "He'd got that far. Now that he's decided it's wise to know more, Smiley's partner, Briggs, finds he can remember more. He remembers that Smiley was following Phipps. No doubt expecting Phipps to meet a payoff man from the Grainger outfit downtown. Briggs remembers that Smiley had something about Phipps's having rented himself a hideout − actually it was a place where he and the senator could go, and the senator could change. Presumably, Smiley saw what happened, decided to shake down Phipps as well as the admiral − and got himself killed."

"And Phipps called you up?" Jerry said. "To tell you Smiley was murdered? Why?"

Bill shrugged. He said Phipps would have to tell them that. At a guess, he had seen Mrs. Haven go into the building, hoped the police would catch her there.

"She was there," Bill said. "She admits that, now. And the elevator man recognized her. She found Smiley, as I thought all along. She − well, she ran. Still afraid it was her father. She called after him, found he wasn't at home. Put two and two together and − well, came up with the wrong sum."

Bill drank his coffee. There was a period of silence.

"Such a dishonest murderer," Pam said. "Dishonest in so many ways." She seemed a little annoyed. "I was tricked," she said. She looked at Bill. "Of course," she said, "I didn't have Blake to tell me he was shaved when he shouldn't have been." She paused momentarily. "Blake's nice," she said. "Where is he?"

At home, Bill told her. Presumably in bed. Bill sighed. Dorian looked at him, and he shook his head. "Have to go back," he said. "Help the boys ask questions." He sighed again. He started to get up.

They all got up. They went out of the café at Charles, said good night to Hugo. Bill and Jerry turned to the checkstand for their hats and coats. Pam went up to the bar to tell Gus good night, and stopped.

Sergeant William Blake was neither at home nor in bed. He was sitting at the end of the bar and he was talking very earnestly to his companion, who had hair of an unusual deep red, who seemed to be listening earnestly.

Pam turned quickly back to the others. She began to talk rapidly about nothing in particular. He's explaining how he happened to put his arms around her, Pam thought. She thought he ought to have the chance.

Although actually, Pam thought, as she led the others out of the restaurant, I doubt whether it will be as hard to explain as I think he thinks it will. Pam, as the person in the lead, nodded to the doorman, who began to whistle.

Because usually it isn't, Pam North told herself, rounding off her thought, as she always liked to do.

THORNDIKE-MAGNA hopes you have enjoyed this Large Print book. All our Large Print titles are designed for easiest reading, and all our books are made to last. Other Thorndike Press or Magna Print books are available at your library, through selected bookstores, or directly from the publishers. For more information about current and upcoming titles, please mail your name and address to:

THORNDIKE PRESS
P. O. Box 159
THORNDIKE, MAINE 04986

or in the United Kingdom:

MAGNA PRINT BOOKS
LONG PRESTON NEAR SKIPTON
NORTH YORKSHIRE,
ENGLAND BD23 4ND

There is no obligation, of course.